The Borrow a Bookshop Holiday

The Borrow a Bookshop Holiday

Kiley Dunbar

hera

First published in the United Kingdom in 2021 by Hera Books

This edition published in the United Kingdom in 2022 by

Hera Books
Unit 9 (Canelo), 5th Floor
Cargo Works, 1-2 Hatfields
London, SE1 9PG
United Kingdom

Print ISBN 978 1 80032 976 8
Ebook ISBN 978 1 912973 47 7

Look for more great books at www.herabooks.com

Printed and bound in Great Britain by Clays Ltd, Elcograf S.p.A.

I

This book is a celebration of storytellers, booksellers and book lovers

and I dedicate it to you, my wonderful readers.

Love, Kiley x

Advertisement: A Novel Holiday Idea

Borrow-A-Bookshop invites you to live out your dreams of running your very own bookshop in a historic Devonshire harbour village… for a fortnight.

Spend your days talking about books with customers in your own charming bookshop and serving up delicious cream teas in the cosy café nook. Get to know our wonderful volunteers (all locals), always ready to offer a helping hand.

After shutting up shop, climb the spiral staircase to your two-bed apartment and settle down to admire the Atlantic views. When your holiday's over, simply hand the keys to the next holidaymaker-bookseller.

Request your booking early. Currently, there is a nineteen-month waiting list.

Small, fully equipped private kitchen and shower room on site. All shop and café takings retained by the Borrow-A-Bookshop Community Charity.

Apply in writing to Borrow-A-Bookshop, Up-along, Clove Lore, Devon.

£380 charge per let for 14 days.

Chapter One

'Gran needs me, sorry,' I say, not making eye contact because I know I've said this a thousand times before and it wears a bit thin with people.

'You really won't come out tonight?' Daniel's looking at me incredulously from behind the yellow lenses of his achingly fashionable chunky sunglasses. 'You only graduate once. We should be drinking champagne 'til dawn.'

'There's plenty of champagne here,' I say, gesturing across the sunny quad at the waiting staff holding their trays laden with bubbly. All around us families are raising glasses and beaming their approval at their graduating loved ones. I'm not really seeing them though; I'm scanning the spaces between the family groups.

'Looking for Mack?' Daniel prods, and I ignore the hint of dismay in his voice. He stops a passing waiter and grabs two tall flutes, pressing one into my hand.

'He'll be over in a sec, I imagine.'

I use Daniel's pointed silence to glug my bubbly and put on a good performance of looking just as happy as my classmates who are all milling around in their cliques, signing each other's graduation ceremony booklets and posing for group selfies.

Only moments ago we all processed out of the university's fancy auditorium and into the July glare. Daniel couldn't get a ticket, even though I wanted my best friend there to witness it all – tickets were limited to three guests per graduate – so he was waiting outside for me, looking handsome as hell in his suit with his dark hair beautifully quiffed as usual. He'd been standing by the doors when we all

3

emerged, flowers in hand – red roses because he knows how much I appreciate anything resembling a romantic gesture from a novel.

Mum and Dad bound towards us over the lawn. They were the last to leave the ceremony and I just know they were having their usual faffy struggle with the footrests on Gran's knackered old wheelchair. Gran's sailing towards us, glamorous as ever, coo-eeing and waving, but I see her get distracted before she reaches us.

'Wait a sec, Roni,' I hear her instructing Mum. She's pointing her walking stick towards the Pimm's table and the sign reading 'free bar' above it, and I watch Mum divert her in that direction.

Dad's looking so proud as he approaches. I'm not really sure how to react. It's so strange being the centre of attention. He's snapping photos of me and Daniel on his big old camera before his hug knocks the mortar board off my head.

'Well done, Jude! You did it! My clever girl.'

'Thanks,' I smile, proud that he's proud. Oh no, he's on the verge of tears again. He's such a softie; I think that's where I get it from. Daniel notices and chips in to save us all.

'Don't you agree we should be celebrating out on the town tonight, Mr Crawley? She deserves a proper wild night after all that work.'

'Nothing stopping her,' Dad says, quizzically tipping his head at me. 'You young ones need a night out now and again.'

Young? The last thing I feel today is young. In fact, if you want to feel old before your time I recommend two courses of action. Number one: dedicate yourself to being a home carer to your lovely Gran. Spend your days nipping to the bookies for her and reapplying her corn plasters and see how young you feel. And two: sign up for a part-time degree in your mid-twenties so that you graduate along-side twenty-one-year-olds just as you're approaching your thirtieth birthday.

I was lucky enough to get a part-time place at the Borders campus of an Edinburgh university so the classes were amazing and only ever a twenty-minute bus ride from Gran and the bakery.

I've never felt more 'mature' than when my classmates would ask me if I had kids (I don't) or whether I wanted to join their nights out at the Students' Union bar (I did, but never went). They were sweet though, and would say things like, 'It's all right, you can bring your husband along', fully expecting me to be a proper, married grown-up like their parents (who probably aren't that much older than me) and not in fact a perpetual undergraduate whose idea of a big day out is 'prize bingo and bacon butty Thursdays' down the Senior Citizens' Club with Gran and her rowdy mates.

'See, nothing's stopping us,' Daniel's saying, and he's nodding at Gran over by the bar. 'Doesn't look like your gran needs you all that much at the moment.'

Annoyingly, he's right. Mum's left Gran to it and is making her way towards us. I watch as Gran chats up one of the uni sports coaches by the bar. She's waving a fag around in one hand and clasping a Pimm's with the other. Fair play to her, the coach guy is laughing his head off. She's offering him a cigarette now. She'll get us all chucked out at this rate.

Gran's like that; gets on with anybody and loves a party. Not like me. Daniel says it's nothing but habit – my love of my comfort zone – and I could shake it off if I really wanted to, and it's kindly meant, I know that, but he wasn't the one stuck at home with caring responsibilities as a teenager. He was free to follow his own life path, like all my other classmates.

I don't really admit it out loud but I know how easy it is to lose yourself when you're safe and cosy, going along with life with no signs of change or escape on the horizon. Letting opportunities slip by becomes your new normal and after a while you barely notice it, not until everyone your own age suddenly seems to be escaping and excelling, leaving you behind.

Anyway, I'm already thinking about how long I need to stay here before I can ditch this cape and hood thingy that I'm all trussed up in and we can pile back into Dad's van and head home where I'll be able to get back to re-reading *Persuasion*.

Jane Austen is one of the greatest loves of my life – alongside our bakery's iced Copenhagen slices, my pyjamas, and of course Mack. I'd left off at the good bit where steady old Anne Elliot thinks Captain Wentworth is drooling over the impulsive Louisa Musgrove, and Louisa's about to toss herself off the Cobb at Lyme Regis and brain herself trying to impress him and…

Mum interrupts my dreams of getting my Austen on at home. 'Well done, sweetheart,' she says, suddenly planting a kiss on my cheek from nowhere. Dad's got his camera to his face again and is clicking away, capturing it all.

'Say cheese,' he calls.

That's when I glimpse them, over Dad's shoulder, Mack and the woman – actually, I'd call her a girl – and they're walking so close it looks like he's towing her. They're nipping round the back of the auditorium, and I'm sure she's tipping her head coyly and twirling her hair in her fingers. Her giggle reaches me all the way across the quad, and just like that I find I'm following them, stalking through the happy crowds in hot pursuit with Daniel's voice, cautioning and grave, ringing out behind me.

'Jude? Jude. Don't! Just, please stay here…'

Somehow, tiptoeing after them, I know my narrow little life is about to get even thinner. I know that whatever I see when I round this corner is going to hurt.

She's still giggling and, wait… Mack's joining in?

And on my graduation day, when I'd finally reached the top of my game. When only an hour ago I was beaming with pride and achievement.

As I prepare to turn the corner and confront them, holding my breath, dreading the sight that awaits me, I think back to when I was waiting in the wings inside the auditorium and what had been my Big Moment begins to take on a sadder, slightly pathetic, appearance in this new light.

I'm next. This is it! I'm going to sail across that graduation stage like a swan. My heart's thumping because it's just hit home I'm about to be the centre of attention for the first time in my life; one thousand eyes will be fixed upon me and everyone's going to hear my name, but I've had six years to prepare for this and I am doing it.

'Jude Crawley,' calls the Dean of Arts over the speakers, and I'm off, up the steps, and I'm definitely fighting back big, proud sobs. 'Bachelor of Arts in English Literature.'

I can hear Mum and Dad whooping at me from their row but I daren't look around, and if I were to catch Gran's eye I know I'd dissolve completely.

The Chancellor's holding out my certificate rolled in a red ribbon and all I have to do is nod at him, grab it and not stumble in these heels.

'Jude Crawley also accepts the Chancellor's award for academic achievement,' the Dean booms and my parents burst into another fit of whistling and yelping.

I'm bowing and he's handing me an actual award, a Perspex star with my name on it. This is *just* like that bit in *Anne of Green Gables*, one of my favourite childhood reads, and I'm Anne Shirley finally getting her Bachelor's degree in spite of nineteenth-century prejudices, only she's got a teaching career ahead of her and her belly button isn't showing because of a damned cloak and hood thing yanking up her shirt and half choking her. That doesn't matter though, because this is *my* moment and I'm beaming through my tears. All that work, six years, and it's finally here.

I try not to glance over to where Mack is sitting amongst the stage party, here in his official capacity as Head of Philosophy: Doctor Rupert Mackenzie-Aubyn – also known as my secret boyfriend, Mack.

'Secret boyfriend' makes it sound sort of illicit. It isn't really. We're only a secret because he's on his way to becoming a professor and although Mack assures me student–staff relationships aren't *strictly* against the rules when you're in different departments and the student in question's a mature student, they're not exactly encouraged.

I shake the Chancellor's papery hand. He's congratulating me on my success and I have no words other than a whispered, slightly snottery 'thank you'.

I can't resist a little peek at Mack to see his reaction and to get another eyeful of him looking all distinguished and owlish in his suit with that brown tie and his little round glasses that make him look like William Butler Yeats, one of my all-time favourite poets.

He's not looking at me. In fact he's staring down at… is that his phone? Nobody smiles at their own crotch like that, not in public with the Chancellor six feet away anyway, so he must be texting.

Well, that's one way to play it cool. Nobody would ever know I've spent many evenings over the last eight months listening to him reading Camus and Machiavelli – and not understanding much of it – as I laid my head across his lap and he ran his fingers through my strawberry-blonde bob.

I remember one time, right at the beginning, when he counted every single freckle on my face and kissed each one, and I'd stopped hating my freckles after that. That was only a few weeks after our first meeting, when he'd first approached me among the library stacks and, after a bit of flirty chat, told me I was welcome to peruse his bookshelves at home if I fancied. I'd blushed and we ended up talking for ages and I missed a lecture so we could go to a bar off campus.

He's not even clapping.

I leave the stage, a little wobbly on the stairs, clasping my scroll and my star award, and feeling a little deflated, if I'm honest.

I know things will be different from now on, though. Now I'm a graduate there'll be no more secrecy, and I can visit Mack on campus and openly bring him his lunch, instead of sneaking into his office under the pretence of being a philosophy student looking for advice about interpreting Plato or whatnot.

Only, the thing is, I'd hoped – in fact, I'd fantasised – that the secrecy would end *today* and he'd be grinning at me from the stage and applauding hard. Maybe he'd be misty-eyed, overcome with pride and relief that now we're out in the open.

I know I'm not the only one thinking these things as I make my way back to my row through the packed auditorium and I see Gran, tiny and adorable in her best dress, little pink jacket and matching hat, sucking on a Murray Mint, her eyes boring into Mack up on stage.

Mum and Dad don't seem to have noticed. Like Gran, they haven't met him yet so they may not recognise him from his picture on the uni website that I've shown them. Gran's got a memory like an elephant though, so I know she knows who he is.

My parents are sniffing and wiping their eyes and doing thumbs-up signs at me as I pass. I hold my award up for them to see and Dad snaps a photo. They're prouder than I've seen them since the day I got my acceptance letter. Apart from that I don't think I've actually done anything for them to be proud about.

I know they're grateful that I help clean up at the family bakery at the end of their long days' work, and they're always telling me how they'd be lost if I wasn't Gran's carer. I protest that it's fine, never wanting them to feel guilty about it, and I tell them yet again that we're family so we stick together no matter what, but I know how much they worry about me. They knew that my greatest ambition had always been to study English at university and it was them who encouraged me to give it a try. They know how big this is for me – the first self-improvement, just-for-me kind of thing I've ever done. They saw how much determination and courage it took for me to do it in the first place, but I did it – a few years later than most, granted, but I enjoyed every second of my degree. In many ways it's been my first and only excursion into the real world.

I find my seat again. The Chancellor has finished handing out degree certificates and is giving an address about how this is 'only the beginning' for us graduates. I don't feel as though he's talking to me, though. This is actually the end of my adventure. Now I've stretched my wings and scratched the itch that was my love – no, my *obsession* – with English literature, I'll be heading straight back to how things were before, and that's fine by me, honestly.

I'll still be looking after Gran, keeping her company, making her meals and reading to her. Mum and Dad will still work from three until three every day in the bakery downstairs. I'll go in and clean the place like I do most afternoons – earning my keep at home – and then we'll all settle down to evenings in front of the telly with my parents exhausted and ready for bed by half seven and Gran doing her online bingo. Only now, instead of studying at night or occasionally sneaking off to Mack's at nine o'clock, there might be the prospect of more romantic dates on the horizon. Or *any* dates, for that matter. Mack and I have never actually been out in public together yet.

I try not to sigh at the lovely possibilities this opens up: kissing under street lights on snowy walks this winter or holding hands in the cinema queue pretend-bickering over whether we should order salty or sweet popcorn, and he'll let me have my way because salty is the only option for cinema snacks, and we'll laugh and look at each other in a soppy way that'll leave anyone seeing us under no illusions that we are *the* most starry-eyed couple of all time.

Then there'll be holidays – or more likely stolen weekends away, although they won't be easy to fit into our schedules, I imagine, what with Mack working all hours at the uni and Gran's medication to keep up around the clock and the fact she'd be totally lost and lonely without me if I were to nip off to a couples' resort for cocktails, spa treatments and fancy dining with Mack. But maybe we'll be able to get away over the Bank Holidays when the bakery's shut and Mum and Dad can take over my responsibilities at home.

Oops! Everybody's suddenly standing up and we're all clapping for some reason. Wake up, Jude! Ah, we're supposed to applaud our lecturers, thanking them for all the attention they've given us during our studies. I'm whistling and clapping exaggeratedly, arms up over my head when Mack finally glimpses at me and, in the hubbub of the erupting auditorium, he throws me a lusty wink that heats my blood and now it's me having to look away, blushing.

When I look back, he's poised and elegant again. His sleek golden-blond hair, now turning a little dusty with age, is swept aside like a real-life Ken doll. He adjusts his glasses and coolly crosses his legs, observing the graduates lining the front rows. He's smiling – well, as much as he ever smiles at work.

He's very serious in public. 'Gravitas,' he calls it. 'Important to maintain my reputation as a serious philosopher around the faculty.'

Only I know that he's amusing in private when he's relaxed and we've opened a bottle from his never-ending wine supply (only ever the best Barolo from his vintner brother in Oxford). He gets rosy-cheeked and lets me loosen his tie and I'll cook while he rehearses his lectures for the days ahead. After dinner, we'll lazily kiss and nod off on the sofa.

Nobody here understands how personable he is in private moments like that. Nobody knows how his family are all vintners going back generations and that he's gone against the grain – the family's rebel academic. Only I really know him and his life.

Anyway, it's all academic now. We'll be showing each other off all over the place soon and I'll get to meet his intimidatingly posh parents. Once he tells them I exist, they'll be dying to see me, won't they?

All those future romantic dates, public declarations and fancy occasions are a big consolation for my studies coming to an end and life settling back into its old routines of caring, cleaning, cooking and nipping out to put a bet on one of Gran's dead certs. Things are about to get much simpler at home now that I won't be pulled in umpteen directions at once with the logistical problems of fitting in my reading, essay writing, and attending lectures. Yep, it's going to be good.

The clapping's stopped and I sit down again, accidentally bumping the girl beside me. I smile my apologies. She was in one of my classes – Restoration Theatre and the Comedy of Manners 101 – but she doesn't seem to recognise me. Olivia, I think her name was. I don't think we ever spoke much beyond hellos.

I didn't really make any proper friends on the course. I suppose I had a reputation as a bit of a swot, never able to go out for a drink after class, always getting firsts in our assignments and making sure I had all the reading prep done – and with pages of handwritten notes too.

While I devoted myself to giving this degree my best shot, most of the younger students had other priorities; messy relationships and parties, uni societies and shop jobs, summer breaks overseas and gap-year planning.

I was more focused. I had to compartmentalise my life. There was time for studying and there was time for looking after Gran, and not much left for anything else outside of that, other than nipping next door for a brew in Daniel's kitchen while he filled me in on the latest gossip at the Borders General Hospital where he works.

It's a shame Daniel's not here in the auditorium. He'd be grinning at me across the room and communicating daft, unintended innuendo he'd found in the Chancellor's speech just with the look on his face and we'd be trying not to laugh out loud and spoil things like the two twins sharing one brain cell that we are.

I scan my eyes along the row at my classmates, all of whom are listening wide-eyed to the Chancellor describing the exciting lives awaiting them. I wonder if I'd have had a better chance of making friends if they had an inkling about me and Mack?

Perhaps then I'd have a reputation for being secretly wild and risk-taking, a daredevil romantic in an undercover love affair with a glamorous genius – like something straight out of *Madame Bovary*. They probably saw me as a bit boring, if they saw me at all. Well, they'll soon know just how exciting Jude Crawley really is, once Mack makes it known we're together and word gets around. I can't wait.

–

After being so happy and hopeful this morning, it burns a hole in my heart all the more to catch Mack pressing the girl against the wall round the back of the auditorium and watch him whispering in her ear between hungry kisses trailed up her neck. His glasses are steamed up and squint on his face and she's *still* giggling and tugging at his tie and ruffling his perfect hair.

Is it weird that in this moment I'm thinking about how I don't remember him kissing me anywhere outside of his flat or his locked office with the blinds pulled closed? 'Not worth the risk,' he'd tell me in a whisper, pulling away whenever I tried to sneak my hand into his as he pretended not to know me in the corridor or in the queue for coffee or in the big multi-storey car park on campus where I'd wait for him after his classes.

I suppose this girl must be worth the risk.

I watch them lost in their clinch for a moment, my feet frozen to the spot. Neither of them even notice me and I'm not surprised, given the way she's rummaging inside his tweeds.

Instead of storming over there and demanding to know how long this has been going on, I find I'm crouching behind the big, stinking wheelie bins, which are buzzing with wasps, with my hands clamped over my mouth to keep the sobs inside. But they do notice when Daniel comes racing round the corner.

Through welling tears I watch my friend's expression change from alarm to anger as he discovers the pair of them. I hear the girl yelp in surprise and Mack mutter something about things not being as they appear; that he's only helping a student with a knotty philosophical quandary.

Daniel ignores him and reaches for me, scooping me up and guiding me away. For a millisecond I catch the look on Mack's face, his nose screwed up in surprise and, I think, disgust that I was hiding behind the bins all along. 'It's not what you think,' Mack says once more, and I get a glimpse of his expression dissolving into panic. Maybe he thinks I'll make a scene and endanger his precious promotion.

'Dignity,' Daniel whispers quickly, keeping his eyes set dead ahead where Mum, Dad and Gran are waiting for us, their faces all concern and confusion. 'We're going to Anne Elliot this,' he adds in a hiss, and that's all he has to say.

I immediately sniff away my tears, straighten my back and we walk, heads held proudly, through the crowds of my oblivious classmates and away from Mack and his latest secret girlfriend.

In the back of Dad's van as we head home to Marygreen and the flat where I was born, above the bakery where I grew up, I dissolve in a heap of tears and regret on Daniel's shoulder and surrender my dreams of having a tiny slice of a life I can call my own after graduation.

Chapter Two

Daniel's being an angel, of course. He brought round his duvet and we've settled in for some serious comfort eating and snuggling – easy when he still lives next door. He's yet another of the millions of singletons like me living in our family homes as our thirties approach with little hope of affording a place of our own. Nurses aren't paid a tenth of what they're worth so moving out isn't exactly likely for him any time soon. His parents have long since retired from running their Borders clothes shop empire and now they spend their summers at their holiday home near Land's End while he takes care of things at home.

He'd made a few detours on the way round to my place too, God love him: to Marcia's chippy at the end of the high street (tiny Marygreen's *only* shopping street) for our Mackageddon Celebration Supper (the name was Daniel's idea – I'm not ready to laugh about it yet, and I seriously doubt I ever will be) and he's bought a bottle of cheap plonk from the corner shop. Ten out of ten for best-friending.

I made sure Gran had everything she needed for the evening (she was busy on a Zoom call to her craft circle, talking about their latest yarn-bombing project, so she was happy enough) and me and Daniel burrowed into our duvets on my bed and made short work of all the carbs and booze.

He didn't even ask which DVD I wanted picking from the shelf; he went straight for my trusty copy of *84 Charing Cross Road* and after scoffing our chips, we tore into a bag of Cadbury's giant chocolate buttons and the comfortingly familiar opening titles rolled.

If you haven't seen this movie, or indeed read the book it's based on, you're missing a treat. Who wouldn't love a story about a real-life antiquarian bookshop and a correspondence between an American book-lover and an English bookseller that spans a lifetime? *Ah!* It really is lovely and speaks to my love affair with books.

I don't just mean the stories *inside* books, I mean the books themselves and the unfathomable loveliness of holding them in your hands, poring over the handwritten inscriptions and pretty bookplates, sniffing the pages and wondering who owned them before you.

If I wasn't needed at home – and if I had endless money, as opposed to next to no money – I'd do nothing but tour the world's bookstores and treat myself to treasured first editions and scruffy, well-thumbed, neglected paperbacks from years gone by. I'd have to take Gran with me of course. She'd love that. We're pretty much inseparable.

Anyway, me and Daniel have stayed in our nest watching bookish movies and eating rubbish all evening and now I'm feeling vaguely human again. Mum felt sorry for me and helped Gran with her bath and then I brought her usual nightcap (ice-cold Baileys – double measure – and a big wodge of our bakery's fruitcake) and now me and Daniel can drink tea and speculate on who the girl Mack was practically humping in broad daylight might have been.

I had a ticklish notion at the back of my brain that I'd seen her somewhere before, and around the bottom of the second bag of chocolate buttons it strikes me.

'She's the girl from the coffee shop on campus! I'm sure of it. I can picture her in her little brown apron and everything.' This discovery gives way to a wave of disgust. 'She's only a first year. I'm sure she told me back in the autumn that she was doing English like I was.'

She must be only eighteen or nineteen, I reckon, and ever so sweet and smiley. Too sweet for Mack, that's for sure, that serpent in leather elbow-pads. He hasn't called, by the way, and I don't think he's going to either.

'So much for Dr Mack and his *gravitas*! Grab-an-arse more like,' Daniel says grimly, hoping I'll laugh. 'Wonder what the uni bosses would think about him shagging Freshers?'

All I've got in response is a wry smile and a shrug. That student's just a kid really. It's not her fault she's been swept off her feet by a gorgeous, powerful man. What excuse do I have for getting swept away at twenty-nine?

'I really thought we were destined for great things, or at least normal couple things, like this,' I say, indicating the cosy bubble I've made with Daniel. We're huddled together, clasping our mugs, close and conspiratorial. We're confidants and utterly comfortable together, me and him, and we've been like this for years.

'Oh yeah, this *really* is couple goals,' Daniel says with a smile and a roll of his eyes.

Will it shock you if I tell you that, apart from Mack, Daniel's the only other person I've ever been with? Don't go rolling your eyes at me for falling for my next door neighbour. You'd understand if you'd seen how adorably handsome he was at sixteen or if you'd grown up among the very slim pickings in our little Borders town. It's not exactly a hotbed of eligible guys.

There were some other local lads, at school and in the years after, but nothing to set the world alight. It didn't help that it was difficult for me to get out on dates, and even the sweetest ones didn't want to wait around for me, missing out on their twenties when everyone else was out every weekend in Kelso and Peebles, or even Edinburgh and Glasgow, at clubs and parties.

Even getting out to the local pub was a rare occurrence, unless the whole family went for dinner or something. Boyfriends don't want to put up with that sort of unavailability. Except for Mack. Or at least I thought so, while I was busy convincing myself he was the big Love of my Life that I'd been waiting for, like they tell you in the novels. Every time I felt rotten about neglecting him he'd reassure me it was fine, he understood, and he'd remind me we had the rest of our lives to go places and do couple things, and I'd think myself so lucky to have found him. Turns out we had the perfect arrangement – for him and his other clueless girlfriends, that is.

Daniel was a model boyfriend, of course, back in the day; so kind and considerate, sexy too. He looks adorable lounging beside me now

17

in his striped pyjamas and a black sleep mask keeping his hair back. He didn't even *ask* if he was staying over, he just turned up with his toothbrush and aforementioned emergency supplies.

'You'll find your Captain Wentworth one day, Jude,' he's saying, 'and he'll be loyal and patient and all the other good things you deserve.'

I sigh, trying not to weep again. I'm at risk of considerably lowering my standards after Mack. I don't need grand gestures and romance; I'd settle for someone who texted me in their lunchbreak to ask, 'How's your day?' It would mean someone was interested in the little boring details of my life. It would be nice. Mack never once asked anything like that, I'm realising. Instead of admitting this to Daniel, I say, 'Whoever he is, I hope he's good at duvet dens and midnight feasts,' and we both smile at that.

This was our childhood speciality long before we got together – pillow forts and sleepovers. My parents never seemed to mind Daniel staying over. He was, after all, only Derek and Jean's dorky boy from next door.

Once things got serious at high school, Mum gently suggested that letting us share a room maybe wasn't very responsible, and Daniel's parents had agreed, but pretty soon after we broke off our adorable teenage love affair (all getting steamy in his bedroom and listening to My Chemical Romance on repeat) the cosy sleepovers resumed for a while – before Daniel went off to uni.

'We haven't done this for ages,' I say. 'I've neglected you a bit while I was studying for those finals.' My brain pipes up to remind me it was more likely because I was saving every spare second I had for Mack and I wither a little more. 'Sorry I've been a crap friend, Daniel.'

He greets this with a dismissive, '*Meh*, you've had a lot on your plate,' and puts an arm out for me to snuggle into him, still cocooned in my duvet. I wrap him inside it too and reach my arms round his back and his tummy. He's so solid and warm, it's an instant dopamine hit, but I can't stop thinking about the way Mack was kissing that girl, even when I screw up my eyes and try to shake the image out of my head.

'What is it?' Daniel wants to know.

'Well, I… I suppose I'd got used to telling myself that Mack was just reserved and not the mad passionate type, but that's definitely not what I saw from behind the bins this morning.'

'It looked like he was going to eat that poor woman's head,' Daniel shudders dramatically. 'Slobbery!'

I have to agree with him there. Mack never once slobbered over *me* like that. We had our fair share of decent enough intimate moments, but thinking about them now, there was never any time to luxuriate in each other like they do in romance novels, and no snuggling up and sleeping in each other's arms afterwards either.

'I thought that maybe our love was so deep it remained unspoken, you know? Like it was buried very, *very* deep under those lovely waistcoats and Savile Row shirts I used to lug back and forth to the dry cleaners for him.'

'I didn't know you were doing that. You kept that quiet,' Daniel says.

I know he's peering down at me but I can't meet his eyes for some reason. I squirm a bit, almost on the verge of making excuses for Mack, wanting to say he was so dreadfully busy and important, and I didn't mind helping him, really. But he's right, I kept it secret.

Subconsciously I must have known I was being taken advantage of, and Daniel would have spotted it a mile off if I'd said anything. I try to gloss over the little ashamed feelings that ignite in me and I think of all the good stuff that distracted me from the red flags; the flirty texts inviting me round his place, the way he'd fan out the takeaway menus and let me order for us while he uncorked another fancy bottle and lit the candles, and how deflated he'd be when he realised he couldn't make yet another of the opportunities I'd set up to meet Mum and Dad or to join me alone for a romantic lunch off campus. 'Judith, I'm so sorry, another meeting's come up,' he'd say, looking stricken and guilty. 'You know what the Dean's like. Look here, I got you this,' and he'd slip me a box of the chocolate truffles I once said I liked or a lovely new edition of the book he was currently reading so I could share the experience with him, and we'd talk about

19

it late into the evenings round his flat when he was finally free, and he'd get a wolfish look in his eyes and take the book from my hands and lead me to his bedroom. *Hmm*, looking back, there were plenty of red flags – like the texts he was always getting.

Glumly, I tell Daniel about them. 'He always was a bit secretive, looking back. I'd put it down to him having a lot on, what with him angling for a professorship and everything… but the texts would arrive at all hours and he'd slink away to read them and I'd hear him furtively texting back. I always assumed it was other night-owl academics asking searching intellectual questions or wondering what time the morning meeting was supposed to start.'

I was so determined this was it. The One. The kind of True Love heroines in novels find before they hit their thirties. The kind that lasts a lifetime. I was so busy kidding myself, I let myself get played.

I glance warily up at Daniel's face, but he's still not judging. He's nodding and crumpling his lips sympathetically. He's no stranger to this kind of thing. His last girlfriend cheated on him with Deltoid Dave, the town's sports centre manager with the deliciously thick thighs who always smells of chlorine. I squeeze Daniel a little tighter, take a breath and go on.

'Some nights when I arrived at Mack's place, he'd tell me there were members of the faculty unexpectedly round for drinks or he was working on a big research bid so I couldn't come in, and he'd promise to make it up to me the next day, which he always did – dinner at his, flowers maybe – and so I'd just accept it and get the bus home again in the dark.'

It's only now my brain choses to replay a scene I'd packed away in a memory box marked 'Nothing To See Here: Only Perfectly Innocent Boyfriend Behaviour'. It's from the night I turned up at Mack's door with a spare toothbrush, some knickers and PJs and I asked him if I could have some drawer space to keep them in since I was staying over so often.

Mack had looked at the toothbrush still in its plastic packet in my hand and said, as cool as you like, 'Judith, it's not as if you *live* here now, is it?' He'd arched a lovely blond brow and smiled like I was a naughty girl and he was humouring me with his light disapproval, but it worked. I shoved my stuff back in my bag and carted it all back here again.

I'll keep that memory to myself. Daniel already knows this is a new low for me, no need to overdo it. But now the lid's off that memory box there are humiliations bursting forth from it and parading across my vision, all gaudy and grotesque now I'm finally grasping the fact that Mack well and truly took advantage of me.

He certainly got more out of me than he ever put in to our… well, was it even a relationship? In return I got the illusion of a lovely life: the expensive wine, the wonderful old leather-bound tomes piled everywhere in his artfully shabby home. It looked a lot like the bookish, cerebral existence I used to dream of as a skint baker's daughter growing up in Nowhere-in-the-Sticks, and the conversations and the grown-up sophistication really hooked me, convincing me I'd found my place in life.

I could kick myself now. There was me, thinking we were daring bohemians, living a life of ideas and discussion, hiding our love from uncaring, authoritarian university governors; but it turns out I was just one in what is probably a long line of clueless students he shagged. But I'll bet there were none more willing and docile than me.

I think of the new bride in Daphne du Maurier's *Rebecca* – another of my absolute lifelong favourites, and a book I retreat into when in need of some glamorous, gothic thrills. Maxim's bride was happy to sit at her handsome, aristocratic husband's feet and have him absent-mindedly stroke her head like she was one of his dogs, and now that pathetic image has popped into my brain I erupt into tears while Daniel rubs circles on my back.

'Imagine waiting for so long to get to uni only to be hopelessly distracted by a bad man so it all ended in humiliation,' I sniff.

'*Uh*, it ended in you getting a big, shiny award, don't forget.' Daniel points to the star by my bedside. 'You're being too hard on yourself. Mack looked legit, like a young Indiana Jones, only more anaemic and homely, you know? Who'd have thought under all that gabardine and paleness there'd beat the heart of a scumbag? And you're not the only person to fall for his dandified nonsense, are you?'

'And not the last, I imagine,' I throw in, cringing at myself. 'Do you know who I feel like? I'm Jude the Obscure.' This comes out with a big, self-pitying sob.

'Never heard of her,' Daniel shrugs and my jaw rattles off his chest.

'Thomas Hardy's last novel?' I say, sitting up again. 'Jude's a man, by the way, and all he wanted was to go to uni. He strived and pined and waited for his chance and one day he finally went for it, but he was fated to be a lowly stonemason, you see? He was *born* to it. He should have accepted his fate but instead he fought against it. And you know, he might have succeeded but he kept getting distracted from his ambitions by his libido and his insecurities. In the end, all he ever succeeded in doing was making himself and everyone around him thoroughly miserable.'

'That sounds hideous,' Daniel grimaces. 'Remind me not to watch *that* adaptation. I'm guessing he died of consumption without a china pot to piss in like all the other Victorians you're obsessed with?'

'Close enough,' I say.

Daniel's not a book-lover as such, not like me. His passions lie elsewhere – in his job which he's properly brilliant at (he's on his way to becoming a senior staff nurse in the next few months) and he loves following designer trends, looking for rip-off high-street pieces that he somehow throws together on his lovely, solid frame and looks a million dollars in for just a fraction of the cost of the catwalk originals. He really does look runway ready at all times, even now in his stripy flannels. Having said that, he's not averse to *Pride and Prejudice* binges with me when things get tough.

It took us both a while to realise Daniel was as interested in Mr Darcy emerging from the lake in his wet shirt as I was, and even longer for him to articulate that he was definitely interested in both my heroes and heroines. That was around about the time we morphed into the inseparable friends we are today. I remember the night it happened, too.

It was the summer Gran had the first stroke. I was about to turn eighteen, and we'd just got to the bus stop after our school leavers' ball. I was reaching for him, after downing our eighty-seventh sneaky lemon Hooch of the evening – I don't know, it may as well have been, we were so inappropriately hammered – but when our lips met there was just… nothing, except maybe awkwardness. We'd both squinted and blinked at each other and had another try just to be extra sure, but still nothing. So we shrugged and laughed, a little abashed by this sudden, strange shift in feeling as it dawned on us that somehow we'd grown out of our status as childhood sweethearts.

It hurt a bit at the time and now I try not to dwell too much on the fact that we've seen each other naked and had some actually really sweet and oh-my-goodness-hot moments back in the day.

Whatever it was that suddenly cooled between us, it must have happened at roughly the same time as my bombshell realisation that my parents would need me to look after Gran, who'd just moved in with us, and that we couldn't really afford for me to go to uni right away.

That summer I accepted that my teenage years were well and truly over, and I packed them away, embracing my fate as a good girl who puts her family first, and gladly too. Daniel left town to start his nurses' training soon after (three years at Edinburgh Napier – God, I missed him!), and that truly was the end of me and Daniel as an adorable couple.

We were something bigger than that, it turned out. We were soulmates, and even if I can't say I was a young and reckless Fresher straight out of high school or a gap-year backpacker exploring the bookshops and libraries of the world – my deepest, most secret dream – or anything like that, I will always be able to say I had my lifeline, Daniel, and my lovely family, and I wouldn't swap any of that for another iota of teenage freedom.

It's dark, it's late and we're both getting sleepy, so I pull the covers up over us and we lay ourselves down for the night.

'Daniel?'

'*Hmm?*'

'You're the best.'

'Don't I know it,' he murmurs, and soon I hear his breathing settle as he drifts off to sleep, exhausted from his run of night shifts at the hospital recently.

Just knowing he's next to me helps me switch off my brain which has been delivering a long lecture with PowerPoint slides all evening, entitled, 'An illustrated history of all the completely obvious ways gullible, naive Jude was manipulated by Dr Mack the snake', and I let myself fall asleep amongst our drained wine glasses, cold tea dregs and chocolate wrappers in our big bubble of comfort.

Chapter Three

Here we are, five days later and life's gone back to the way it was before enrolment. Mum and Dad are busy as usual creating delicious treats downstairs in the bakery, Gran's been nothing but comforting and diverting, full of ideas for things to do at home together (gin rummy, anyone?), and Daniel's beautiful red graduation roses are fading now, just like my memories of Dr Rupert Mackenzie-Aubyn.

I'm actively trying not to think about him, forcing myself instead to attend all the more closely to Gran. It occurred to me in a particularly guilty moment of self-reflection that I might have been neglecting her too while I was writing up my final year essays and spending more and more time at Mack's place waiting for him to look up from his grading and notice I was still hanging around.

I'm angrier with myself than with him, if I'm truthful. He's just a suave, greedy, selfish cheat doing what comes naturally to him. It wasn't really his job to look after me and he never once promised that he would – not in so many words, anyway. He would smile at me and flirt in that well-bred way he has and I'd hear all kinds of unspoken promises but maybe they were all in my head. I was star-struck that somebody so intellectual and posh and glamorous could fancy me and I let all that stifle my misgivings about why we only ever met up on his terms and when it suited him.

It's made me worry I'm a snob. How could I have been so befuddled by his fancy ways and his bookish appeal? Am I really that easily impressed? Anyway, it's all been a timely reminder that looking after myself is *my* job and I've badly let myself down. Safe to say, I am never, *ever* letting a sexy, sneaky, secretive snake in the grass take advantage of me again.

To make up for being a crap granddaughter, I've been busy. I called the mobility shop and ordered a replacement wheelchair – one without wonky foot rests – and I've booked Gran in for a mani-pedi with Treena the hairdresser next time she's here doing her perm, and I've renewed all Gran's magazine subscriptions which were close to lapsing, and I've discovered a new bean soup recipe to try out because the doctor said she's supposed to be getting more fibre, and yeah, like I said, life's gone back to normal, and that's OK. Honestly. This is fine.

It's true that, very occasionally, the little voice inside me that's been straining to make itself heard since I was seventeen is whispering away, telling me that I could do more, see more, be something bigger and brighter than this, but I can't pay it any attention. This has been my life for so long that all the missed opportunities barely hurt anymore, and I long ago accepted the fact I'm lucky to be here with Gran and that nothing's going to change any time soon.

Gran's a bit listless this morning though, and I've suggested calling her nurse but she's having none of it.

'I'm not ill,' she huffs when I try to plump the cushions behind her on the armchair. 'I'm just fed up.' She's been saying this more and more recently, and there's something of the petulant teenager in her expression when she does.

'Well, what shall we do? You've got an hour until you can eat after taking those tablets, but you can have a cup of tea? And we could watch *Countdown* and try to find filthy words again?' She loves that normally, but no, it's not working. 'We could go down the Border Arms in a bit, see if Aunty Anne's doing her hotpot for lunch?' I know this'll be approved, which it is with a quick nod, but still, Gran's not her usual chirpy self.

'Crossword?' I suggest. Gran exhales and shifts in her chair. 'What is it? You can tell me? Is it your bunions?'

'Judith, love?' she says, tentatively.

'*Hmm?*'

'You know Bernice and Jill?'

'Of course,' I shrug. They're Gran's best friends and would be *very* hard to forget. They're both athleisure-wear enthusiasts, crochet queens, got mouths like longshoremen, and they sweep the boards every time there's a darts tournament at Aunty Anne and Uncle Mike's pub, and they've been utterly devoted to each other for over sixty years. Plus, every time I've ever seen them they have a packet of Starburst for me, even in the days when they were still called Opal Fruits.

'Well… umm…'

Gran's getting tongue-tied and I'm panicking a bit. You can't be too careful when someone's had two strokes.

'Do you want me to call Dr Stevenson?'

She waves a hand, getting a bit annoyed, I can tell. She's told me before, ever so gently, not to stifle her. So I sit back a bit and wait.

'Bernie and Jill are moving in to that new retirement complex…'

'New Start Village?' I say, thinking of the big hoardings by the gates which have been pasted over with enormous images of youthful-looking elderly people living the good life; all false-teeth-grinning over dinner, and grinning over bowling, and grinning in the pool. 'The place that looks like a weird sports cult recruiting seniors?' I say. We've laughed at this before, but Gran's serious now.

'They've finished building it, and half the yarn-bombers are moving in this August. Got most of the East wing booked out already.'

It's clicked now. '*Ah*,' I say, 'and you're worried they'll disappear into that place and you'll be lonely? I'm sure they'll have visiting hours and I'll go with you and—'

'No, dear. That's not it. I want to move in too. Here, look at this.' Gran produces a leaflet from down the side of her chair.

'*Are you ready to start a new life at New Start Village?*' I read. '*Relocate to your luxury shared living complex and indulge in unlimited cruise-style dining, cocktail hour and afternoon teas, every day.*'

I glance up at her and she nods for me to go on, saying, 'Have a look at the entertainment page.'

'*Enjoy a variety of evening entertainment options including karaoke, live bands and dancing…*' I start skipping bits, the list is so long. '*Our Pilates, Yoga, and Shiatsu programmes run daily… spa offers hairdressing and manicures, massage and mud therapies.*' I fold the leaflet again. 'Gran, we can do all this stuff together, you don't have to move out. I can arrange—'

She lays a steady hand on mine but it's not comforting me and I've got a big well of panic building up in my chest. 'We have fun, don't we, Gran? I'm good at looking after you? We look after each other, don't we? And—'

'Judith. It's time. I've watched you this past week with your broken heart and no dreams left. That's not right, not for a young woman. I've got a life insurance policy maturing this year, so I can afford to move out and finally give you the space you need to do your own thing.'

I can't help but sniffle and my shoulders are heaving, trying not to let my heart burst. She's on a roll now and isn't stopping.

'You've been a wonderful, *wonderful* granddaughter to me. You've taken me to all my appointments and seen me through my physio, and look at me! I'm all the better for it.'

I stare at the leaflet on my lap. I don't need to look at Gran to know that she's right. She's got roses in her cheeks like she used to, and her mobility's improved so much in the last year or so she only uses her wheelchair on long trips out.

'If I don't go now, I'll start heading downhill again and we don't want that. More importantly though, Jude, *you've* got to go out there and live your own life.'

'But I love hanging out with you,' I cry.

'Me too.' Gran's teary-eyed now, and she's not supposed to get upset, what with her blood pressure. 'I asked your mum to ring them and they've got a unit available for me at the end of the week, and it comes with a free gym pass and Netflix.'

I can't help laughing at the hopeful note in her voice as she says this, but my heart hurts like I've never felt before. I know it's a done deal but I'm not giving up without some bargaining. 'This has been my life since I was seventeen and I didn't ever want it to change. I want to look after you forever… be your friend forever.'

Gran fixes me with a look I feel right in my soul. It's a look that says, *Jude, I'm eighty-three. I haven't got forever.* So I give up bargaining and I feel my life as I know it slipping away.

'I'll only be down the road, you can come see me anytime – stay over, even. There's a wing for guests, you know? It's not prison; it's *Retirement Community Living.*' She jabs her finger at the leaflet. I'm nodding and reaching for the tissues. 'We had a lot of fun, Jude, didn't we?' she says, gently.

'We did,' I say, and I really mean it. 'Remember that time we yarn-bombed the police station railings? That was amazing.' I wipe my tears away. Gran's laughing fondly too. 'In fact it was one of the best nights of my life. I'll never forget Hilda Flint in her mauve balaclava stringing her crocheted coppers all along the street, and it was my job to wrap the yellow and blue woolly bunting around the gate posts, do you remember? Nobody ever knew it was us, even after the ITV news crew turned up.'

'Who'd have thought we'd make the six o'clock headlines?' Gran says.

The panic's subsiding slightly now, but the ache hasn't shifted. 'What will I do without you?' I say.

'You'll *live*, dear. You'll live your life.' Her eyes are sparkling as though she can see it all before her; my future, bright and exciting, but all I can see is blank nothingness; no plans, no job, no boyfriend, and now that Gran's off to master the arts of tai chi, pot throwing and watercolours at New Start Village, no purpose either.

Chapter Four

'Just the crusty bloomers today, Marjorie?'

'Better give me two cream buns as well; the grandkids are coming.'

'Oh, lovely! How's little James's asthma these days?'

I've been listening to Mum chatting with the customers all morning while I try to make myself appear useful behind the counter, but Mum and Dad have got such a well-refined system I know I'm only getting in the way, and it's hot and stuffy in here too, now August is here, which isn't helping matters.

It was lovely watching them working together first thing this morning though; I so rarely get the chance to see it, and it was reassuring to be reminded that nothing's changed in all the years they've been doing this.

Bread and rolls are always the first task of the morning – that's very much Dad's job, and they're always cooling on the big racks by five. Then it's gingerbread men and, in the summer months, delicious strawberry tarts. Mum whips those up in what looks like minutes and they're ready by six while Dad produces a big batch of perfect choux finger buns which he deftly pipes full of whipped cream (I was responsible for the whipping bit this morning) and he finishes each one with a shiny slick of milk chocolate on top. Somehow Mum's always there with her tub of sliced almonds ready to receive the tray of Copenhagen slices as soon as Dad's got them iced, and she sprinkles the slivers on top while Dad opens the fridge door ready to take the tray back, and *voilà*, the morning's baking is done.

They emerged triumphantly up the steps from the oven room into the shop just before seven, their bakers' whites, faces and hairnets dusted with flour, both of them gasping for a brew (also my job this morning). The display cabinet by the till was fully stocked by seven thirty when Mum turned the sign on the door to 'Open', just in time for the milk delivery.

Even once the shop's open everything ticks over like clockwork as they move easily around each other, humming along to Borders' radio, concentrating on their individual tasks, not communicating with words but perfectly in sync. They've got their choreography down better than any of the K-Pop groups me and Daniel watch at night on the Arirang channel – something we've done a lot since Gran moved out at the end of last week.

''Scuse me, Jude, love,' Mum's saying now, hands on my shoulders, manoeuvring me out of the way so she can pass Mrs Weston the pile of Mills & Boon books she's been keeping behind the till for her. They do a big book swap every few weeks. I'm reminded that there's really only room for two people behind the counter.

At one time Dad ran the place with Grandad, but when he died suddenly, far younger than my dad is now, a new apprentice baker had to be recruited and well, that was Mum, straight out of school. Back then Marygreen was just a busy High Street, all flats over shops. Nowadays Marygreen is hemmed in by new-builds and there's a lot of commuter traffic at rush hour and not a lot of shops left – at least, not a lot of interesting ones. The florist, stationer, clothes shops, and Miss Bunton's sweet little bookshop all closed long ago.

Anyway, that's how Mum and Dad fell in love – over the currant buns and floury barm cakes – and they're still just as devoted to one another as they were when I came along. Gran moved in when I was tiny and she looked after me during shop hours, then seventeen years later I was the one looking after her.

Maybe you think seventeen is a bit young to become a carer? All across the country right this second there are kids, tiny ones – primary school age, even – helping to look after adults, hardly any of them even recognised as carers and given no support whatsoever, so I consider myself lucky that my caring responsibilities came along when I was old enough to cope, and of course Mum and Dad were always just downstairs in the bakery or asleep upstairs, so I was never really alone.

Anyway, there I was, aged seventeen and in charge of the prescriptions, doctor's appointments, and all the other stuff too. We've lived pretty quietly ever since, not leaving our little town much, not one of us setting sail for adventure.

'Sorry, don't mind me,' Mum says, squeezing past, giving me a little reassuring rub on my arms as she goes, trying to make me feel as though I'm not horribly in the way.

They've barely needed me in the bakery in the past, only on days when one of them was ill, and that's hardly ever happened. So far this morning all I've managed to do is keep their brews topped up, sweep the floors, and wipe down the big oven. Today's decision to 'help out' feels especially futile because I could fit all that cleaning into my usual three o'clock wipe down and that only takes me an hour max. So I slink even further back towards the fridges and make myself look busy rearranging the little juice cartons as I listen to Dad happily working the till and calling comments over his shoulder, chipping in brightly with the customers' conversations.

They're happy, my parents, and perfectly at home, even if they do seem to have the same three conversations over and over again: the weather, the roads, and reiterations of the same small town gossip the customers have heard over at the butcher's or at the corner shop on their way here.

Mum must have heard me sighing to the milk cartons because she turns and says, 'Jude, you've been very helpful indeed, but why don't you go and have a break? You could visit Gran again if you're at a loose end?'

'She's on the New Start Village magical mystery coach trip today, remember?'

'Ah yes, so she is,' Mum says breezily. 'Well, go check the post. Maybe one of your job applications got a reply?'

'I think they'd email rather than write a letter,' I mutter, feeling like a sullen teenager getting under everyone's feet and in front of the entire queue of customers too – one of whom is my old high school maths teacher, Mrs Patterson. She's raising an eyebrow at me.

I never was any good at maths and Daniel and I used to muck about something rotten in her classes. She told us once that we'd 'amount to nothing without a solid grounding in mathematics', but Daniel spends all his days doing actual applied maths working out dosages and prescriptions, and he's in charge of the staff rotas for his team, so Mrs Patterson was wrong about him. Maybe she was right about me, though. I slink out the back door and upstairs to our place.

Nope, not one email in my inbox. I applied on spec to all three of the county's libraries and our one bookshop, a big corporate thing, all celebrity bestsellers and hardbacks, but still an utter treasure trove for people like me, fifty minutes' bus journey away at the retail park.

It's hitting home that I hadn't actually put much planning into a career after my degree, thinking that I'd be looking after Gran for many years to come.

What am I supposed to do with myself now? That's been my mantra for days.

Daniel and I had a brainstorming session over his kitchen table last night and made a long list of job options. Most of them required special training or a Master's degree or something else that would take time and money. Even tutoring kids for their English Higher exams isn't a possibility without any teaching experience. 'There's always dog walking?' Daniel had said, looking optimistic. 'Or babysitting?'

'Or I could get a paper round?' I replied, flatly.

'A job's a job,' he shrugged, and I looked back at our list. I'd written:

- *English tutor*
- *Bookseller*
- *Librarian*
- *Book conservation type of job (does that even exist? Probably not, sounds too lovely to be real)*

Our list may as well read 'lion tamer' or 'hot air balloonist' for all the likelihood I have of launching into any of those careers at twenty-nine. I found myself thinking that I could always try to get a loan and launch myself into more training of some kind. It was all just a bit overwhelming, to be honest.

Daniel, sensing my panic, topped up my wine glass and changed the subject but that only made things worse. 'Have you thought about what you want to do for your thirtieth?' I couldn't help spluttering at my wine.

I had planned on dinner with Mack, so he could meet my family at long last, somewhere smart – and conveniently near his house so he'd be more likely to agree to come along in the first place. Hadn't that idea burst like a bubble!

'My thirties are on hold until I've got my future worked out,' I told Daniel, and even though he threw me that eye-rolling, ironic expression he does when he thinks I'm being over dramatic, he didn't say anything else, and he helped me drown my sorrows along with four of the day's unsold chocolate eclairs.

So, here I am, no further forward with my job hunt and booted out of the bakery because I'm in the way even there.

Trying to think positively, I tell myself it's only been ten days since I sent out my CV and there may be news on the way. I just have to be patient and keep scanning the job alerts online, but what do I do in the meantime? I can't just potter around the house all day.

I decide I'll make something nice for Mum and Dad's dinner so it's waiting for them at three when they're done. They eat so early in the afternoon. In fact everything in our house runs three hours ahead of real time. I look through the cupboards. Bolognese? No, lasagne.

My preparations are cut short by the doorbell and a letter that needs to be signed for. I bring it inside and tear into it, feeling a little buzz of nervous energy as I pull out the papers asking myself why a library or a bookshop would send an invitation to a job interview by recorded delivery.

That's when I notice it's not for me at all. It's for Mum and Dad, and it's from that big developer, the company that built New Start Village and bought up Daniel's parents' clothes shops. They've been trying to buy as many of the shops on the high street as they can. The greengrocer and the post office have already been redeveloped (now they're a trendy barber shop and a bottled craft ale place with flats above), and here they are offering Mum and Dad a whopping amount of cash for *our* shop and house.

> *Further to our discussions, we await your response to the offer of £250,000 for your premises, to include Crawley and Son Bakers and the three-bedroom apartment above. Cash transfer will take place on 13th August dependent upon return of the enclosed paperwork, signed and witnessed, and with it your agreement that all occupants will leave the property vacant within one calendar month of signing.*

I read it again just to be sure. 'Our *discussions*?' Mum and Dad *know* about this? I know they've been talking about retiring for a while now, but selling the bakery and our home in one fell swoop?

Staggering to the sofa, I've already started berating myself for being cross. I should be pleased for them, and I am – well, I will be in a minute, once I catch my breath.

This is their 'out', the opportunity to retire they've been waiting for. If they sell up, for the first time in their lives they won't be phenomenally skint in spite of grafting every day except Sundays for thirty-three years.

They won't have to look across the street at the long queue snaking out of Greggs at lunch times, agonising over whether sticking to making Grandad's lovely traditional bakes was really a good idea.

They can take all those holidays they've always talked about but never been on. Come to think of it, Katie from the travel agent did drop round a 'winter sun' brochure the other day and I thought it was weird at the time.

No more three a.m. get-ups for the pair of them. Dad's forever saying how much harder it is to face the alarm clock in the morning, especially in winter.

I turn over the letter in my hands, along with the formal-looking paperwork that's attached. No need to take it downstairs to show Mum and Dad right this second. They're busy, and I know what they'll decide anyway. They're going to grab this opportunity and go for it, start living for themselves as opposed to living to work.

I pull Gran's old blanket over me on the sofa and curl up on my side, thinking of her words, 'you must *live* your life'.

It seems events are conspiring to shove me out of my cosy nest, my comfort zone. I feel like *Alice Through the Looking Glass* and everything is sickeningly distorted and out of reach. Maybe if I close my eyes for a while, when I wake up things will be back to the way they were, with me and Gran together again in our gingerbread-scented home, and all our routines running like clockwork – predict-able, cosy, and safe.

Chapter Five

I didn't go down to the bakery this morning. Mum said I should probably have a lie-in after our long talk last night. They both stayed up 'til gone nine – which is unheard of for my parents – and Dad wanted to finish the bottle of bubbly he'd bought to celebrate signing the paperwork.

At first I couldn't face a glass but as they chatted about all the things they'd planned to do but put on hold over the years, and Mum's eyes shone under the kitchen lights, and Dad burst into happy, relieved tears twice, I couldn't help get swept up in it too.

None of us talked about where I'd live or what I'd end up doing after the sale. I think Mum and Dad assumed it went without saying I'd be welcome to move in with them, but there was a hint of strain in the air at the unsaid words.

Maybe they were waiting for me to say, 'Guess what, you guys, I'm moving out – I've got a flat and a job lined up!' but that wouldn't be true, so we all just kept sipping the bubbly and when I came back from changing into my PJs I caught them waltzing around the kitchen even though there wasn't any music. They were laughing together quietly, giggling almost, and communicating all their excitement for the future with their eyes. I sneaked off to my room, leaving them to their celebrations.

So now I'm in bed, the summer morning light is harsh on my tired eyes even with the blinds shut and there's a horrible drilling sound coming from somewhere outside. I stumble out of bed to see what's going on, only to find a hardhat-wearing bloke up a ladder immediately beneath my window fixing a sign to the outside wall. If I crane my neck I can make out the words.

Acquired by New Start Developers
Opening this Christmas: Luxury Vaping Supplies Store
Rental flats above: Three self-contained designer units to let

They don't hang about, do they? In a matter of months the only home I've known will be gutted and partitioned off to make a new shop, three teensy flats and a tonne of cash for New Start Property Developers.

I don't expect the big sobbing sound that erupts from somewhere under my heart and at first I'm startled to hear it over the relentlessness of the workman's drill. I'm all for plonking myself down where I'm standing and just howling like an injured wolf, but my mobile's ringing.

'Gran?' I answer, not even looking at the number. It's almost time for our ten a.m. chat so who else is it going to be?

'Judith?'

It's not Gran. Of course: she's got a cookery lesson today. 'Who's this?' I've said the words when it clicks. I know exactly who it is even though this is the very first time they've ever rung this number. It's Mack, and he sounds gentle and quiet, speaking almost in a whisper.

The traitorous little cutpurse in me, greedy for something that's not mine, betrays me and my heart leaps. He's had second thoughts. He's dumped that Fresher and come back to me! I'm struggling to hear the little voice in my head reminding me he's a spineless oil slick of a man.

'It's Rupert,' he says, and his low whisper makes me shiver. I'm unsure if it's the good kind of shiver or not; my feelings are churning like a tornado.

I resolve to try and sound sensible and sophisticated. I'll be the woman he wanted me to be back before my graduation.

'Oh, you all right?' That didn't come out quite as refined as I hoped it would.

'Yes, *umm*, listen…'

Oh my God, he really does want me back! I can hear it in his voice.

'A letter arrived today, addressed to the both of us. It's from Borrow-a-Bookshop in Devon?'

'Oh, OK.' I pause and force myself to think. Now my heart starts pounding because I'm realising what this means. 'We've made it to the top of the queue?' I ask, feeling a sudden thrill of nerves and excitement recalling the way I felt responding to the advert all those months ago, having only just found out it was possible to actually rent a bookstore and live in it for two whole weeks.

I'd literally squealed when I saw the advert in Gran's magazine and got totally carried away, dreaming of travelling all the way to the Devonshire seaside and selling books, imagining me and Mack behind the counter together, getting his undivided attention, living the bookish, cerebral life I'd always dreamed of.

Gran told me I had to at least apply, and since there was such a long waiting list the whole thing hadn't felt like a real possibility at the time, so I went for it, paying the money up front – clearing out basically all of my childhood building society savings – the only way to secure a place on the bookshop's waiting list.

Mack's voice reaches me through the dizzy feeling that's overtaken me. 'A couple have pulled out, so the bookshop's ours from Saturday morning if we want it, but I've to let them know our decision by the end of the day.'

He said 'ours'. He did, he said 'ours'! We're a 'we' again, just like that? 'Right, I, *umm*… so what do you want to do? Are we going?' I say.

Mack's breezier now. 'To be honest, I'd forgotten all about it, and I've admin to do here, of course, but…'

'Yes?' Damn me and my annoying optimism.

'We *could* go.'

The phone feels a bit slippery in my hand. I have to sit down on the carpet. I lean back against the wall and am immediately aware that the workman has swapped drilling for heavy hammer blows on the other side of the brickwork. Each strike reminds me that not only is my family home sold and I've nowhere to go, but I've no job here or anywhere else. I *could* go to the bookshop for a fortnight. *We* could go.

He's whispering again. 'Two weeks by the seaside reading books sounds rather pleasant.'

I register the little hint of desperation – or flirtation? – in his voice.

'I've got a lot of reading to catch up on for this research project and you could enjoy yourself prettifying the shop all day and in the evenings we could—'

He's cut off at his end by a woman's voice saying, 'Rupert Bear, where *are* you hiding yourself?' and I hear his hand covering the mouthpiece, trying to muffle the exchange that comes next, but his voice is clear enough for me to make out the false jollity.

'As I was saying, Chancellor, the bid's coming along nicely. I have a feeling we'll be successful and we can arrange my sabbatical for this time next year…'

The hammering outside my window suddenly stops and in the silence I hear a different beat; my blood rushing and pulsing in my head. My eardrums seem to throb as it gets louder and I realise I am absolutely bloody livid.

He's not alone. Of course he isn't. He's whispering not with tenderness but because he's trying not to be overheard. To think I was almost sucked back in as though Mackageddon never happened, as though I didn't learn a single thing from Anne Elliot.

He's back now, saying, 'Sorry about that, you know how it is…' and I know for sure some poor, hoodwinked girl has just been hustled out of the room. Some girl just like me. My mind's racing now.

Of course he'd forgotten that I applied for a chance to run the bookshop. He was barely listening that night as I hunched over my crummy old laptop writing the application letter – old school style, no online presence for this bookshop – chattering away about how lovely it would be to be a bookseller by the sea and how romantic a fortnight's holiday would be, fantasising about working together all day and exploring Clove Lore together all evening.

I told him all about how I'd never even been to Devon, let alone stayed in a sweet little harbour village with a dreamy bookshop. I remember enthusing for at least an hour and he'd nodded once or twice, throwing me cursory glances over the frames of his specs. I'd been so wrapped up in the idea of us living a bookish life, however temporary, I'd failed to see *yet again* that this man simply couldn't care less about me and my dreams.

'Who is it this time?' I practically spit the words.

'I beg your pardon?' he says, haughtily. I can't believe he's going to try to brazen this out.

'Who are you seeing this time? Tell me she's at least a postgrad and not some poor Fresher with stars in her eyes and a complex about smart-looking men in wool suits?'

'*Hah*,' he laughs, as though I'm such a funny little thing. 'I don't know what you're talking about, Judith.'

'Rupert?' I'm not calling him Mack, he doesn't deserve my cutesy boyfriend name.

'Yes?'

'I'm going to report you to your best pal, the Chancellor.'

For a moment I hear him waver, considering whether he should press on and try to wheedle a fortnight by the sea surrounded by literary treasures and the chance of a few shags with one of his old secret girlfriends, or risk exposure in the faculty. Then he gives up.

'Judith, be reasonable,' he hisses stiffly.

'And if you don't send that poor girl home right this second and promise to keep your hands off the student body for the rest of your career, I might accidentally forward this phone call to the *Daily Mail* and then your precious standing in the department will be well and truly fu—'

'You recorded this?'

That's got his attention. This is the first time I've ever heard him lose his cool, and no, of course I haven't recorded our call. I'm not a TV detective and I don't think Mum's hand-me-down Nokia from the turn of the century is quite up to the job of catching a sad old perv in the act, but from the way he's panting and swallowing I know he *thinks* I have and soon that girl will be shoved out onto his driveway. Poor thing.

41

Little does she know that, thanks to me, she's narrowly avoided being passed over at the end of term for one of her pals in another subject area.

'Judith, you mustn't... I mean, please understand...' He's spluttering and muttering away, full of panic, but I'm not listening. I'm sinking.

How has all this happened? One minute I'm Gran's carer and Mack's girlfriend dreaming of our future together (albeit a fantasy future he never actually promised me), the next I'm single and unemployed, not even a student anymore. And all it took was one call from Mack dangling the promise of a dreamy bookshop escape in front of me and I was almost drawn in again! No sooner was my heart pounding with excitement than the illusion faded. There's no future for us, there is no 'us', and worse than that, there's no bookshop holiday. I feel far worse about this than I do about this confirmation that Mack and I are completely over forever. It's not like I can go on my own, is it?

Mack's still wittering on, telling me how I have to understand that for a man in his position it's impossible to conduct relationships in the usual way, what with him being so over-worked and stressed and so often thrown into the path of temptation.

'Temptation?' The word makes something click in my brain and I throw it back at him.

'Well, you know, these undergraduate girls, they're so flirtatious and dead set on getting what they want—'

'Which is?' I butt in.

'Well, a... mature mind to guide them...'

'*Ugh!* So that's how you saw me? Immature? A flirt? An opportunity to flex your brainpower and your ego in front of an impressionable student who doesn't understand she's being diverted from her studies by an old lech exploiting his position of power?'

'I didn't hear you complaining when you were borrowing my books or drinking my wine, lying in my bed—' His voice is so calm, a familiar dry monotone... I realise it's his lecturing voice.

'Stop right there,' I say, and I'm surprised how commanding I sound. It gives me a little fizzy feeling of power and… joy, I think. 'I don't need you. I never needed you, or any of the fancy trappings of intellectual life that you gather around you, or your sweet talk when nobody was in earshot. I don't need any of it.' In my head I'm doing the world's fastest cost/benefit analysis weighing up how I can regain some pride right here and now in front of Mack against the fact I'll be a puddle of anxiety and shock later on. Sod it, I'm going to say it anyway. I've decided.

'Rupert, I'll be going to that bookshop, and I'll be going *alone*. Make sure you tell them that, as soon as you hang up. *I* paid the three hundred and eighty quid. *I* made the booking in *my* name, albeit they've got your address and phone number because like a gullible fool I tricked myself into believing we were an actual couple with an actual future. No, this is *my* dream. You said you'd forgotten all about it, just like you'd forgotten all about me. Tell the bookshop Jude Crawley accepts their offer and I'll be there on Saturday afternoon.' This bit makes my voice shake, but now I find I'm standing up again, straight backed and head held high. 'And Rupert?'

'Yes?' he says begrudgingly.

'Never call me again.' I hang up, shaking and elated and ready to weep all at once.

Chapter Six

Once I'd calmed down again, a big part of me was hoping Mum and Dad would say no, I couldn't have the van, and no, I couldn't go off gallivanting to Devon to prettify a bookshop when I was needed at home. Yet, they didn't. In fact, Dad got up, marched straight over to his coat by the door and dug the van keys from his pocket saying, 'No bakery, no need for a van, is there?'

'Of course you should go. It sounds very exciting, Jude,' Mum said, rummaging in the fridge for the rolled Victoria sponge that hadn't sold earlier that day, and we all sat round the kitchen table and talked about it over tea.

'Don't you need me to help with the move?'

'All taken care of, love,' Mum reassured me, so that's that.

Mum and Dad are only going along the road to one of the new-build two beds with views over the green belt so it's not a big trek or anything. The removal lorry's arriving on Monday morning, the sixteenth, and by then I should be settled in Devon.

'We'll get your things moved into your room, and you can unpack when you get back from your bookshop. It's only two weeks, not forever. Think of it as a well-earned holiday,' said Mum.

There's been a lot of talk of holidays in the last few days since the sale paperwork arrived from New Start Developers. In fact, I had to witness a staggeringly long runway show only the night before as Dad modelled his new summer clothes – the highlights were his neon orange board shorts and white knees and Mum had her turn too, twirling in a series of new floral sundresses. They've embraced retirement already and are all set for their upcoming month-long Greek islands cruise. They'll be gone by the time I get back from

Devon. It's been lovely watching their excitement, actually, even if it's all happened breathtakingly fast.

Getting passport photos taken at the key-cutters down the road the other day was a truly momentous occasion for all of us.

'Imagine getting to fifty-five and never having owned a passport,' Dad had marvelled, turning the strip of pictures over in his hands.

I had mine done too because Mum said I should be prepared for any eventuality, but I can't see how it'll get put to use any time soon. Devon's already *way* out of my comfort zone as it is, let alone hopping on a plane to some exotic destination.

So, to sum up, no, they don't need me. It's a feeling I'm becoming increasingly familiar with this summer. Even Daniel got over my bookshop news pretty sharpish and came straight over when he finished his shift, bringing a suitcase for me to borrow.

'What's this?' I said, opening the door.

'In case you change your mind. I'm here to witness the packing.'

'Change my mind?'

'*Mm-hmm.*' He wheeled the case past me and bumped it up the stairs into my room. As usual he's got me pinned pretty accurately. I'd spent a few sleepless nights catastrophizing about all the things that could go wrong and hoping I'd get a phone call to say there'd been a mistake and the bookshop wasn't mine after all. In fact, that would have been a massive relief, if I'm honest, but Daniel wasn't having any of that. After he had filled me in on the latest instalment of his long-running battle of wills with a young trainee nurse, Ekon-something-or-other, fresh out of college and not enjoying taking orders from the only slightly older Daniel, he went through the clothes I'd picked out for my trip with a critical, amused eye.

'There's the seven and a half hour drive to consider, first of all,' I told him while he ransacked my wardrobe. 'And it'll probably be closer to ten hours in our old banger of a van. And that's *if* I even survive the drive and I don't accidentally end up on a ferry to Calais or something. You know I'm not great with maps.'

He just laughed at my driving concerns so I switched tack. 'Then there's the till and the money side of things,' I confessed. 'Maths anxiety is *A Thing*.'

Daniel was tipping out a bag of old t-shirts onto my bed and picking through them like the fashion maven that he is. Cruelly, he chucked most of them onto what he'd designated the charity shop pile. I quickly rescued Mum's ancient Siouxsie and the Banshees t-shirt and shoved it behind me for safe keeping.

'Tills do all the counting for you though. How can you go wrong?' he shrugged. I could tell that a split second later he was struck by the memory of me ballsing up the money last Christmas when I was needed in the bakery to help with the Christmas cake orders while Mum went on a rare shopping trip with Auntie Anne. Somehow I managed to lose about fourteen quid that day and even when Dad went through the till receipts he couldn't figure out how I'd managed it.

'Granted, your command of numbers is… inimitable,' he said, 'but honestly, how much money's a little bookshop going to take in one day? You can't make much of a mess of a few quids' takings, can you? You can repay any disparities with your wages anyway.'

'That's the thing,' I cried. 'There are no wages. Any profits go straight to the shop charity, they're not mine. So I'd literally be swindling the shop if I made mistakes!'

'You're going a bit blue, Jude. Can you breathe, please?' He's so matter-of-fact, it would be annoying coming from anyone else. Stuff like that comes easily to Daniel but he's never judged me for being hopeless with arithmetic. 'Listen, you're capable and competent, you'll be all right. Just have a backup calculator by the till and make sure you write down everything you sell on paper, to be on the safe side.' He'd come to sit beside me, bringing a bundle of clothes with him. 'What's *harder* to sort out, Judith Crawley, is the mystery of your wardrobe. Consider please, Exhibit A.'

He was holding up four pairs of what I call my 'Oxford bags'; loose trousers in tweedy materials or cotton, a sea of wide-legged beige, twill and pinstripes. He dropped them on my lap. This was followed by two waistcoats, one that used to belong to Grandad – pretty sure it was part of *his* father's demob suit (it's got a gorgeous, snatched Forties-style waist) –and another I found in a charity shop.

I'd bought them after watching *Annie Hall* and falling head over heels for Diane Keaton's seventies androgynous style. I even raided the wardrobe for Grandad's ties and wore the whole thing combined with skinny shirts and Mum's brown leather belt and – I'm embarrassed to admit this now – a taupe, nineteen-eighties bowler hat that used to be Daniel's mum's and was destined for the bin until I rescued it.

Looking at my everyday wardrobe chucked on the floor now it's more reminiscent of a scarecrow than Diane's cool Anglophile style, but six years ago, starting uni, it conveyed exactly the preppy, straight-out-of-the-pages-of-*Brideshead Revisited* look that I was aiming for, even though my never-behaves-itself flicky bob and five-foot-not-very-much curvy frame belie the fact I'm not the willowy, quirky aristo' I wanted to portray myself as.

That's exactly how I rocked up on my first day at uni, thinking everyone would be sartorially experimental like me and I was horri-fied to find my classmates all wearing leggings or sweats, but I'd stuck with it – ditching only the hat. It was A Look and I'd invested the only money I had in it and I've worn it every day since.

'Can I say something?' Daniel was humorously biting his lip and doing that amused-with-himself head wobble thing that he does, so I knew he was going to say it anyway. 'This whole bijou, button-down shirts and brogues business? Do you *really* feel like yourself in it?'

'Well, sort of…' Yup, pinned, as usual. Now that Mackageddon (the word seems to have stuck) had me questioning everything I'd previously thought was glamorous and appealing, I was beginning to realise those clothes were wearing me and not the other way around.

'You don't really want to stay here, do you?' Daniel said suddenly, giving me a level look. 'Passing up the first opportunity for a bit of fun that's come along in ages?'

I sighed and let my shoulders slump. 'I've never been anywhere on my own, and I'm almost thirty, it's pathetic… and it's scary.'

Daniel nodded. 'All those years you gave to your Gran, well... they're over now. She's off doing her thing. It's your turn. You know, I always wanted you to come to Spain and Ayia Napa with the nursing lot, and that time I went to New York, remember?'

Of course I remembered. I'd longed to go too but it was never an option for me, so I'd told myself, and everyone else, that I was needed at home, possibly more than I really was, especially recently when Gran's been so mobile and fit. Maybe I was using her as a bit of an excuse, towards the end.

Daniel had squeezed my hand and smiled. I'm sure he knew what was going on in my head.

'Let's see what we can do with this stuff, eh? Maybe you'll find your style this summer, if you just let life happen to you a bit, go with it?'

I'd nodded and felt sure I was going to cry until I saw Daniel rummaging in the half-packed suitcase and pulling something out. 'Seriously, Jude, braces?' He twanged them straight into the charity shop bag.

'Hey! I liked those.' This was met with an incredulous laugh and so I'd rammed the bowler hat down onto his head and we laughed away the rest of the day, trying new outfit combinations and working on something that better suited a bookseller, literature lover and holidaymaker-slash-brave-adventurer setting out alone for the south west coast.

And that's how I ended up here, at three a.m. on a Saturday morning in the middle of August, standing by Dad's van, engine running, suitcase in the back, ready to leave.

Daniel's looking approvingly at my outfit, even though I'm absorbed in snivelling into a tissue right this second. It was actually my idea to combine my old band t-shirts with the waistcoats and the now gorgeously tailored and turned-up Oxford bags (thanks to Daniel and his clever sewing machine skills). I've ditched the brogues – too clumpy for summer and too smooth-soled for safely navigating the steep, cobbled streets of Clove Lore. Instead I'm in my trusty old

Converse, the white high-tops I've had for years, and I threw on an old grey The Cranberries t-shirt to complete the look.

'I've got something for you, for the journey,' Daniel says, producing some ancient cassettes I instantly recognise. Mix tapes I made for him on Mum and Dad's clunky old stereo when we were just kids. 'Going through all your old t-shirts reminded me of these. Thought they might keep you calm on your epic drive.'

That was a definite wobble in his voice as he handed them over. He's as sentimental about these things as I am. I scan my teenage handwriting on the cassette and smile at the playlist: emo favourites from fifteen years ago alongside songs my parents loved by The Cure, Blondie, and Gary Numan. By the time I was in sixth form their taste had rubbed off on me and now they're an indelible part of my life's soundtrack.

I rest the tapes on the dashboard where I'll be able to reach them as I drive and I pull Daniel in for one last hug. He can't meet my eyes when we pull apart and luckily Dad's here now, hurrying me along, but also not wanting to say goodbye.

'You'd better get going. You've got everything?' He gives his big blue bakery van a pat and says, 'She's full of diesel. That'll get you to at least Bristol, I reckon.' He gulps a bit and glances inside the back of the van. 'I've secured the sacks. Just don't take any sharp bends at speed or you'll end up covered in flour.'

I glance inside too. He's given me the last of the bakery's flour, eggs and sugar, and there's a ginormous tub of marge in there beside my suitcase. I've got a bookshop café to run, remember?

That fact's been weighing on my mind at nights because the only thing I was ever any good at baking was Grandad's scone recipe – handy if you're running a café in Devon – but I've only ever made a dozen at a time before and those were just for Gran and her pals to eat. I imagine I'll have to make far bigger batches than that at the bookshop… or will I? It's all a mystery until I get there and see what footfall's like. Maybe I won't get a single customer all fortnight. On the bright side, I'll have plenty scones to live off.

'Take this,' Dad says, just as Mum joins him, still in her pyjamas. She slips under his arm. Dad hands over a scuffed, floury notebook. 'My dad's recipes, the ones we used in the bakery. They're all in there, in case you want to branch out. Scones are on page three.' I watch Dad's chest heave a bit at that. I've never seen this little book before and I clutch it to myself.

'I'll take good care of it,' I promise. That sets Mum off sniffing into Dad's shirt sleeve.

I'm too nervous about the drive ahead to cry any more so I give everyone a tight hug and say my farewells with a cold feeling of dread in my stomach. It was hard enough saying goodbye to Gran yesterday at New Start Village. Thankfully it was cut short by the two o'clock mojitos coming round on a trolley and the whole place erupting to the sound of Wham!'s 'Club Tropicana' over the speakers. The last I saw of her she was snaking through the recreation room door in a very slow conga, flirtatiously telling one of her pals – Kenny Simpson who used to run the post office – to mind where he was putting his hands.

I manage to get my seatbelt done even though my hands are shaking and I slam the van door shut. Dad shouts in the open driver's window, 'Mind you don't get any egg wash down the sides of your scones or you won't get an even rise.'

Daniel's got his fingertips steepled over his wobbling bottom lip and my voice cracks when I shout out, 'I'll be seeing you,' over the noisy engine.

I pull away, waving an arm out the window, too nervous of crashing to glimpse back in the mirror at my little family blowing kisses and calling out, 'Good luck!' from the pavement outside the little bakery that is now no longer my home.

Chapter Seven

Palm trees! There were palm trees everywhere, all along the coast. And every now and then I'd catch a glimpse out the corner of my eye of something glittering. Turns out it was the sea, and I *swear* it was a tropical turquoise shade. I've never seen anything like it (it's an hour and a half's drive to the coast from Marygreen, and the Scottish water's always a sensible navy or slate grey). This part of the world is something else.

I can safely say I was beginning to enjoy the drive at last as I hit Devon and turned down towards the coast, even if my nerves were still rattling from the congested carriageways and drivers roaring past me and beeping angrily because poor old Diane really can't go much over sixty. Oh, that's what I named Dad's van, around about Penrith when the motorway madness was kicking in.

I really feel like Diane and me have bonded now, after all the singing along to Daniel's mix tapes and that half hour where I cried over the steering wheel in a Wolverhampton lay-by and a nice police lady made me jump when she banged on the window and asked me if I was all right.

She checked my driver's licence and looked me over like I had two heads and eventually gave me some tissues and poured me some tea from her Thermos. It was a momentary blip, I told her; I was emotional because this was a big day for me for all sorts of reasons. I was leaving home for the first time and determined to prove myself making a go of running a shop I'd never even set foot in, and I'd made a promise to myself to get stuck in to village life and meet new people and stop holding back from trying new things and even though I was nervous about cashing up at night alone I'd try my best and... that's when I'd stopped wittering. The police officer was giving me a weary look like she regretted stopping for me, so I smiled and told her I'd be OK from there.

The sight of her waving me off and giving me a flash of blue lights as I joined the slow lane again really got my head straight for the rest of the drive, and now here I am. In Devon. And it's pissing it down.

I don't know where the sun went but I haven't seen it since around about the time I learned there was an actual place called Westward Ho! with an actual exclamation mark. That's where I stopped for chips and scoffed them in a Tesco Express car park because I was ready to pass out with hunger. I don't know what that place name's all about but I love it. More places could use punctuation for added drama. Milton Keynes? has a ring to it, and three little dots could really build some anticipation for visitors to Yorkshire's Thornton-le… Beans.

Anyway now I'm here, still sitting in Diane and I can't seem to peel my hands from her wheel somehow. The rain is pelting off the windscreen and it's suddenly gone quite dark even though it's only three in the afternoon. Diane's wipers couldn't cope with the downpour so I turned her engine off.

We're straddling two parking spaces in this National Trust car park; she's just that wide, what can I say? I hope it doesn't get us a ticket.

The sea wall's blocking the view of what must be a rainy harbour or beach. Over the noise of the rain beating on the windscreen I can just about hear the sounds of a fierce tide sloshing across rocks.

I know I've got to find the bookshop where Mr de Marisco, the owner, said he'd be waiting for me but he was expecting me about, oh, at least two hours ago, and I wouldn't be surprised if he's got annoyed and wandered off to get some lunch at last.

From my limited experience with bookish types – well, OK, with Mack – I know they can be cerebral and brooding and don't like to be kept waiting or to be distracted from whatever their pet project is that day.

I suppose it *was* nice of Mack to forward me the email from the bookshop owner with the arrival arrangements. I had told him not to contact me again so at least he's not being vindictive or anything.

I didn't report him in the end. Knowing he's on campus shitting himself every time his inbox blinks with a message from his old mate the Chancellor is enough closure for me to be getting on with for now. So, why can't I get out of the van?

When I see I don't have a signal on my phone to ring Gran and tell her I've made it, the relief at getting here in one piece gives way to a sudden sense of my extreme remoteness from my family and I feel the prickle of tears.

I've never been this far from home and from Daniel. Part of me is wishing myself back there and into my pyjamas. Then I think of the boxes lying packed up in what, come Monday, is no longer my childhood bedroom. Three cardboard boxes of books, a Perspex star award, and some worn old clothes doesn't seem like much to show for a life.

I try not to think of the removals lorry that'll be pulling up on Monday morning, and how Dad will probably cry when he gives away the keys to his father's bakery and I won't be there to comfort my parents. My brain almost said 'when they need me most,' but actually, that's simply not true. My folks have got each other and a new home and holidays to look forward to and Gran's got all her mates around her, and Daniel's off conquering the world of nursing and keeping his unruly trainee in check. And I've got… well… I look over my shoulder into the dark recesses of Diane's back seats… I've got a sack of flour, a humungous tub of marge, two dozen eggs, a suitcase of old clothes and Grandad's recipe book. Oh no, here come the tears again.

Chapter Eight

There's a little break in the clouds so I haul Daniel's suitcase out of Diane and reach for my bag, (which is actually just a bookshop tote full of treasured books that I couldn't bear to leave at home) and my wallet and phone.

I spot a faded sign on the back wall of a building towering over the car park. Shaped like a pointing hand, it reads '*Up-along*' so I guess that's where I'm going.

Dragging the suitcase up the grey stone steps towards an archway under the building isn't especially easy but I'm trying to be 'present' and take it all in.

There's ozone, wet sand and salt and delicious cooking smells in the air and I hear shushing waves and the cries of gulls. I can't see the birds anywhere but somehow I feel as though they're watching me struggling with my case and laughing. A few spots of rain hit me and I don't like the lowering look of those clouds. There'll be another downpour soon, I reckon.

Once I'm under the archway I'm presented with another signpost. This time it's got arms pointing in every direction.

> Harbour and The Siren's Tail Pub

> Up-along, shops and visitors' centre

'Right! Obviously,' I say aloud. 'Glad I know where the donkeys are kept.' I'm shaking my head, chuckling in bewilderment when I step out from the archway and— just *wow*! I thought I'd seen seaside views before, but this?

To my left a great arm of sea wall reaches out into choppy, summer-storm water. The wall is giving a protective hug to the boats bobbing on their chains in the tide, and out at the end of its stone arm stands an imposing inn, rising out of the sea, all whitewashed walls and red geraniums in boxes beneath every one of the many little windows that must be guest bedrooms. Even though there's nobody to be seen standing by the windows I have the uncanny feeling of being observed.

In front of me the waves slosh up a sloping shore of grey pebbles where gulls jump and flap, picking over stones at the water's edge. There are lobster pots, nets and buoys, and men washing down boats.

The grey beach seems to stretch on and on away from me for miles in a long, pebbly curve watched over by the towering rocks all topped with what looks like a treacherous, windy, green coastal path.

To my right – that's where my feet are already wanting to lead me – is the steepest street I've ever seen, only a couple of metres wide in parts and on each side stand white-walled cottages with little front gardens snaking all the way up the hill.

'Up-along,' I mutter to myself.

As I climb on the hunt for my bookshop, passing a few tourist families in kagoules on their way down to the beach with crabbing nets and buckets, I peer into the tiny gardens all packed with bright, clashing flowers that I don't know the names of. There are quaint little timeless touches everywhere I look: pale pink and lemon roses on trellises around the cottage doors; a milk churn on a doorstep full of flowers; an old bicycle tied to fence railings and wrapped in flapping floral bunting with a hand-painted sign over the crossbars that says, 'Harbour Mouth Cottage B&B' and 'No Vacancies'. There's a red post box that must be Victorian by the looks of it and ornate gas lamps all the way up the street, and *ooft*, this incline's making my knees ache!

How can anyone actually live here, making this climb day after day? The cobbles stretch on up ahead of me; they're slippery after the rain so I find myself holding onto the garden railings and hauling myself up. Two blokes in yellow overalls and wellies trek effortlessly past me and I wonder how they're managing it. They must be locals. Look at them bounding up the hill like it's nothing!

By the time my wheelie case has tipped over on at least five occasions I'm ready for a sit down. There's a narrow cottage that is, I'm delighted to discover, a little ice-cream shop in front of me, but the door's closed and there's a sign saying, 'Back in Ten Minutes'. I can make out the little rack of tourist postcards behind the lace curtain on its door. I take a moment to lean on the shop's gate post, dreaming of a Mr Whippy with raspberry sauce and a flake like the ones I'd have on summer trips to Eyemouth with Gran when I was little. Maybe I'm hallucinating, what with the climb, and maybe the air's thinner at this altitude, because I'm sure I can hear the chimes of an ice-cream van now.

Glancing back down the street I realise I almost missed this wonderful view of the entire bay and the brooding grey horizon. I want to wait right here and take it all in but there's a storm cloud shaped like a big black boxing glove billowing in so I'd better stop stalling and find my shop.

'Jude?'

My head snaps around at the sound of my name and I wipe at my mouth in case I was drooling at the thought of the phantom ice-cream van. 'Oh, hello!'

The owner of the voice is looking expectantly at me as though I should know him. He's probably in his late sixties and has long sandy hair tied up in a messy kind of man bun which is all windblown – in comparison to his immaculate beard which looks like it's no stranger to product and is used to getting a thorough brushing every morning.

'I'm Jowan de Marisco, the bookshop owner?'

'Ah!' We shake hands. 'How did you know it was me?'

He's smiling now, looking every inch like some kind of Breton pirate with his well-salted, weather-beaten complexion and crinkling bright blue eyes. He's in baggy olive corduroys and multiple layers of plaid cotton and fleece and has an ancient-looking scarf the colour of faded coral round his throat and, I swear I'm not making this up, a single pearl drop earring in one lobe. All he needs is a parrot on his shoulder to complete the look. He nods to my tote bag.

'Who else would be arrivin' in town with a bulging bag of books?'

I laugh. 'You got me! I had to bring some old favourites, just in case. Is that weird, bringing books to a bookshop holiday?'

'I understand,' he says, and I start to pick up his lovely, grumbling West Country accent, thick like clotted cream. 'I'm the same with John Donne. Read any?'

I scan my brain and all I can turn up is a poem about a flea that I read in my first year at uni and I can't say I was very impressed by it. '*Umm*, not a lot,' I confess. 'Sorry I'm late, by the way.' I'm mumbling about Diane's problems with scaling even the lowest hills and needing to refill her twice on the way down but he's just squinting at me.

'Late?' He shrugs, like he's never heard the word before. 'You're 'ere, aren't you?'

'Well, that's true…'

'The fellow not 'ere yet though?'

It takes me a moment to figure out what's going on. Mr de Marisco is glancing down the street looking for an invisible someone following behind me. For Mack? 'Uh, no, I thought you knew he wasn't coming?'

He juts his bottom lip, confused. 'Ain't he? Oh.'

My mind's working away ten to the dozen. What does that mean? Didn't Mack tell him I was coming alone? Mr de Marisco doesn't seem that bothered but he obviously sees me wigging out and blurts out an explanation.

'He was in a rush when we spoke, I think. Fidgety-sounding sort of fellow. Secretive? Didn't like parting with details about himself. I hope you don't mind him. Any trouble, let me know. A'right?'

He's giving me a cautious glance and I'm *really* confused now. 'I'm holidaying alone, so I'll be fine, thanks. He won't be troubling me, Mr de Marisco.'

'It's Jowan, please. Show you to your bookshop, then?' he says, still squinting in confusion but hiking a thumb up the hill and taking my case from me.

I suppose Mack *would* sound strange to Jowan. They're total opposites on the Man Scale: Ten being this big, bristly, rugged Devonshire man with a fading blue anchor tattoo stretching across the back of his hand; Zero being Mack, pale and elegant and a bit sickly looking in that aristocratic way, with all his indoorsy interests, refined manners and annoying habits, like the way he'd call his expensive watches his 'timepieces'.

'*Eugh!*' I can't help vocalising it and my spine shivers as I shake the memory of sneaky, lying Mack away.

'Beg' pardon?' Jowan turns, alarmed.

'Oh, *uh*, swallowed a bug. Ugh, *yuk*.' I'm not much of an actor, but he buys it. I fall behind his long strides, still peeking in at the gardens as we climb, when suddenly Jowan takes a sharp left turn down an alley between two cottages and I see the weathered old board on a wall saying Borrow-a-Bookshop is twenty metres this way. Doorsteps and window boxes, sleds and plant pots line the narrow route and I skip a few steps to keep up.

''ere we are,' Jowan says with a crinkle-eyed smile, though we're still winding along the cobbled path which is widening out now into a little, airy square, lit overhead with two crossing strings of white bulbs, and at its centre a palm tree in a big terracotta pot. I glimpse occasional hints of blue sea and dark sky between the grey tiled rooftops peaked like wonky wizards' hats. 'Binbags out on Tuesday nights, mind you cover 'em with the blanket or the gulls'll have 'em ripped apart and rubbish strewn everywhere, the buggers! Milk and clotted cream delivery every morning, except Monday and Thursday.

Spare key's kept at the Siren if you need 'un. Volunteers'll pop in most days to help you out, see if you've got any problems. I'll call in now and again too, but you can find me at the B&B Down-along if there's trouble. S'where I live. My mobile number's taped to the till if you need me.'

'Down-along?' I say.

'Ah, yes. Street's called Up-along if you're down at the harbour, and Down-along if you're up at the top of the village. Question of perspective.'

I'm nodding as though that's perfectly sensible but internally screaming '*what*?' Jowan's instructions keep coming though so I have to try and concentrate.

'Gold key's the front door, silver key's the cash box. Take the money upstairs at night and stow it under your bed. Not that we get many burglars round 'ere, but still. Oh, and Aldous only eats jam scones, cheese sandwiches and chicken soup, no point trying anything else, many have tried, all failed. Right, 'ere we are.'

I'm about to ask who the hell this Aldous is and will I be expected to make chicken soup for just one customer – I doubt there's a recipe for chicken soup in Grandad's baking book – when we stop at the white steps of a squat, wide cottage, and there, behind a bay window that once upon a time must have had straight frames but now they're slanting – like everything else in Clove Lore – are rows of books on display. I peer in at them. The glass looks about two hundred years old and is warped and bubbled with a greenish tinge like seawater so it's not easy to make out the titles.

I'm a little dizzy all of a sudden, but Jowan seems used to this kind of reaction and he smiles indulgently as he gives me the last of his welcome spiel. 'It's your bookshop to do as you like with. Remember, every guest changes the display by the till on their last day to reflect their own reading tastes, and you must leave it for the next bookseller to keep in place during their fortnight – nice little tradition we have 'ere, a legacy of your stay. You'll see Charles and Enid who were with us before you loved spy thrillers and espionage, so that's what they've left for you. Otherwise, do as you please, same goes for the café.'

I'm nodding and hoping I remember all this.

Up three wide and wonky stone steps is the shop door, painted a glossy sky-blue. A bell tings as Jowan unlocks it and lets it swing open.

'She's all yours,' he says, and I think I must have floated up those steps.

Of course I'd Googled my destination and discovered it was recently declared the 'Most Instagrammable Village' in England by a national newspaper, and I read the TripAdvisor comments from previous guests – only three reviews, all five stars and all raving about the sea views, the helpful locals, and the fun of playing at bookselling for a fortnight. I even found some photographs of the bookshop interior online, so I knew this place would be stunning, but now that I'm standing on the 'welcome' mat, frozen to the spot, open-mouthed, trying to take it all in, I realise none of those accounts of Borrow-A-Bookshop had done it justice.

'Why don't you lock the door and give yourself time to 'climatise?' Jowan says, and I nod and mumble my thanks. I'm dimly aware of him chuckling as he walks away, the keys still in the lock, and I have a tiny spike of panic that he really has left me to my own devices.

I want to call him back and ask him a thousand questions about how someone actually goes about running a bookshop, but I suppose that's the point of this mad experiment; I'll have to figure it out for myself. Isn't that why I wanted to come here? To prove I can do something more than prettify the place, to show Mack and everyone else I've got the gumption to go it alone, even if just for a fortnight. That, and the fact I can inhale old-book smell for two weeks and be part of something new, a community of a kind. Not that the place is full of people tripping over each other to make friends with me, at least not with a storm coming in. Clove Lore feels as though everyone's battening down hatches and hiding. It's so quiet, quieter even than Marygreen with all its boarded-up shops and scaffolding, and that's saying something.

I pull the keys free, step inside and let the door close behind me.

Chapter Nine

At first I drift around trying not to touch anything and just having a really good marvel at the place.

There are shelves from floor to ceiling lining the walls and table 'islands' with towers of books piled up on them. Here and there are little nooks and dead ends with chairs for customers to secrete themselves away with a book, and there are lovely little windows, some of them just glazed portholes, with only enough room for a plant pot on their sills. Threadbare rugs cover the floor and everything is just a little dusty and faded in the nicest way and every surface seems to be made of ancient-looking wood.

I stagger a bit making my way through the shop since every floorboard, overhead beam and shelf seems to have absorbed a hundred winters' cold and damp and a thousand spring storms and it's all dried out again over a hundred parched summer months until no surface is level. I'm convinced if I were to drop a bag of marbles in the middle of the shop floor they'd run off in every direction and disappear into umpteen mouse holes, cracks and gaps.

I'm quickly discovering that everything creaks, too. The vertiginously warped floors and the creaking sounds give me the feeling of being at sea in a strange old ark full of books.

I have to flick lamps on as I go, to illuminate all the dark cubbyholes and crannies.

Nothing is bright, except for the dried flowers in clay jugs that are dotted around the shop. Everywhere else there are the colours of old mahogany and lead paint in sage, faded burgundy and ochre. Then there's the leather and cloth book bindings – also a sludgy palette of greens, reds and black. The whole effect speaks to me of times long ago, the easy passing of the seasons, and hours happily lost engrossed in books Up-along – or is it Down-along when you're in the middle of the slope? Whatever. This place is heavenly! Happy chemicals buzz through me. This must be what pure joy feels like.

-

The spiral staircase creaks as I drag my case up, huffing and puffing as I go because I was not expecting a workout at the end of my long day's travelling. Bathroom, avocado-shell green. Nice and retro, spotlessly clean.

Behind a flimsy sliding door is my bedroom which, it turns out, comprises two single beds shoved together and a few hooks on the wall for clothes, and that's it. There's no room for anything else up here under the pointed hat of the roof. But there is a lovely big box window with a long cushioned sill inside to curl up on, and there's a view of the stormy sea and sky. A perfect reading spot.

I snap a few selfies on my phone and send them to Daniel with a heart-eyes emoji and he instantly pings an 'OMG!!!' back at me.

My stomach starts telling me it's time to find something to eat. Going down the spiral staircase is easier than going up I find, but just as creaky.

I trip over the raised threshold and into the little sunken kitchen area at the very back of the shop and my heart swells even more. Well, I say 'kitchen'… There's a crazed Belfast sink with no plug, an old gas stove with a tin kettle – the whistling kind – on the hob, and there's a metal tea caddy with '1/6d' printed on the lid. That's it, it's officially nineteen fifty-two in here.

Mercifully, there's a modern fridge in the corner and a table set for two by the window with a view over higgledy-piggledy slate rooftops below.

I clear away one of the place settings, wondering if this was the work of the previous guests, the spy-novel fans? Like everyone else they were expecting a couple to move in for the fortnight.

'It's only me, I'm afraid,' I say to the cool air as I put the dish away in a lemon-yellow cabinet that looks like it's been here since the middle of last century. I'm struck by the thought that this must be the café kitchen as well as the place I'll make my own meals. 'Not much of a café set up,' I mutter to myself, peering out at the shop floor. There are a few chairs scattered around the bookshop but nothing resembling an actual cosy café. I resign myself to making my scones in here and to the fact I'll likely only have a few customers looking for food in the coming days. What a pity.

The realisation only takes the shine off my happy new situation a tiny bit. Filling the kettle, I still find myself sighing contentedly. My nerves have calmed considerably now that I'm here among the books and nobody's watching me settling in. I can take the rest of the evening to adjust and unpack, no hurry whatsoever.

As the gas ring whooshes into life beneath the kettle, I'm trying really hard not to think about how much Mack would have loved this place. He'd raid those shelves and leave with bags full of lovely old books and he'd probably only ever read a handful of them. And there it is once again – the pang of humiliation at being taken in by him, and my embarrassment about being so green. He must have taken one look at the stars in my eyes and known I'd fall for his privileged baloney. He had the readymade bookish life I longed for, all afternoon tea and lazy evenings reading poetry on antique armchairs. But that wasn't mine. And, looking back, it was all illusory. I didn't belong there. I haven't really belonged anywhere other than at home with Gran.

But this bookshop is soaked in old-timey bookishness; it's just the kind of place I used to dream about visiting as a kid and – I can't help squealing a bit as this thought really hits home – this *is* all mine.

I revel in the strange feeling that I might actually belong somewhere for once (even if it is just for a fortnight). My name's in the guest ledger by the till. I'm fully paid up. This really is my little kingdom and I don't have to please anyone but myself for fourteen whole days.

The kettle whistles, pulling me out of my thoughts, and I'm happy to find a carton of fresh milk in the fridge alongside two strawberry tarts. There's a Post-it note stuck to the dish.

With love from Charles and Enid. These did a roaring trade in 'our' café!

Enjoy your stay, x

p.s. We found Aldous to be far less troublesome than we were led to believe. Just keep him supplied with chicken broth and cheddar butties and he'll pretty much keep himself to himself.

Aldous again! I'm not going to let whoever this picky customer is worry me right now. Not when there's a fresh pack of Devonshire cheese in the fridge and a loaf in a brown paper bag (nice one, Charles and Enid!) and my stomach is growling with hunger. I have everything I need to survive the night.

I've just got settled on a kitchen chair with my cuppa and am about to take a bite of my doorstop sandwich, when I hear it — a sort of sniffing, scuffling sound. I hadn't had this place pegged as haunted (it's got such a cosy, calm feel to it) and I'm not going to give in to the panicked thoughts racing through my head which are saying, *what if it's rats? Or mice? Mice are marginally worse than rats because they're so tiny they can poo in the sugar bowl or run right up your pyjama sleeve while you're sleeping!*

That's when I peer through the kitchen door into my shop and notice the messy jumble of rags dumped on a pile of blankets in one of the larger window alcoves overlooking the sea and I leave the sandwich and cross the shop floor to inspect it.

Is it an abandoned art project? Some kind of felting or macramé? Whatever it is, it's getting shoved in a cupboard or, better yet, chucked in the bin. I'm only feet away when I realise the bundle of beige scraps is definitely the source of the noise and it's moving. Snoring, in fact.

'A dog? How did you get in here?'

It's only now I notice there's a largish cat flap in the shop door.

I give the scruffy bundle a tentative poke and it shifts, revealing a pale brown nose and snuffling nostrils, but it doesn't open its eyes.

I'm on my way to the till to grab Jowan's phone number to ask whether he's left his mutt here and somehow hasn't realised (how is that possible?), when it strikes me.

'Oh no.' I turn back, reach for the blue collar around the dog's scruffy neck and reveal a nametag baring the legend 'Aldous'. How could I not know the shop comes with a resident dog?

Ah! Mack! Were there other emails from the bookshop trust he was supposed to forward to me? Maybe it didn't occur to him that I'd like to know I'd be sharing my holiday with a scruffy… 'Well, what breed of dog *are* you, Aldous?'

He doesn't answer and I back away into the kitchen again. I watch him sleep for a while. Only once I'm halfway through my sandwich does he move, stretching in his raggedy bed. He lifts one lid and eyes me lazily, spots the sandwich in my hand and immediately hops off his window perch.

I surrender what's left of my meal to him, but when I try to pat his matted head he backs off and turns for the door, taking my sandwich out the cat flap.

—

And that was the last I saw of Aldous all evening. I heard him return just after eleven. God knows where he'd been, but in between unpacking my things, phoning Gran and reading the bookseller's information folder Jowan left for me by the till, I'd rather forgotten about him.

I'd left him some bread and cheese in a dish and topped up his water bowl which I found under the kitchen table, and as I brushed my teeth upstairs I could hear Aldous wolfing his food and then climbing back onto his spot on the window ledge with a grumpy sort of sleepy snort.

Jowan's folder told me, *Aldous is a Bedlington Terrier. He is (possibly) thirteen years old, doesn't care much for people and is rather set in his ways. He walks himself so mind you don't obstruct his doggy door. He keeps his own hours. Don't worry if he's late coming home. Under no circumstances are you to attempt to brush him. At last count he had eight teeth but I wouldn't risk a bite if I were you. The vet grooms him quarterly and that's trauma enough (for the poor vet). Also, please don't remove or wash the items of clothing he sleeps on, they belong to him.*

Sure enough when I'd checked, I found what must once have been a nice mohair jumper now trodden into a messy nest. 'Remove it? I wouldn't touch it with tongs!' I said, and carried on settling in.

And now I'm in bed with the window open behind me and I'm listening to the shushing of the sea all the way down on the beach. The rain's still falling steadily and it's completely dark outside.

I let my eyes close and my mind turns to Marygreen and Mum and Dad packing a suitcase for their first proper holiday. Gran told me they'd been like teenagers when they'd visited her today. I'm glad they're happy, even if they too must be a bit shocked at the rapid turn of events life has taken in the last month. How can we have gone from our steady, plodding routines to everything suddenly unrecognisably different and new so quickly? The bakery sold, a new house, Gran living independently at last, my degree over, Mack moved on.

It's as though someone threw our old life up into the air and all the pieces somehow miraculously fell, right side up, neat and tidy. Every piece except me and my life. For now, there's this. A little hiatus. A fortnight where I can't really do anything about the future. I'll just have to enjoy the here and now, making the most of my bookshop escape, before my life comes crashing back down and I have to turn the pieces into something meaningful and new. For now, this bed's warm and cosy, the sea is shushing me to sleep, and I'm utterly exhausted. My eyes are as heavy as my tired body and I let myself drift off to sleep.

–

I'm not sure what started first, the half-hearted growling from Aldous downstairs or the sound of something metallic scratching at the locked shop door. I immediately jump up and secure the little hook lock inside its fastening on my bedroom door, sealing myself in.

The shop door creaks open. I grab my phone and am weighing up whether I ring Jowan or the police. Who'd be fastest to respond? Where's the nearest cop car likely to be, anyway?

I can hear a whispering voice. 'Hello, little guy, you must be Aldous.'

I notice the scruffy mutt isn't growling anymore. He's probably been slipped a poisoned Bonio. That's how they do it, you know? Burglars. They pacify the guard dog and then take out the occupants one by one before rifling through their wallets. Well, my wallet's got four pounds fifty and a Body Shop reward card in it and there's no way I'm dying for those!

Oh shit, they're on the stairs. There's actually someone climbing up the spiral towards my room.

I give up on phoning anyone, I'd be better off screaming out the window, but when I hang my head outside I realise there's nothing out there but the rooftops and the rain's falling so heavily I doubt anyone will hear me. Still, here goes, I'll just have to yell for help and pray one of those fit fishermen I saw earlier is passing by on their way home from the Siren.

'Anyone home?' A voice – definitely a man's voice – calls from the other side of my bedroom door. I'm pretty sure my heart is failing and I'm close to being officially dead from fear. 'Excuse me? Are you in there?' the voice says again, and even through my panic, I think he sounds a bit tentative and not hugely murdery, but still, if I reply, he'll know for sure I'm a woman on my own in here, and that door's pretty flimsy, even with the little hook fastening it shut. He could easily get through it with one big kick.

'Are you in there? Jude?'

I'm standing behind the door holding a hairbrush in the air as though I could backcomb this burglar to death. 'How do you know my name?' I screech in a pitchy voice, trying to sound as much like a muscle-bound WWF wrestling star as I can – as opposed to a girl from the Borders whose lifetime exercise regime consists of those three online Fitsteps classes I did in twenty-nineteen. 'That's not you Jowan, is it?'

'It's me. Elliot? I only just picked up my key from Jowan's B&B. He was pretty surprised to see me. He said you'd told him I wasn't coming?'

'*What?* How could I do that when I don't even know who the hell you are?'

'I'm the replacement for the other occupant who dropped out. Remember?'

'Honestly, you're going to have to start making sense or I'm calling the police.'

'What? No, don't do that!' I'm glad to hear the panic in his voice. 'Listen, I'm the other holidaymaker. Somebody from the bookshop charity thingy rang me the other day and said you'd had someone drop out of your booking and would I like to take their place? They rang you. The person they spoke to said that wouldn't be a problem? So here I am.'

'What?' *The person they spoke to?* My mind stops racing when I realise who's behind all this. Mack. He didn't bother informing me about this replacement person, of course, the vindictive little sod. It all makes sense now. This is what Jowan was talking about earlier when he asked if 'the fellow' was arriving with me.

I lean closer to the door and shout back. 'How can you replace my... boyfriend when there's only one bed? That's ridiculous.'

I read somewhere once that men are less likely to molest a woman they know has a boyfriend – it's some sort of cavemanish respect for another man's property kind of thing – so this little white lie is justified.

'*Uh?* But the advert says "two-bed apartment".' The murderer's voice falters. I think he's genuinely as confused as I am. 'Listen, just point me to the other bedroom and we can talk in the morning.'

'There *is* no other bedroom.' I look again at the two single beds pushed together that fill the little room. 'You're not coming in here!' I yelp, grabbing my robe and throwing it on in case somehow this guy's got x-ray eyes and he's currently getting a peep at me in my Snoopy PJs.

'Look,' he says, wearily, and I hear him slump down onto the floor at the other side of the door. 'I've travelled a long way in the rain to get here, I'm soaked through and I just want to get dry and get some sleep. Where do you suggest I go?'

'Go back down to Jowan at the B&B, he'll have a bed for you.' That's when I remember the 'No Vacancies' notice I spotted this afternoon on the bicycle chained to the B&B railings.

'I paid to stay here, though,' he says, and I hear what I'm guessing is the back of his head thwacking the door as he leans back on it, exasperated.

'But this is *my* bookshop,' I tell him. 'My booking, not yours.' I'm here alone to do some cathartic growing and a bit of healing, not to shack up with some stranger.

'You should have said that when they rang up then.'

I think of Mack using his charming, smarmy voice, telling whoever rang up that Jude would be *delighted* to lodge with another person. He's pushing it, the bloody creep. Then again, maybe Mack honestly thought there'd be another bedroom too? I try to be charitable and give my ex the benefit of the doubt. After all, I thought there were two rooms here. Just like this guy did, this…

'What's your name again?' I yell.

'Elliot, and you don't have to shout. I'm pretty sure this door's plywood.'

'Is that some kind of threat?'

'*What?* No, of course not.'

'I still don't get why you're here. You'd better start explaining quick…'

'OK, OK. I've been on the waiting list for a solo slot at the bookshop for ages now, but they prioritise couples, so I'd given up hope of ever getting here. Then last week they called me and said the chance had come up to share with someone else. I took it and they refunded your half. I thought they went through all this with you on the phone?'

'They didn't ring me. They rang my ex, OK?' There, the cat's out of the bag now. I didn't think to check my bank account, not expecting money to go *in*, an unusual occurrence for me these days. The thought of the one hundred and ninety pounds I'd stumped up for Mack's half of the holiday – he never did pay me back – suddenly boosting my finances for the fortnight is almost enough to cheer me up. Almost. 'He's not here because we broke up,' I say.

'Oh.'

'Exactly,' I reply, slumping against the door too.

When he talks again, I jump a little at how close his voice is through the thin wood. 'So what do we do now?'

'I don't know.'

'Listen, sorry I frightened you,' Elliot says and his voice is deep and hoarse. 'I thought you were expecting me. I thought there were two bedrooms. I... I can go ask at the pub if there's a bed there. It'll be closed by now, I guess, but somebody might still be up...'

A great rumble of thunder makes the walls quake and the rain responds by falling twice as hard as it was before. I'm going to have to relent, aren't I?

'You said your clothes were soaked?'

'Yeah,' he confirms, gruffly.

'There's towels in the bathroom, and hot water for a shower.'

'You don't mind if I stay?'

I do mind. I really, *really* do mind. This is *my* bookshop and *my* adventure and somehow Mack's managed to spoil it by sending me some bloke who... hold on a minute. A queasy thought strikes me.

'Jowan was talking about you earlier.'

'*Hmm?*' the voice behind the door says, a little nervously, to my mind.

'He said you were cagey, that you didn't like giving away details about yourself.' I thought that was weird at the time when I mistakenly believed Jowan was describing Mack because he *loves* talking about himself. I think I hear a sniffed laugh through the door and I stiffen. 'Who are you? Like, what do you do for a living? Where are you from?'

'*Umm*, well, I'm... I'm a teacher in a veterinary school.'

'You hesitated!' I spin round and accuse the door.

'What? No.'

'Yes you did, you hesitated.'

'I'm just cold, that's all. I'm shivering here.'

71

'How did you get here?'

'Train, then another train, then an Uber, and then I walked. The village roads are all gated off at night, so I was dropped off at the visitors' centre. The bookshop's further than you think down that hill.'

'You're really a vet?'

'*Umm*, yes.'

He definitely hesitated that time. 'You didn't say where you're from.'

'I have a flat in Cambridge. Are you done with the inquisition?'

Cambridge checks out. His voice is definitely posh, but there's a roughness undercutting it, nothing like Mack's plummy RP. It's gravelly too, like Tom Hardy playing someone a bit classy.

'Who knows that you're here?' I ask, though I'm not sure how this is supposed to make me feel better.

'Well, Jowan knows, obviously, and the bookshop charity, and *uh*, well, that's it.'

'No family?'

'No, I didn't get a chance to tell them, *umm*...' His voice tails off. 'Do you mind if I make us some coffee? I really am freezing.'

'I'm not opening the door,' I say, alarmed all over again. 'Go make yourself one.'

I hear what sounds like boots heavily scuffing the floor and he's up and walking away. The light spills under the door frame once more and I wonder how big this guy is, that he was blocking it out so well.

Pressing my ear against the door, I listen to him in the kitchen. He reads aloud the Post-it about the jam tarts (both scoffed long ago, around about the time I was drawing the avocado bath and sipping my third cup of tea) and I hear the fridge door opening and closing, the kettle whistling, and pretty soon he's back upstairs.

'I made you one too, just in case you changed your mind,' he says, and dammit, I really would like a cuppa. 'I, *uh*, brought some KitKats with me.'

Am I going to be murdered in my own room because I couldn't resist the offer of a free KitKat? 'Just leave them at the door.'

'OK, I'll go dry off in the bathroom.'

I flatten my ear against the door this time as I listen to him retreat and slip the bolt inside the bathroom. That's followed by the buzzing of the strip light coming on and the water running.

I take my chance to slide open the door and make a grab for the brew and biscuit, giving myself enough time to clock a pair of black DM boots lined up outside the bathroom beside a bulging khaki rucksack (no other luggage; this guy's travelling light), and a dripping black hooded jacket over the banister. I resent his stuff being there, taking up space, being in the way.

There's a scent in the air, which I only just catch as I slink back around the door into the safety of my room. It's something gorgeously sweet and musky, like roses and patchouli but not the hippiefied kind, the expensive kind. He smells nice. So what? I want him gone first thing. I slide the door shut and lock it again.

After a while spent deciding whether it is safe to drink the coffee and wondering if he's slipped something in it, I conclude it's probably just made from the jar of Mellow Birds I saw in the little yellow cabinet earlier, and I split the KitKat and get dunking. Soon enough, I hear Elliot step out the bathroom door and rummage inside his backpack.

'What are you doing now?' I shout.

'If you don't mind I'll change and then I'll sleep downstairs tonight? I won't come up again. Just stay in your room. What do you say?'

I'm thinking.

'If you want me to go, I will. That Uber might come back for me.'

'It's the middle of the night in one of the more sticky-out bits of rural Devon,' I say.

'So I can stay?'

'Any funny business and Aldous will have your extremities off.'

I hear a little sniffed laugh again, deep and amused, and I feel a tiny bit ridiculous. I haven't heard a peep from Aldous since Elliot arrived. I imagine he's long since over the excitement of our new flatmate and is snoring peacefully again on his windowsill.

'Aldous looks like a killer,' Elliot says as he goes downstairs, heavy-footed like he's trying to make extra sure I know he's leaving me in peace. 'Night, then,' he calls from the bookshop.

I hear a clatter as a pile of books is knocked over, followed by some low, grumbled curse words and a shouted, 'Sorry, just some books! It's OK!'

I can't help giving a tiny laugh at that, and I climb back into bed, still shaking a little from the adrenalin of the unexpected intrusion, and maybe the late night coffee has something to do with it too. I'm mentally congratulating myself on sticking up for myself and my plans for my dream holiday and wondering if this is a new, tougher me, unafraid of voicing my needs. I ask myself if this Elliot guy has spent the last thirteen years caring for others and letting their life slip slowly by. Is he newly dumped and humiliated and almost (sort of) homeless? I doubt he needs a solo break as much as I do. I'm midway through these thoughts when the old, familiar guilty feeling comes creeping back in, except this isn't my usual sense of being torn in two, wanting to dutifully help my family while swallowing my dreams and my pride and secretly, guiltily wishing I could have more from life. No, this is just plain old shame at being badly behaved.

The feeling won't leave me. I was hostile and petulant, grasping onto my bookshop like it didn't also belong to this stranger too. That isn't like me. I'm stubborn, yes, but not unkind. This is what Mack's done to me. He's made me cautious and bitter, sniping and untrusting.

I settle down, restless now, wonder how on earth Elliot's going to get any sleep tonight – he doesn't even have a blanket – but nothing could make me unbolt the door and go check on him. In the morning, when there are people out and about around the village, I'll talk to him, tell him gently why he can't stay, explain how there's been a mix-up and this is all Mack's fault and Jowan's misunderstanding, and maybe he won't mind leaving, once he knows what this break means to me. Maybe then I can get my bookshop holiday started at last.

Chapter Ten

The next morning there's no sign of last night's intruder. His boots, jacket and backpack are all gone, and for a moment I think I've dreamt the whole thing. Aldous is asleep in the window. Does he do anything else?

I've slept far longer than I wanted to. I should have been up and baking hours ago, but months of tiredness seemed to have hit me all at once and I eventually slept a long, blank sleep.

The rain's gone too so I open the shop door and breathe in the cool morning air, all sea-salty and fresh. No sign of the milk or clotted cream on the step like Jowan said. Somebody's brought it in, I guess. Could one of Jowan's volunteers have been in already? Do they even have keys? I don't want any more surprise visitors; one was quite enough, thank you.

The sky is a wonderful light blue and the cobbles in the little square before me are gleaming in the sun. What with the white walls of the surrounding buildings – the backs of little cottages, I think – and the red geraniums in pots here and there and the palm tree that stands in a terracotta pot at the centre of the square, the whole scene feels positively Mediterranean. Not that I've ever been to the Mediterranean, you understand, but this is what I imagine it's like. I rest a hand on the doorframe and smile thinking how my lovely little bookshop has weathered the decades here and is now settled, slumping and slanting, enjoying its cosy old age by the seaside in its little cobbled square.

I check my phone and it's just before nine. I'd better think about opening up the shop. Maybe it's OK to open late since it's Sunday?

The little niggling worry that's been prodding at me since I arrived yesterday really makes its presence felt now. I know I can't put it off any longer. I'll have to figure out how to master the till. Last night I found the cashbox Jowan mentioned stashed under the bed and inside there was thirty-six quid in change, which I'm guessing is the float for the till. If I can just keep the money straight for thirteen days I'll be so proud of myself, but experience tells me I'll struggle.

I'm sinking into the familiar anxiety yet again and wondering if it's too early to ring Daniel for a bit of reassurance when the figure — no, when the Wall of Man — appears before me, crossing the little square in the morning sun.

I have to let my eyes take him in bit by bit because he's kind of huge. The first thing that strikes me is the broad chest and even broader shoulders with a waist that suggests this man has a set of 'hip dips' to rival Tom Daley and is a classic 'V' (look it up online if you don't know what that means, and don't blame me if you have to delete your browsing history).

He's mostly cheekbone and long dark hair that's splayed messily over his shoulders and then there's long legs in loose dark pants that instantly have me averting my eyes, but not before I notice he's heading straight for me holding two takeaway cups. He's not exactly smiling; he's giving me more of an appraising grimace.

'Morning,' he says, stopping at the foot of the shop steps. God, his voice is deep. 'I got us some coffee up at the visitors' centre after my run.'

'Elliot?'

He gives me a look, not unkind, just incredulous, that suggests this should have been obvious, and that's when I notice the silvered scar dissecting one of his dark eyebrows. It looks recent and as though it hurt.

'I got an Americano and a cappuccino, didn't know what you'd like.' He's making a move up the steps so I awkwardly reverse into the shop again.

'*Umm*, cappuccino. Thanks.'

77

He puts it in my hand as he passes me, his height making me feel positively miniature – even more so than usual, I mean.

'And I got this for Aldous.' He pulls a dog chew from his pocket. 'They had a big jarful up at the coffee place.'

Aldous doesn't even open his eyes when Elliot places the chew next to his snout and attempts a gentle pat on his scruffy head. The dog's nostrils flare as he sniffs the gift, then shifts his head away to avoid it.

'Ah, he doesn't like it,' Elliot says. 'Maybe he's still full from the breakfast cheese sarnie I made him? He didn't want to come for a run with me either this morning, poor little guy.'

My holiday-crasher has his back to me now and I swear he's blocking out the sun from the windows at the back of the shop. This guy must be over six foot. It's kind of intimidating.

'Jowan says Aldous does his own thing... So, *umm*,' I pipe up, thinking we really should be addressing our booking mix-up. 'Listen, shouldn't we...'

'The note in the kitchen said he mainly eats chicken soup?' Elliot whips his head round to face me, and I can't help laughing.

'That's what people tell me too. He's not your regular kind of dog.'

'They didn't have any chicken soup up at the visitors' centre.' He's shaking his head and looking amused, but the uncomfortable atmosphere in here is enough to cut it short. 'Anyway, *uh*,' he says. 'What do we do now?'

'I've got to open my shop,' I say, emphasis on the 'my', and I watch Elliot's brow crinkle before he takes a slow drink of coffee.

I take the opportunity to square up, standing feet hip-width apart and trying my best to keep my chin up. I want him to go, remember? Even if it does make me feel like a mardy old cow. Wanting to meet people in the community and enjoy welcoming them into my shop is one thing, living in close quarters with a man I don't know is entirely another. I clear my throat, feeling fully a foot and a half shorter than this guy. 'Thing is, Elliot. I've been looking forward to this for months now—'

'Me too,' he interrupts, giving me a level look.

'But I need this. I… I don't have anywhere else to go.'

Elliot just nods and gives an abrupt shrug as though he's saying 'me too' again.

'I just want to be on my own,' I say, and it comes out a bit desperate. 'Besides, there's still the problem of the bed situation. So you can't stay here, even if you wanted to.'

'Even though I've paid my money too, and made the journey, and I'm here now, and I want to stay?' he says, and there's something so reasonable and dry in his voice that I find myself getting annoyed. He already thinks he's won.

'Look, I've got stuff to do, I can't stand here talking. I have to get the sacks of flour from my van down at the harbour, and there's scones to bake, and…'

'You bake?' he says.

I nod. 'A little.'

'That's good. I could help out with that. I mean, I've never baked before but I can learn.'

I tip my head. 'You said you came in an Uber. Can you just call them back and, I don't know, get going?' I think of the money in my bank account and wince at the thought of parting with it, but needs must. 'I'll give you your half of the booking fees back. There must be a cash machine somewhere round here.'

'There's one at the visitors' centre.'

'OK, great! Well then—'

'Jude,' he cuts me off and comes closer. When he sees me take a step backwards he freezes. 'Look, Jude, I really want to stay.'

I huff out a breath and my shoulders stiffen.

'I can help out around here. See?' He walks over to a bookshelf and plucks a dusty novel from the top shelf. 'I'm good at reaching things, right?' He half smiles as he says this and I have to hide the fact I found the way his mouth moved completely delightful.

'There's a step ladder right there,' I say, stolid and unmoving.

'OK, I can lug the stuff from your van. It's a long way up the slope from the harbour. You said there were flour sacks? Those can't be light. I can go fetch them for you.'

79

'There's a sled by the shop door for transporting stuff like that.' I'm not giving in. This guy has to go, and not just because I might want a little solitude after busy days in my shop, but because I don't know him from Adam. He's turned up here with the sleek black hair falling over his cheekbones and a scar over his eyebrow, and he's saying he's got nowhere else to be, and he's *supposedly* a vet teacher but what kind of teacher has muscles like that and walks around looking deadly in baggy pants and a sweat top like he's fresh from boot camp? No. I've read *All Creatures Great and Small*. No vet was ever muscle-bound and hot like that – if you like that sort of thing, which I don't.

'I can serve? I'm good with people,' he shrugs, lowering himself into a chair in the middle of the shop.

'Are you? You scared the life out of me last night.'

'I'm sorry about that. Listen, I can work the till, and help with the stock taking and money side of things? I was always good at that kind of stuff.'

I pause. I sip my coffee. 'That doesn't fix the bed problem.' I'm so stubborn. Daniel always tells me that.

He leans forward, elbows on his knees and hangs his head slightly, and I'm surprised to find myself suddenly panicked he might actually leave. What the hell is that all about? The thought of someone taking responsibility for the money – or more specifically the cashing up – must have been properly appealing for a moment.

I'm asking myself if I've lost my mind when he says, 'I can lug a mattress down into the shop at night. There'd be plenty of room for me to sleep if I move a table or two. Aldous can keep me company. What do you say, little guy?' We both glance at the sleeping dog's hunched shoulders and curved back; he doesn't move a whisker. 'See, *he's* thrilled. And I'll keep out of your way, Jude. You wouldn't know I was here.' That half smile again, just a curve at his lips but I feel myself caving in. *Argh!*

'Who's your favourite author?' I say.

'Huh?'

'What do you like to read?' *Not Catcher in the Rye, not Catcher in the Rye, not Catcher in the Rye.*

80

'Well… I like, uh… let's see. Paulo Coelho? *Umm*, what else? Ursula K. Le Guin is amazing. *Uh*, you really put me on the spot here. Last thing I read was *Wuthering Heights*. That was pretty awesome. Bleak but awesome.'

Half an hour later and Elliot's on his way back up the hill with a spring in his step, my van keys in his pocket, and a sack of flour over one shoulder and the sugar, eggs and marge together in a bag bumping off his thigh. He puts them down on the shop counter as if they're as light as air.

I've filled the cash tray inside the till using the float and counted it twice and written the total on a notepad so I can be extra sure things stay straight, and I nod in his direction.

'You OK? Something wrong with the money?' he says.

'Nope. It's fine,' I say breezily and slam the till shut.

'Serve our first customers while I was gone?'

'Not one,' I say. 'I haven't turned the sign yet though.'

'Do you want to do the honours?' he asks, and for such a big guy there's something unexpectedly light in his deep voice that shows his excitement.

As I'm reaching for the sign, he stops me, saying, 'Is that your phone? You'll want a picture of this, hold on.'

So, as I flip the sign from 'Closed' to 'Open' I hear him snapping away, and I smile awkwardly. 'Right, we're open.'

'We are,' he says, and I catch a little smile at the corner of his mouth again that tells me he really has been looking forward to coming here for ages, just like me. 'So… the café?' He nods at the flour.

'Oh, right *umm*.' I panic a bit. I haven't really given it a second's thought since I arrived, what with all the excitement. 'We'll just have to muddle through with what we have: a teensy kitchen and a few chairs scattered here and there in the shop. The advert mentioned a "cosy café nook". So much for that!' I shrug, a bit disappointed, if I'm honest.

'You haven't seen it?' he asks, amused again. 'Grab the keys.'

He strides for the door and I follow him outside. Round the side of the bookshop there's another set of steps and another door with glossy sky-blue paint. He stands back and lets me unlock it and step inside.

'Here it is, our café,' he says.

A sullen little voice in my head wants to correct him, saying, 'it's *my* café', but I don't say it out loud because I'm too excited at the sight before me and I quickly forget my tetchiness.

It's exactly how I'd imagined a seaside tearoom attached to a tumbledown bookshop would be. Lace curtains on café rods at the windows, four little round tables and a counter. There's a filter coffee pot, a big silver urn, lots of little silver milk jugs and a jumble of mismatched chintzy china cups and saucers on shelves behind the counter and three empty cake stands with domed glass lids.

'OK,' I say, nodding. 'This is OK.' I slip behind the counter and push my way through the beaded curtain into a back room scarcely big enough for one person, where I find shelves stocked with jars of jam. There's just enough room for the fridge and double oven. I'll have to mix my scones on the counter top in the café, but that's OK.

Even with its tiny proportions I recognise the familiar feeling of cosiness and industry, just like our bakery back home. I know I can do this already. In fact I'm grinning as I turn to shout to Elliot to bring the baking ingredients through and I'm met by his chest in close-up. 'Oh!'

He's holding the strands of the beaded curtain aside and filling the doorway, glancing around the little kitchen too.

'Sorry,' I squirm, and he lets me squeeze by, and that's pretty much how the rest of the morning continues. I show him how to bake scones from Grandad's recipe book and he fills up the room; he sits on a café chair to write the prices on the chalk board, accidentally snapping two pieces of chalk in half and laughing drolly at how this kind of thing happens to him all the time, and I trip over his feet as I shake out the tablecloths. Everywhere I go, there he is.

I'm feeling claustrophobic by the time the heat from the oven and the morning sun elevates the temperature in the little café by at least a thousand degrees and that's when Elliot pulls aside a curtain on the other side of the café revealing a low door that links to the back of the bookshop. Tying the curtain back, he crouches to squeeze through the door and I can't help but feel relieved that the space has suddenly opened up and I can breathe again.

I prop the café entrance door open and let the sea air in, trying not to think about the dorky way Elliot stooped to get out the room and how I can hear his boots clomping on the bookshop floorboards next door and I'm wondering if, contrary to first impressions (that this guy is tall, shifty, dangerous, and... *dammit*, handsome), he's actually a bit of a big clumsy nerd. Either way, he's still an interloper in my escapist fantasy of seaside bookselling and I'm going to steer clear of him as much as I can.

The seagulls start calling to each other and lining up on the outer wall of the cottage garden opposite the café steps and I fix them with a stare and tell them they're not allowed any of the scones, which are now looking fat and golden beneath the glass domes on the countertop so don't even *think* about coming in here.

Elliot's been for a shower – what kind of bookseller drifts off for a shower mid-morning and leaves the shop unattended? Proof, if it were needed, that we're not going to get on at all. He pops his head through from the shop, strands of damp black hair falling over his light eyes. What is that colour anyway? Golden brown? No, light amber. Is that even an eye colour? I look away sharpish.

'Any customers yet?' he asks.

I shake my head. 'You?'

'Not one, and it's almost ten. Wanna swap? I'm pretty sure I can serve up a mean cream tea and you can get to know your bookshop.'

That's all he has to say. I tell him there's a huge supply of clotted cream in the fridge – and he laughs, telling me he knows as he was the one who brought it in off the step early this morning – and I leave him to read his book in the café.

He's plucked a battered copy of *Drums of Autumn* from a shelf, which makes me wonder if he's read the first three *Outlander* books already – because that's the fourth in the series – and I try not to think about what this says about his reading habits and his personality, but dammit, I'm begrudgingly impressed. When he reaches for reading glasses and slips them on – the frames are thicker over the brow like a nineteen-fifties newsreader and just the perfect shape for his face – I'm annoyed to feel myself wilting at the sight of him. I stumble over the raised threshold under the doorframe as I hurry to leave him to his time-travel historical romance and I stake my claim once more to my bookshop.

Chapter Eleven

'Ornamental teapots?' I say, and the old lady blinks at me expectantly. She arrived with the rest of her bus tour group five minutes ago and they're swarming through the shop, touching everything and carrying bundles of books to and fro, and never actually coming to the till to pay for any of them.

'That's right. Present for my daughter-in-law. Collects them, and books about them. Got any?' Her accent's hard to place, Londonish maybe, putting me in mind of *EastEnders*.

'Well, *umm*, I don't know, to be honest…'

'Hornsea pottery, then?' She's more abrupt this time.

'*Umm*.' I scan the shop hoping to remember seeing shelves devoted to crafts, but it's not ringing any bells.

'It's my first day, you see?' I'm explaining, and she's crumpling her lips at me, losing patience, when Jowan appears bringing the sunshine and fresh air of Clove Lore with him and I'm flooded with relief.

'Nothing on Hornsea,' he says, softly, 'but there's some nice old Meakin trade catalogues at the back under the sign that says "House Beautiful", third row down.'

I watch the lady's expression melt into a charmed smile under Jowan's gentle gaze and she shuffles off amongst the shelves.

'Thanks, Jowan. I haven't quite got to grips with where everything is yet.'

'You'll get there,' he reassures me. 'So, the fellow arrived late last night, everything OK?' Jowan squints around the shop looking for Elliot. He's obviously still not convinced he isn't a bit shifty.

'He's in the café, and from the sounds of it he's doing a roaring trade already.' There's been a steady thrum of chatter and cutlery clinking for a while now and every so often Elliot's deep voice makes its way to me out here. I let him get on with it, happy to focus on the task at hand – running my bookshop. 'I, *um*, I didn't actually know he was coming. My ex didn't pass *that* development on to me. Didn't mention Aldous either.'

Jowan's eyes widen. 'Ah!' He stares at me, probably trying to decide what to do next. 'Are… those things going to be a problem? I *uh*, I can talk to the charity committee, see if we can move one of 'em, or both of 'em? Be easier to move the man than the dog, mind.'

'Oh no, don't,' I protest, worried more for Jowan, who looks deeply concerned at the idea of evicting Aldous, than I am about my already surrendered fantasy of a solitary holiday. Maybe he thinks I'll kick up a fuss, one-star the place on Tripadvisor. I rush to reassure him. 'It's fine, now that I'm getting used to things. Honestly. But, Jowan?' I ask, tentatively. 'There was one thing I was wondering. Is Aldous really OK sleeping in that window and fending for himself around town all evening? Wouldn't he be happier at the B&B with you?'

We both look over to his spot on the sill where Aldous is snoring loudly. There are a couple of bluebottles trapped in the window and buzzing around his head but he doesn't seem to have noticed.

'Tried that,' Jowan sighs. 'He couldn't settle, howled all day long and broke his heart, he did.'

'But why? You'd think he'd be lonely here at the shop, away from his owner?'

Jowan's eyes crinkle and he smiles but there's sadness in it. 'This is his home. Isolda and I lived here since before we were married. It was her bookshop, you see? And her mother's before her. Isolda brought Aldous here as a rescue puppy and we had years together, our little holy trinity, she called it. But my wife passed away, two and a half years ago now, Christmas Eve it was. Poor little fella's been pining for her ever since. I think he's waiting for her to return. In truth, I think we all are. Isolda was the kind of woman you couldn't believe would do such a thing as die, but it happened all the same.' Jowan's eyes dim but his lips still curl into a smile beneath his bristles.

Don't cry, I tell myself, but there's a lump in my throat. I've a horrible tendency to burst into tears at other people's sad stories when it's *their* pain I should be focusing on. I gulp and we both look at Aldous again. 'I'm so sorry,' I say.

The ladies in the shop are clucking over recipe books now and I doubt anyone's going to buy anything at this rate, but that's OK, Jowan wants to show me something anyway. He takes a book down from a shelf, above which is painted the words, "*Death is an ascension to a better library*". John Donne', in a gold curly script. Jowan hands me the book.

'Did your wife paint that?' I ask.

'She did. She loved Donne, loved this shop.' He smiles as he instructs me to turn to page one hundred and thirty-eight.

I do as I'm told and there's a passage marked down the margin in the lightest, spidery pencil. I find I'm reading aloud but getting choked up again as I do.

> *When one man dies, one chapter is not torn out of the book, but translated into a better language; and every chapter must be so translated; God employs several translators; some pieces are translated by age, some by sickness, some by war, some by justice; but God's hand is in every translation, and his hand shall bind up all our scattered leaves again, for that library where every book shall lie open to one another.*

Jowan's eyes are sparkling again when I meet them. 'Aldous and I are just waiting for our scattered leaves to be bound up again…' He tails off, reaches for the book in my hands and returns it to the shelf. 'This one's very expensive, on account of my not wanting to sell it. It was Isolda's favourite. But it's there for folks to read should they wish.'

That does it, I really am going to cry. Jowan doesn't seem to mind the tear on my cheek. 'But you live at the B&B now?' I press, with a sniff. 'You didn't want to live here in your bookshop?'

'Isolda forbade it, worried I'd haunt the place, mooning around, frightening the customers. It was her idea to share the shop with other booksellers, let them get a taste of how happy we were for twenty-five years. So I moved back to the B&B my family have always run. But Aldous, he won't budge.'

'The clothes!' I blurt suddenly. 'In his bed?'

'Yep, they were hers. Bring him some comfort, I hope. It was the vet's idea.'

I suddenly get the overwhelming urge to cook chicken soup for the poor bereft mutt. Jowan pulls a tissue from the box on the counter and hands it to me. 'No crying in here, Jude. This is the happiest place on the coast. Don't go feeling sorry for me.'

'Just these, please!' The voice cuts our conversation off and I'm faced with my first real customer. Not the teapot lady, but one of her group. She's holding her purse open ready to pay. I try not to look at Jowan as I ring up the books. Each has a price pencilled inside the cover page, but as I jab the numbers into the till I find the digits start to swim a bit. This always happens when I'm faced with lots of numbers, but it's worse when I'm being watched.

'Need a hand there, Jude?' Jowan's already around my side of the desk, and there are more women queueing behind the first, all with a book or two in their hands, all looking impatient and making sure I'm aware their bus leaves the visitors' centre in twenty minutes.

Jowan reads the prices aloud to me while I hit the keys and I only mess it up and have to start again three times, which isn't that bad, is it?

Eventually, they are out the door, carrying away their treasures. It all happened too hurriedly to write down what they bought so I'll have to rely on the till being correct for today. 'Thanks,' I mumble, knowing full well Jowan's peering down at me, wondering why I can't simply read prices and then make my fingers type those same numbers into the keypad without losing track of them or hitting the wrong keys and getting flustered.

I'm saved by the lumbering appearance of Elliot, looking a mixture of ridiculous and impressive in a little white apron, his hair tied up messily at the back, long strands falling down over his ears and neck. He's taken the glasses off, which seems a shame.

'I come bearing scones! Morning, Jowan. Will you stay for one of Jude's scones? She's from a baking family, you know? Here, you can have mine.' He seems more chipper than I've seen him so far. Maybe he's cut out for running a café by the sea.

Jowan takes a bite and, nodding approvingly, makes his way to the door. 'Very nice. I'll be off then, if there's nothing you need me for?' There's a little wistfulness in his voice that makes me think he'd quite like to stay, but he leaves anyway, and all the time he was here Aldous never once lifted his head to greet his owner.

The morning passes in a jumble of long, quiet moments where I try to familiarise myself with the stock, mixed with frenetic bursts of activity when tourists suddenly arrive at once and queues form quickly because I'm being slow at the till.

I don't know how I'd have coped on my own running the café as well as the shop, and every time I hear the café door open I'm grateful someone else is there to take care of it all.

I only made twenty-four scones this morning and Elliot calls through to let me know they've all sold out by half-twelve so he's running a barista service of only tea and coffee for the rest of the day so I make a mental note to triple my quantities tomorrow, even though that will mean getting an earlier start on baking.

As I'm thinking I've got a handle on this bookselling business, the bell over the door trills and a tall, imposing blonde bursts in, dressed in tweeds, hunting boots and a wide-brimmed waxed hat. 'Get your gun!' she calls out jauntily before disappearing out the door again.

I'm still gaping at the door when she reappears carrying a banana crate piled high with books and I rush to help her inside.

'Are these for me?' I ask, settling the box on the front desk and she informs me in very well-bred tones that of course they are.

'Your pricing gun's under the desk.'

'But where did they all come from?' My eyes must be as big as saucers.

'Oh, you know, house clearances, sales, charity donations, that sort of thing. I help Jowan find new stock, and in return he helps me with the Christmas harbour lights committee.'

I'm shaking my head and looking none the wiser, making her roll her eyes pityingly at me as though I should somehow know all this stuff.

'I'm Minty. Proprietor of Clove Lore House and Gardens?' She shakes my hand briskly but I couldn't say that information helped me much. 'Come up and have a look around the grounds one day. Tell the visitors' centre you're from the bookshop and they'll waive the ticket fee.' She reads my expression and gives me another exasperated look. 'The whole village is part of my family's estate. You must have driven past the big house on your way down to the village? It's open to visitors in the season. National collection of camellias?'

I don't want to tell her I neither noticed a big house nor knew about its existence, so instead I thank her and set about rummaging through the box and enthusing about how a crate of used books is a better present than a fancy box of chocolates any day. That's when Elliot comes in, knocking his elbow on one of the shelves while peeling his apron off, which in turn makes his hair fall loose. It's quite something to behold.

'All locked up, I can help out in here now it's gone three, oh, hello.' He stops in the middle of the shop, filling the space. 'Sorry, I didn't realise you had a customer.'

The woman looks a little put out and I try to introduce her but make a mess of it. 'Elliot, this is, *umm*, the lady from the big house…?' *Did she really say Minty?* I have to give up. I'm terrible with names; they never seem to stick in my mind. Names, phone numbers, important dates – they have a habit of slipping away from me somehow.

'Araminta Clove-Congreve, Minty to my friends.' She's looking at Elliot as though he's fallen from the sky somehow, and I get the impression she is definitely not inviting him to be her friend or to call her Minty. Elliot offers his hand to shake, but she doesn't take it. 'Have we met before?' she asks him distractedly.

'I don't think so.' Elliot's eyes dart around and he begins to back away. 'Well, it was nice to meet you,' he says, shuffling off up the spiral staircase.

Minty watches him go, still narrowing her eyes. 'Well, yes, right.' She smooths her hands over tweedy jacket pockets and collects herself. 'I'll be off then. That's the last of the books, for now. Toodle-pip.'

The door closes and I'm left alone in the shop with the sunshine casting a bright triangle of light into my little spot behind the till. Elliot doesn't seem to be coming back down any time soon and I wonder if he's fallen asleep up there, he's so quiet. But I don't mind. I have a whole confection of books to sort through before closing the shop. So, I grab my gun and reach inside the box.

This is where I come into my own. I might not have the best memory or a head for dates and numbers but what I am good at is knowing who wrote what, and I can recall the plot of a book or details of an author's life without an iota of difficulty. That stuff's imprinted indelibly in my mind.

The pricing doesn't take long. I'm just guesstimating how much they're worth and not one of the titles gets priced at more than ten pounds. It's shelving them that's tricky.

First I tackle the nearly new hardbacks, all biographies, each of them fresh and fat, not a dog ear or faded cover in sight. They all go on the top shelf under Isolda de Marisco's hand painted sign, 'Life Writing'.

Then comes a cornucopia of crime paperbacks, unapologetically shiny and colourful, stuffed full of fusty old detectives looking for clues, chalked lines and grizzly morgue scenes. I squeeze most of them into the shelf marked 'Police Procedurals'. I don't quite know where to put the bundle of SAS-inspired action adventures so I add them to the general fiction shelves which sprawl all along the far wall that leads to the low café door.

Next, there's a handful of Young Adult books; their spines a rainbow of colour. I find a spot for them on the edge of the children's section, though I feel they deserve a special spot all of their own. Then I shelf two big, blousy bonkbusters involving sexy equestrians, followed by stodgy political dramas penned by a shamed MP.

Then come the treasures, choked with dust that makes my skin itch. Clad in covers of burgundy and emerald, mahogany and even gold cloth, these are books printed more than a century ago. I wonder how many shelves they've lived on during their long lives. I don't recognise any of the authors' names. There are slender volumes on aesthetics, three decker novels reminiscent of Oscar Wilde's Miss Prism, and a decorous collection of poetry by a minor war poet, everyone long since dead.

I add them to one of the table top displays alongside the dour temperance pamphlets rubbing up alongside Rabelais. I can do what I like, remember? This is my shop. The whole thing takes longer than I thought, and it's almost six when Elliot appears on the stairs.

'Are you done? I was reading upstairs in the window seat, lost track of time.'

His voice makes me jump. I'd forgotten he existed. He's wearing his glasses again and is holding the same book I saw earlier.

'Elliot! I was miles away. I *uh*, I guess we can close up? I'll just put this empty box out by the bins.'

After his shower this morning he'd changed into black pants which are baggy like a boxer's, or maybe a dancer's, and now he's zipping up a grey hoodie over a light t-shirt. The thin fabric's stretching over his arms. 'I'll cash up,' he says.

Those three little words provoke a surprisingly large amount of relief and gratitude, and I leave him to count the day's takings while I tidy up, praying the money tallies with the till's records, which I'm delighted to learn, it does.

Take that, Mrs Patterson! See? I *can* do maths. I can run a shop and manage the money, no problem. I'll ring Daniel later and let him know he was right, I was worried about nothing.

'So, *uh*, should we… get something to eat?' Elliot says, as he hands me the cash box to stash under my bed for the night.

Running up the spiral stairs gives me a moment to think about it. There's no food in the kitchen fridge, and no shops nearby to get any groceries, not that I saw on my way Up-along yesterday anyway. 'Is the visitors' centre café still open?' I shout down to him as I smooth my hair in front of the bathroom mirror.

'No, closes at five, that's the village pretty much shut to visitors for the day,' he calls back. 'Except the lucky ones staying at the pub or the B&B. You, *uh*, you want to go to the pub?'

I hadn't planned on dining out, let alone eating in the pub with a total stranger, and not one who looks like a model-slash-part-time-wrestler, and will get us stared at by the entire population of Clove Lore (which is probably about fifty-three people, a score of cats and dogs, and possibly a few olde-worlde pirates, if Jowan's anything to go by), but there's a little money in my bank account and my stomach growls about only having had a scone and some coffee all day and I relent. I quickly brush some powder over my shiny bits and sweep on a bit of tinted lipbalm.

'Okay then,' I call, trying to sound casual. 'I can spare an hour, maybe. There's lots to do in the shop,' I shout back, and I hear Elliot putting another cheese sandwich in Aldous's bowl in the kitchen, promising him he'll buy some real dog food and muttering about Jowan not looking after his pet properly. Maybe he laughs too, but when I get downstairs he's looking serious.

'Ready?' he asks, and from the atmosphere in the shop I'd say neither of us are really ready, but we lock up anyway.

Chapter Twelve

Clove Lore in the early evening summer sun is, let me tell you, one of the prettiest sights I've ever beheld. Elliot walked ahead of me, saying if I slipped on the steep cobbles he'd be able to break my fall, and so, as I take cautious, crab-like steps, I take in the sunlit flowers and greenery, refreshed after last night's rain, the gleaming whitewashed walls of the cottages with each sparkling facet of their leaded windows aglow, and the clear blue sky with the wonderful glittering deep blue of the sea glimpsed between houses. I can't avoid also glimpsing Elliot's back and his long, thick-thighed legs powering him down the hill. Every so often he rakes his hair back and turns round to check I'm OK.

Yes, Clove Lore really is stunning tonight. This was a good idea, getting out of the shop for a while, getting orientated in the village a little more.

We hit the harbour within minutes, passing the defunct lime kiln and the red doors and flying flag of the lifeboat station. Down here the buildings (storehouses, places for smoking and salting herring) tell the stories of generations of fishermen, but they all look like family homes and holiday lets now, their gardens and balconies frothing with summer flowers.

The Siren, when Elliot holds the door open for me, is busy and everyone – except the oblivious tourists – turns to look at us as we enter. Jowan's by the bar talking with Minty and the two lads in waders, the ones I saw yesterday. Jowan raises his pint glass at us as we come in. I'm sure I see Minty's jolly demeanour shift to something more unsettled, suspicious even, as she watches Elliot stride past.

'Let's just grab a quick bite and get back to the shop, OK?' I say, feeling every inch like an exhibit in a museum.

'Yup,' Elliot agrees and he steers a course for a table in the corner. Once we sit down I realise, delightedly, that our little window is directly above the water – in fact, the whole corner of the building seems to be jutting out over the sea as if held up on stilts. The window's open and the fresh salty scent of the sea makes my stomach growl again.

'Scampi and chips?' I say, scanning the menu, aware that we're still the whispered talk of the bar room.

'I'll stick to the veggie pasta.' Elliot's shifting uncomfortably in his chair and holding the menu up as if to deflect the stares.

'You're vegetarian?'

'Carb loading. I work out a lot.'

'Was that where you went this morning?'

'I ran up the slope to the visitors' centre then along the coastal path for an hour.'

'All that before you even got the coffees?'

'I like to run, clears my head.'

He's got his nose buried in the menu again and I admit, I'm starting to despair about making small talk with this guy. I really should have brought a book.

'I'm definitely getting fries though, and a milkshake,' he throws in over the top of the menu, which helps settle me a bit.

A man, probably in his late fifties, approaches our table, notepad in hand. His salt and pepper hair is cropped short and his grey eyes smile the unfazed smile of a landlord who welcomes everyone to his pub and who has seen it all over the years.

'You're the Borrowers then?' he says, and I get the chemical whiff of cigarettes off him. 'How's life at the bookshop?'

'Good thanks,' I say, smiling. 'We're finding our feet.'

'Busy today, was it?' He directs this towards Elliot who he catches glancing towards Minty and Jowan still huddled by the bar.

'Oh! Yeah, steady stream of café customers all day,' Elliot replies, collecting himself.

'You'll be in Clove Lore for our Sleuthing Club a week on Monday. Fancy it? Eight p.m., all the sandwiches you can eat.'

'The *what* club?' I say, rather liking the sound of the sandwiches.

'We read a crime novel once a month and meet to dissect it. Usually turns into a bit of a rabble by nine and the book gets forgotten, but we try to stay on topic for a while. You'd have to read Vera Lancing's new book before then, though, *The Heart That Shattered*.'

My mood lifts instantly. 'I've heard that's really good. Count me in. I can download it on my phone and read it in a week, no problem,' I say, before we both turn expectantly to Elliot.

'Uh,' he says, blanching. 'I'm not one for crime stories.'

'Pity,' the landlord says, his eyes narrowing at Elliot's strange manners. 'We love a mystery here at the Siren's Tail. Some of the club members are super sleuthers, Minty especially. There's not a red herring can put her off and not a clue she misses. She always knows whodunit long before the rest of us.'

I notice Elliot's staring across at Minty again and his face is assuming the same stern, serious set it had this morning.

'Well, I'll definitely be there, *umm*?' I throw in, trying to prompt the landlord's name while drawing attention away from Elliot and the awkward atmosphere he's creating.

'Name's Finan,' the landlord says, shaking my hand, 'and over there's my wife, Bella.' We turn to the bar where a woman in a low-cut dress printed all over with pink rosebuds dries glasses.

The proprietors of the Siren are a good-looking couple, and somehow matching, as though you could pick them out as a twosome in a crowd. Bella waves back at us with a smile before serving her customers.

I tell Finan our names but Elliot keeps his eyes cast down, and he looks a little absurd with his thick arms folded over his broad chest. He's wishing he could somehow shrink, I reckon.

It must be difficult, being so striking and so obviously *present* in any room. I'm tiny and can go wherever I want without anyone paying much attention to me. Getting served at a busy bar was always next to impossible for me – not that I've stood at all that many bars in my life.

I watch Finan decide to ignore Elliot's silence, and he politely takes our food order. Just as he's leaving our table I call him back and ask for a glass of wine instead of juice. I don't drink much, but sitting here with Elliot being so quiet and kind of stern-looking made me do it.

'So…' Elliot says eventually, after our drinks arrive, and it looks like the effort pains him. He's been watching me with growing panic in his eyes as I struggled to think of anything to say other than trite comments about our day at the shop. 'You're *Scottish*?' he manages, and the pitch of his voice makes me stifle a little laugh into my glass.

'Borders, yeah,' I say with a shrug. 'Ever been?'

'*Hmm?*' he raised his brows.

'To the Borders?' I say, a little desperately.

'Ah! No.' Elliot drums nervously on the table's edge with his index fingers before realising what he's doing and putting his hands awkwardly in his lap.

Silence again. Laughter erupts from the table behind us. It's a big party of tourists, an entire family by the looks of things. They're having a lovely time.

'So, you're a teacher?' I say.

'*Erm*, yeah. Taking a bit of a break over the summer, you know?'

'You mentioned a vet college, or something?'

'*Umm*, kind of.'

Well this isn't getting us anywhere. I'm relieved when my scampi arrives and he's presented with a steaming bowl of pasta and we each have an excuse to be quiet for a moment.

I glimpse at him stabbing at the farfalle and eating like a man half starved. Most of his milkshake disappears with one long slug at the straw too.

I don't stare at his lips as he sucks – that would be weird, obviously – but for a millisecond I caught how they looked and something flipped in my tummy, which does nothing but remind me of why I wanted to be *alone* on this break. I don't need any distractions like that.

I stare at my chips, remarking how good they are about three times more than a normal person would and I think Elliot smiles but I'm not looking at him to know for sure. The wine is good too. The wine is definitely helping. I might order a second glass.

'Have you been to Clove Lore before?' I'm proud of myself for coming up with this scintillating nugget.

'*Mmm,*' he swallows, surprised at my sudden efforts. 'Once, when I was a kid.'

'With your parents?'

'Yeah.'

'What do they do? Are you from a family of vets?'

'Uh, well…' I watch him take a few more stabs at his pasta before he answers. 'Mum's a local councillor and Dad's… in agriculture. So… yeah, no vets.' He shrugs and sets about eating again, except he's less enthusiastic this time. 'Tell me about you,' he says.

'What?' I'm not used to anyone taking an interest. It throws me.

'You know, where you're from? What you like doing? Interesting hobbies?'

'Interesting scars?' I blurt out, indicating with the end of my fork the silvered line that interrupts one of his beautiful dark eyebrows. It's out before I realise what I've said. 'Oh, my God, I'm sorry. Obviously, that's none of my business.'

He's glowering at his plate, his brows pinching, and his mouth setting sternly.

'I'm sorry,' I say again.

'It's nothing, just a stupid scratch,' he mutters.

'At work?'

'Yeah, sure. At work.'

'Declawing a tiger, were you?' Why can't I stop? For Christ's sake, Jude! He smiles, but not with his eyes, and I drop the subject. 'So, my hobbies?' I say, determined to save this and get to the bill-paying and leaving part of the evening as quickly as possible.

I tell him about my love of books, my only real hobby, and after a while he stops eating and just listens, watching me get more and more enthusiastic.

'So yeah,' I ramble. 'I ended up bringing a big bag of books from home, which I don't think is *that* weird. Is it weird?'

Elliot just smiles.

'I don't even own that many books,' I confess. 'Most of my favourite reads I found at the local library, and if I *really* loved something I'd renew my loan over and over again for months, reading it umpteen times. Nobody seemed to mind. I don't think the residents of Marygreen were queueing up for a copy of any of my favourites, if I'm honest. It's not a big reading town.'

The waitress comes back and Elliot quietly orders us more drinks while I give him the lowdown of my top books. I'm in full sail now and enjoying myself. *Tess of the D'Urbervilles* (poor woman dies because of an undelivered letter and a bad man); *Jamaica Inn* (poor woman discovers her bad uncle likes wrecking ships and slitting throats); *Frenchman's Creek* (rich, bored woman goes on an adventure with a hot French pirate). 'Ah, I adore them,' I enthuse. 'I could recite whole passages verbatim if that was ever required. It hasn't come in handy yet, but you never know.'

As I speak, something surprising happens. I watch Elliot's expression burst into a grin, a proper bright-eyed, whole-hearted type of grin, and it knocks me breathless for a fraction of a second.

I try to recover. 'You love books too? I mean you must, wanting to stay at a bookshop and everything?' I say, and I suddenly feel bad about hogging the shop all day, confining him to the café. I wonder if he can tell that's what I'm thinking.

'Books were my life as a kid – books and my pets,' he begins. 'My family were always very busy; parties here and there, events and dinners, always working, even in the evenings. I read a lot for company and, when I was nine, they bought me two puppies of my own. I used to read to them in the library.' He's smiling at the memory. It looks as though he's forgotten I'm here.

'You were allowed to take two puppies into your local library? Try that in Marygreen and you'd be out on your ear!'

'No,' he snaps out of the daydream. 'It was, *uh*, our library at home.'

'Oh!'

'Every nerdy kid's dream, right? A library of their own.'

'Literally my biggest dream,' I say.

'Except most of the books were locked behind glass, too precious to touch. I read what I could though. There was a Conan Doyle collection I was allowed to read. Smashed my way through those. Then I discovered Gerald Durrell, you know, *My Family and Other Animals*? I used to dream about having a menagerie of animals like he did. One year my parents gave me a whole shelf full of Observers books. You know the ones I mean? The little volumes on every topic under the sun? Geology, dogs, trees, wildflowers? The birds and their eggs ones were my favourites, I carried them about with me all the time.'

'You love books *and* nature,' I say, and my voice does something husky and wobbly that I didn't intend.

'That's me in a nutshell.'

'And working out?' There I go again with the blurting. He laughs a little, thank God, and looks down at his chest, dark strands of hair falling forwards and, I swear I'm not making this up, I am *sure* he flexes his pecs – not for my benefit, it's like he's just checking they're there – and he's looking all shy and kind of pink under his summer tan. When our eyes meet next we both stifle laughs and my cheeks burn a little.

We're saved from further nerdery by the distraction of a scratching sound at the pub door and a solemn little woof. We watch as Bella places a bowl of something on the floor by the bar and then opens the door.

'Aldous!' Elliot cries, as the raggedy mutt pads inside and tucks into what has to be his favourite treat: chicken soup.

Bella doesn't try to pet him, she just carries on with her job, and nobody in the bar pays the dog any attention – except for the bewildered tourists who don't look too pleased to share a meal with the Littlest Hobo. When he's finished noisily sloshing the broth onto the floorboards – I'd estimate only half of it ended up inside the dog; it can't be easy drinking soup with only eight teeth – he turns for the door and waits sullenly for Elliot to spring up and let him out onto the harbour again.

This place, I tell you, it's certainly got character.

—

'It's OK, you can go first,' I say, squirming.

We've met at the bathroom door. I'm clutching my jammies and my toothbrush to my chest and feeling ridiculous.

'No, it's fine. I'll take the mattress downstairs now. Is it OK if I go in your room to get it?' Elliot hikes a thumb at the bedroom door.

'Sure, knock yourself out.'

Once I'm safely inside the bathroom, I freeze, listening to him grunting and breathing as he drags a single bed mattress down a spiral staircase. He's swearing under his breath but if anybody's built for heavy lifting, it's Elliot. I'd offer to help but I'd be useless and I'd get in the way. I hear him shout, 'Holy shit!' followed by a bit of clattering and bumping, letting me know the mattress has reached the bottom of the stairs with or without Elliot.

It's not like I'm in the wrong for asking him to sleep down there. Where else could he go? And I was here first, remember? He's still the interloper. Even if he was helpful today running the café and everything. This definitely wasn't how my trip was meant to shape up, and I've still got major reservations about all this.

On the way back Up-along after dinner (no dessert; we split the bill fifty/fifty with a tip – Elliot did the maths, thankfully), I broached the subject of how we'll handle this bookstore rental, and between us we laid out some ground rules. It went like this.

'First off, we can't keep eating out together. I definitely can't afford it,' I told him. 'We need to get some groceries and we can look after our own meals, OK?'

'Like being in student digs again? Will you label your beans can and marker-pen a line on your milk bottle, make sure I'm not stealing it?'

Elliot had laughed, but it's all right for him. He clearly has money, or at least he comes from a family with money. I've got next to nothing in my bank account and need to freewheel until I can get back to Marygreen and find a job.

'I'm just saying… we don't need to eat together at night. You can do your own thing.' It came out sounding meaner than I'd intended.

'Got it,' he said with a nod. 'While we're making rules, I've got one.'

'OK?'

'Let me handle any phone calls that come in.'

'Uh, all right. Why?'

He was silent for a moment, looking down at his feet on the cobbles as we climbed. 'I'd just prefer it that way. OK?'

'Is this about the money?'

'*Huh?*'

'You think because I can't count, I can't talk to customers?'

'No, that's not what I'm saying.'

'Good.'

'I'm just saying, let me handle the calls, please.'

'Fine, whatever,' I relented.

'You, *uh*… you can't count?'

'*Tsk*, no. Everybody can count.'

'But you just said…'

'Look, everybody has their own thing they worry about.' Hoping that was an end to the matter, I made the left turn into the passageway leading to our shop, breathless with the climb and trying to keep up with Elliot's strides.

He followed me in silence for a moment before saying, 'True.'

I'd climbed the shop steps and got my key in the door by then. 'I'll bake cakes every morning, and you sell them, all right?'

'Right. Can I at least spend *some* time in the bookshop? We can swap every now and then?'

I sigh. 'Yes, we can swap.'

'But if anyone comes in asking for me…' He stopped himself mid-sentence.

'Yes?'

'*Uh*, it's OK. Forget it.'

'Are you expecting someone to come in looking for you?'

'No.'

'But…'

'Forget I said anything. Nobody's gonna come.'

There was a growl in his throat that stopped me pushing for more and I dropped the whole subject. And that's how we established our ground rules, such as they are.

It's taking me a long time to get to sleep tonight, even though my feet ache from standing all day, and my mind's tired, and my belly's full. I can hear Aldous snoring downstairs, even through the locked bedroom door. Somehow, I daren't move in my bed.

It takes me a while to realise I'm replaying something that happened earlier, when we'd walked inside the shop, flicking the lights on as we went.

Elliot had lumbered on ahead of me into the little kitchen and poured two glasses of water. I was locking up and checking Aldous was in for the night, but my eyes wanted to wander back to the view through the kitchen door where Elliot had his head thrown back and was downing his glass of water.

He slammed the glass onto the sink. Everything he does is so noisy and brutish, like he can't help it. I was thinking how hard it's going to be living with someone who turns a simple task like drinking water into a clattering orchestra – nothing like the quiet holiday I'd planned – when I heard him unzip his hoodie and I watched him slip it off over his arms. He slung it onto a chair and set about refilling his water glass, and by then I was open-mouthed and staring, properly staring (not the polite kind, not the kind you wouldn't mind being caught doing) at his broad shoulders and the expanse of skin revealed by the white vest tee. All evening I'd thought it was a t-shirt.

There were tattoos all over the backs of his arms disappearing under the fabric and onto his shoulder blades. I glimpsed something orange and red, and something black and swirling. I couldn't make out the design, but I could see his muscles working as he drank another glass.

By the time he'd turned and called for me, asking where I wanted him to put my water glass, I'd hotfooted it upstairs, grabbed my Snoopy PJs and was having a very stern word with myself about boundaries and respect and how it's not nice to gape at someone's body when they don't even know you're doing it.

Now I'm under my covers, thinking how it's really too hot tonight for thick jammies and I can't shake the image of ink under Elliot's skin, intriguing inscriptions against taut muscle and bone, and I have to throw the window open and let in the cool of the night.

'I am *not* Jude the Obscure,' I tell the stars, huffily. 'I'm *not* going to be distracted from my plan. Two weeks, just me, alone, rebuilding, being a useful member of the Clove Lore community, preparing for the next bit of my life – the good bit. Elliot will be gone in a fortnight, back to his ancestral home or wherever, and I'll be in Marygreen. The new me. Refreshed and ready for anything. No. I will not be distracted.'

I hear the heavy sound of Elliot turning on his mattress and his duvet rustling and then nothing after that, just the sounds of my breathing and the sea lapping at the pebbles down in the harbour. I focus on those sounds and I don't let myself get distracted.

Chapter Thirteen

No sooner were the scones cooling on the racks (three batches – I can freeze some if they don't get sold), than it was time to turn the sign.

I wonder what Monday morning's like in Clove Lore. The weekend certainly felt busy and eventful, but it's still peak holiday time for English schools and I'm guessing the dry and sunny weather forecast will bring people out in their droves today. I wish I had some proper summer clothes to wear, but my old staples will have to do.

I open all the windows in the shop, apart from Aldous's little porthole – he probably shouldn't sleep in a draught, plus, he could fall out into the wild and weedy back yard below.

The shop is beautiful this morning. Shafts of dazzling sunlight illuminate the sparkling dust in the air as I run an ancient vacuum around. Elliot, all in black, bursts through the door at ten to nine, wet from his run, and he's got coffees in his hands again.

'Morning, I'll grab a shower and then I'll be with you. Oh, and I got this for Aldous.' He's left a can of organic dog food on the desk and bounded up the stairs before I can reply, and in his wake comes our first customer of the day.

'Have you got that one with the *um*, whatsit called?' The gaunt man snaps his fingers, trying to summon the words. '*Um*, you know, the mill?' He's young compared to our usual customer base, mid-thirties-ish, and has a lovely soft accent. Russian? No, Polish, I reckon.

'A mill?'

'*Mmm*, cotton mill. And there's a mum, she's dead. And a vicar father, maybe? And a daughter? They end up living by a big ugly mill? You know the one?'

'It's ringing a bell,' I say.

'Yes, there's bells ringing in it! A mill bell, for the workers? And there's a strike, and she gets hit by a stone? You must know it! *Umm*, what else? He's all haughty, and his mum's a nightmare, and he's all like, *stuff you, Mum, I'm proposin'!*' He says this in a terrible Manchester accent (by way of Warsaw) and that's when it hits me.

'Oh my God, *North and South*!' I yell, triumphantly. 'Elizabeth Gaskell.' Told you I was good at this stuff.

'Yes! That's the one! Have you got it?'

'Oh, I don't know.'

We spend a while browsing the fiction shelves, but it's not there. 'Sorry,' I say, defeated.

'Never mind, I'll get it online.'

'Oh, all right then.'

He's about to leave when he turns back. 'I'm Izaak, by the way. Nice to meet you.'

'You're a local?'

'Yes, I'm the estate caretaker. My booth's Up-along between the visitors' centre and the entrance to the estate gardens. Can't miss it. I saw your man out running this morning. Big, isn't he?'

'*Um*, he is tall, yes. He's not mine, though. I mean, we're not together. I don't know him.' I'm wittering now. 'My name's Jude, by the way.'

'Oh!' A renewed interest lights Izaak's dark eyes. 'So, you're single then?'

For a horrible moment I think he's going to hit on me, but his smile breaks into something kinder. 'Better make sure Mrs Crocombe from the ice-cream cottage doesn't find out, she'll be setting up her sweepstakes again, if she hasn't already.'

'What?'

'All newcomers to the village who aren't paired off end up in her tote book. You'll see. Half the Siren will want a say in the matter.'

'What matter?'

'Well, whether you and The Muscles will… you know.' He's winking at me. It's very disconcerting.

'His name's Elliot, and no, we won't be… you know.' I let my annoyance show in my voice, and he draws his neck back.

'No offence meant. It's just Mrs Crocombe's a bit of an old romantic. That, and her daughter's the head teacher at the local school and if the village isn't procreating, the school won't stay open for many more years.'

'I'm not going to populate Clove Lore primary school in a fortnight, thanks very much.'

'You say that, but the Burntislands turned up at the bookshop as strangers, and they live out on the headland now with two kids. They arrived a little over two years ago, and since then Mrs Crocombe's had her book running. You don't have to marry the big fella, any of the locals will do.'

'Oh, well, that's OK then.'

'Best of luck, with the shop… and everything.' Izaak gives an amused little shrug.

'Thanks for dropping by.' I usher him towards the door, just as Elliot bounds down the stairs in a white summer shirt with the sleeves rolled up, unbuttoned over a white scoop-necked t-shirt and dark pants. His hair's wet. He seriously needs to invest in a hair dryer – the glistening locks thing is too much. Even Izaak pauses inside the doorframe to stare at him. I'm glad it's not just me Elliot has this effect on.

'Who's getting married?' Elliot asks as he approaches the desk.

'Nobody,' I say. 'We're talking about Mr Thornton and Margaret in *North and South*.' I give Izaak a firm look.

'Ah, I liked that BBC adaptation. Remember that?'

Of course Elliot liked it. Why wouldn't he? Dammit again! I dive into my take-away coffee cup, catching Izaak's eye as he smirks at me, throwing one final wink as he lets the door close upon him.

'Is everybody in Clove Lore like that?' I say, exasperated.

Elliot just laughs. 'They're fine. They're eccentric and friendly.'

'Except for Minty?'

'Yeah, maybe not her.' Elliot inhales through gritted teeth, and we both laugh.

Outside the shop on the sloping pavement I catch a glimpse of Izaak talking with a short, white-haired woman in a frilly apron with a pink and yellow embroidered ice-cream sundae on the front – that's got to be Mrs Crocombe. Their faces are so animated I know they must be talking about us newcomers at the bookshop. She appears to be writing something down in a notebook. I can make out Izaak spelling my name out loud to the woman. J.U.D.E. The little traitor, and after I looked for his book as well!

'What's going on out there?' Elliot says, peering past me.

'Not a clue,' I say, veering out of his way, not at all enjoying the scent of rose and patchouli that moves with him. Seriously, is that some kind of body lotion? I must get myself some. 'You can man the bookshop this morning, if you like?' I say, for want of anything more sensible coming to mind.

And with that, I escape Elliot's presence for another day.

—

> Hi! Are you on your break yet? It's nearly 3 and the cafe's gone quiet. Sold half my scones today. Yay! How's your day been?

I see the bubbles in the chat box telling me Daniel's typing a reply. I've spent the day serving tea and coffee and putting blobs of jam and clotted cream into little dishes for the tourists, who on the whole aren't as chatty as the bookshop customers but it's been nice listening to the radio and keeping up with the demand for scones.

I've been reading John Donne during the quiet moments (I can't get into it, I'm afraid, sorry Jowan), and Elliot's just popped his head through the little door from the shop to tell me he's sold a grand total of three books, all from the children's section, and all to the same woman, Mrs Crocombe's daughter.

I deduced that was who she was because she told him the books were for the local school library – and when I glimpsed her leaving she had the distinctly harassed look of a woman sent to spy on Elliot and me by their busybody book-keeping mother.

The café's been hot and stuffy all day and my feet are killing me. A little perch on the counter and a chat with Daniel won't hurt, not now there's no customers. My phone pings.

> I've got five minutes. The nurses' station is a HOTBED of angst. Delays on all blood work, two supply nurses gone AWOL and Ekon being a little B all day.

> Oh no, what's he up to now?

> Giving me lip, hanging around me all morning, asking questions he should know the answers to, generally being annoying. He's just left a cookie from the canteen on my desk. WTF??

> Well that sounds like a nice thing to do.

> It's probably laced with lactulose solution because I asked him to work Friday lates for the next two months. I can hear him laughing with the porter in the next bay. The end of this shift cannot come soon enough. You all right?

> I'm good thanks.

> But?

> There's no buts.

A gif pops up of some TV star I don't recognise. They're raising an eyebrow and saying 'Oh Really???'

> What about the guy with the apron? Behaving himself?

> Elliot. He's nice enough. We're keeping out of each other's way. He's in the shop today. He cashes up at night.

> And then what?

Another gif. This time it's one of the Simpsons waggling their eyebrows suggestively.

> And then nothing.

> Is he single?

> No idea. Plus not interested.

I'm really regretting sending that photo of Elliot behind the café counter in his apron yesterday. It was mostly a picture of my scones, his face wasn't even in it, but you could definitely see some t-shirt and forearms. Daniel had immediately messaged to ask for a full description of Elliot saying he knew he was our type just from the look of his wrists. I told him *we* don't share a type, which isn't strictly true. We're both conspicuously swoony for fit nerds but I made the mistake of deviating from that for Mack (who I'll bet hasn't worn a pair of sweatpants or pounded a treadmill in his life – plus he was more 'swanky boffin' than cute nerd) and look where that deviation landed me.

> OK. Don't rule out any out-of-hours encounters with that one. Perfect opportunity for a holiday flingette. Got to go. There's 18 being discharged this afternoon and I've got to sort their meds. Love you, x

> Love you too. And Daniel, be nice and eat Ekon's cookie! x

It's getting late and there's only so much John Donne you can force yourself to read on a stuffy summer's day indoors, so I turn the key in the door and cover the remaining scones for tomorrow. I might make some cupcakes in the morning for a change, with butter icing. There's quite a lot of cash in the café till, which is really pleasing. Shame none of it's for me – that's the only drawback of this working holiday.

I'll leave the day's takings for Elliot to sort. It's a good arrangement. He cashes up, stays out of my way, and everybody's happy.

All I want to do now is get down to the beach all by myself and see what the waves feel like on these achy feet. It's ridiculous that I've been at the seaside since Saturday and I *still* haven't set foot in the Atlantic.

As I slip through the little door into the book shop I'm struck by two things. Firstly, Elliot's shut up shop for the day as well, and secondly, he's tiptoeing towards the sleeping Aldous with outstretched arms and wearing oven mitts.

'*Umm*, what's going on?' I say.

'*Shh!* I'm going to examine him.'

'Why? What's wrong with him?'

'What's right with the poor little guy? He needs grooming for a start. That matting on his legs is horrible. And his breath! You're not the one who has to sleep in the same room as him. And no dog ever subsisted on cheese sandwiches, scones and soup in the wild. God only knows what's going on with his digestion. He hasn't touched that organic dog food I brought him this morning; three quid that cost me, it's the best you can get. Come over and help me hold him.'

'Not likely. The visitor's book says he bites.'

Elliot curls mittened hands on his hips and gives me a pointed look. 'It's not right leaving him like this, fending for himself, no stimulation whatsoever.'

'Oh… all right then! But if he starts getting jumpy, I'm backing off.'

Elliot hands me a mitt and we both sneak up on the dozing dog. For a few moments Aldous doesn't seem to notice we've each got a hand on his fuzzy little body. Elliot tentatively puts a thumb to Aldous's jowls and lifts his lip to reveal surprisingly pink gums and next to no teeth. 'Poor thing. How old did Jowan say he was again?'

The sound of Elliot's voice rouses Aldous who immediately springs up, half terrified, half murderous, making a gummy snap for my mitt.

'I'm out!' I say, raising my hands to safety.

Elliot grapples with the dog for a good few minutes after that, trying to check his eyes while Aldous windmills his head around and around in the most exasperating way. Well, Elliot's exasperated, I can't help laughing. When he spreads one of Aldous's paws out across his palm to check the state of his claws, the poor terrier yelps and screeches like he's under attack, but Elliot persists, calm and steady. 'I really need to feel his abdomen, Jude. Can you hold him?'

'*Uh*, not really.'

The intent look on Elliot's face makes me a bit ashamed. Here he is, trying to help a scruffy, neglected creature and I've contributed precisely nothing to the process.

Elliot lifts Aldous close to his chest, getting him in a kind of doggy headlock so he can't possibly bite anyone. 'Go on, I've got him, you feel his stomach,' he says.

'Must I?'

'Quickly, he's so distressed, his little heart's pounding against my arm. He's not used to being held by humans anymore.'

'Oh... OK.' I edge forward. 'What am I feeling for?'

'Any lumps or bumps.'

Even Elliot laughs at my grimace as I push through the dog's fur, but the mirth is wiped clean away when he sees me react to the tangled knot of lumps pushing at the little guy's belly.

'Oh no!' I murmur, checking again to be sure.

'What can you feel?'

'I don't know, but it's definitely not normal.'

The grave look on Elliot's face tells me my chances of paddling in the wild Atlantic this afternoon are getting slimmer by the second.

Chapter Fourteen

After half an hour spent searching for Jowan all over Clove Lore –
Elliot ran all the way to the B&B and the Siren while I rang Izaak
up at the visitors' centre – it turned out that he's been away from the
village all day at a book auction. There was nothing else for it but to
call a cab.

Elliot wrapped Aldous in a blanket and bounded up the slope
while I dodged the tourists and tried not to lag too far behind.

I barely had a chance to take in the big sprawling visitors' centre
as we passed by, but I noticed the little craft concessions: a pottery, a
fudge pantry, a silk printing shop and a soap and candle maker, maybe
a few other little stores, all set up for the tourists. It was all a bit of
a blur. I rushed past the pasty stall and its mouth-watering savoury
smells with a bit of a heavy heart (and a rumbling stomach) but Elliot
didn't slow his pace. His face was set sternly and Aldous looked even
tinier and more raggedy in his thick arms as we pressed through the
day's departing crowds.

He marched ahead through the car park, past the last of the tourist
coaches and out onto the main road where, thank God, the taxi was
waiting.

The race to the vet's in the next town, which should have been
like a scene in a movie – a desperate dash for medical assistance – was
in reality a frustratingly slow meander along twisting B roads behind
tractors and tourist traffic, but eventually we ended up here, at the
surgery.

Elliot disappeared with a woman in green scrubs, leaving me alone
in the waiting room. I watched the red light over the door flicker on

and the words 'No Entry: In Surgery' appear, and I settled in for a long wait.

That was over an hour ago and even though Aldous has been nothing but a stinky pain in the arse since I first found him sleeping his life away in my bookshop, I admit I've had a bit of a cry thinking about him in there, under anaesthetic, knots in his tummy, his owners unreachable.

When Elliot finally emerges, peeling off scrubs and looking rather pale, I spring to my feet.

'Is he OK?'

'Poor little guy...' he starts.

'Oh my God, no!'

'He's fine. He's had a very bad case of gastric dilatation volvulus.'

'In English?'

'A twisted stomach, caused by excess gas building up. He's probably been in pain for weeks.'

'So you fixed him?'

'We operated.'

'Got all the gas out?'

He pretends to laugh. 'Yes. He's going to stay here for a few days with Anjali. Get some rest.'

The vet comes out of the surgery, finishing up making notes on her clipboard. 'You can get going,' she says, pulling out her ponytail and swishing long dark hair behind her. 'You'd better try to contact the owner again too.'

'We'll find Jowan eventually, I'm sure,' I say. 'Does Aldous need anything? He has a tatty old jumper he sleeps on, should I go get it?'

'No, he needs sterile blankets until the wound heals,' the vet replies.

'We should settle up,' says Elliot, reaching for the wallet he'd abandoned on the chair beside me as he rushed to get into theatre scrubs.

I watch Anjali still his movements with a hand placed over his. 'It's okay. The owner can pay for his boarding and the meds. I'll invoice them once Aldous is on the mend. No surgery costs.'

'That's really kind,' Elliot says, a little lost in Anjali's smile, to my mind.

'We vets have got to stick together,' she says, 'and I... I really admire your work.'

I squint a bit in confusion at this, but feel a sudden compulsion to not stick around and find out what the hot young vet's on about. I also don't want to interrogate what this reaction of mine is all about either. I was never one for the whole green-eyed monster thing, and especially not over some bloke I don't even know and who I'm categorically not interested in getting to know.

I thank her and gather our things, ready to leave.

'We'll ring first thing, see how he is,' Elliot throws in, and we make for the door. I might have dragged him by the sleeve a bit.

Chapter Fifteen

'Do chips taste better when you've just done life-saving surgery?' I say.

'Definitely.' Elliot's eating like a starved man again. He's halfway through his newspaper-wrapped bundle and I've barely even made a start on my gorgeous flaky cod – freshly landed at Torbay this morning, according to the chip shop owner. We'd asked the taxi to stop on the way back because I was getting dizzy from lack of food.

We've got our feet dangling down into the harbour from our perch at the very end of the lowest tier of the Clove Lore sea wall. The sun's about to set and it's definitely threatening to turn chilly but the colours in the sky (wild dark blues and orange) and the heat of our food is helping insulate us. Plus Elliot's sitting surprisingly close to me, and I don't think I mind.

'You sure he's going to be OK?' I say. I'd heard him on the phone to Jowan in the taxi saying as much.

'Hard to tell with a dog that age, but I've seen older dogs pull round from anaesthetic and go on with their lives a hundred times before now, so I'm hopeful.'

'Anjali was hopeful as well,' I say, peering round for Elliot's reaction. He shrugs and takes another bite of fish, the little wooden fork tiny in his grasp. 'What did she mean when she said she admires your work?'

'Oh, I *uh*…' He's definitely grimacing and trying to hide it by taking a big swig from his Coke can. 'I wrote a textbook about veterinary care a few years ago.' He throws the information away like it's nothing.

'No way!'

'Yeah, right at the end of my doctorate. It became a bit of a staple for undergraduates studying vet medicine, and I had a YouTube channel, *Dr Elliot's Day*, where I'd document basic procedures; that had a few followers.'

'How many's a few?' I'm trying hard not to gush but that's seriously impressive.

'A few thousand, not that many.'

I can tell he's being modest. I find myself thinking I'd probably be quite happy to watch him swabbing infected animal parts online, and I mentally tell myself off for being creepy.

'Anyway, that was a long time ago now, people have forgotten.'

'Anjali hasn't. I think she was a bit star-struck. What uni did you go to?'

He laughs uncomfortably. 'Forget about it, OK. People don't know me anymore.' His voice is terse and I see his jaw flex with tension, so I let it go. 'What about you? You studied at uni, right?'

'Uh-huh, English. I loved it. The subject, I mean.' I'm not telling him about Mack, that's for sure. 'I was a mature student. I lived at home, caring for my gran.'

Elliot turns to look at me, scrunching up his empty chip wrapper. 'Is she, *uh...*'

'She's still very much doing her thing. She texted me this this morning.' I show him my phone and the picture of Gran, Bernice and Jill reclining on sun loungers around the New Start Village indoor pool. Gran's in a yellow floral two-piece and matching swimming cap with plastic daisies all over it. 'Stanley the Stud took the shot, apparently.'

'Who's he?' Elliot laughs.

'God knows, and I didn't ask either.' I shudder a bit and Elliot laughs again. It's a lovely sound. I want him to do it more so I tell him all about the yarn-bombers and what we did to the police station that time.

'Family's important to you?' he says when I'm done. 'I saw the recipe book on the counter in the café yesterday.'

'Ah, you saw that.'

'The inscription was nice.'

'You read it? What if it had been my diary or something scandalous like that?'

'You got me! I was curious. It looked so old, and the words, they were so…' Elliot's eyes meet the darkening horizon and his jaw tenses again. I know what words he means: Grandad's inscription for Dad on the first page. I read it over and over again on my first night in Clove Lore. I recite the words aloud into the summer evening.

'*Yeast to grow a family. Sugar to sweeten it. Icing for forgiveness and to cover over our mistakes. Here are my recipes, for you son, when you are old enough. You were the best thing I ever made. Love, Dad.*'

Elliot's gone quiet, so I finish my fish and chips and the feeling of being a million miles from home returns, and I'd been doing so well too. I haven't been able to reach Mum or Dad yet, other than some late-night texts. They're out and about at restaurants and long walks out of town, making up for lost time, I guess. When he speaks, his voice is deeper than before. 'Family's important to you,' he says again. It's not a question this time.

'Yeah, isn't it the same way for everybody?'

'*Hmm.*' His gaze falls down to where our feet dangle above the sloshing waves. 'That's why you went to uni late?'

'Yeah, lots of people do, for all kinds of reasons. My parents couldn't afford for me to go and I was looking after Gran. I'd spent years secretly looking at college prospectuses on my phone and dreaming about being a student. Don't laugh, but I'd watch live city webcams of Belfast and Oxford when Gran was napping. I'd see all the happy students cycling by and I'd try to imagine myself there. In the end I enrolled part time at a campus a few miles from home. That place saved me from drowning, at least that's what it felt like. I never got over my amazement at actually being there. Do you know what I mean?' Elliot smiles but I can tell he doesn't really get it. 'It seems to me your childhood was my actual dream life. Cambridgeshire, a library at home, straight to uni after school, puppies everywhere.'

'I don't know about that,' he says, uncomfortably. 'And my family aren't from Cambridge, that's just where I ended up living and working.'

'Oh, OK.' I remember him saying his parents were often too busy for him. He was lonely. Maybe that's why he's so reticent to talk about himself? He's not used to it.

'So where are you from originally?' I pry.

He throws me a look that tells me he's not inclined to answer, and I don't want him slipping away from me again, so I try to reel him back into the conversation. 'Tell me something happy,' I say.

'Such as?'

I laugh. 'You don't have to look so startled. I don't know, tell me why you ended up here at the bookshop.'

'I thought you wanted a happy story?'

'What does that mean?'

'Nothing.'

For a second I worry I'm definitely losing him, but to my surprise he looks out at the last streaks of orange sunset and starts talking. 'When I was a kid I'd dream about visiting the great bookshops of the world.'

Me too, I want to cry out, but I don't want to do anything that stops him talking.

'Have you ever been to Venice?' he says, glancing at me briefly.

I shake my head. I don't want to tell him I've never been anywhere.

'In Venice there's the Libreria Acqua Alta. You think Borrow-a-Bookshop is eccentric? This place might fall down upon your head, it's so ancient, and there's a gondola stuffed with books in the middle of the shop and outside you can climb a staircase made of books, I'm not even kidding, and from the top there's a wonderful view of the canal.'

'No way!'

'Yes! It even says, painted on the wall by the staircase, "climb these books for a wonderful view", or something like that. It's years since I've been.'

'You've actually been there?'

'Oh yeah. And Shakespeare and Company. That's probably the most famous bookshop right?'

'Yes!' I pitch in, feeling my enthusiasm bubbling up. 'I've always wanted to go there. You've been?'

'I got fleas.'

'What?'

'Yeah, we went to a poetry reading one night in the summer, left the place covered in bites! And the electricity went off while I was there too.'

'Did you visit in the nineteen thirties?'

'Nineteen ninety-nine. Anyway, they're all modern now. You can follow them on Instagram.'

I make a mental note to do exactly that. 'How old were you then?'

'Only small. We went on a school trip.'

'You went on a school trip to *Paris*?'

'I cried every day, I was so homesick, if that helps? I was kinda too young to be packed off with my form, but that's what happened. Went to Disneyland too though, so...' he holds his hands up and levels them, balancing his childhood trauma against a trip to the magic kingdom.

'Elliot, how old are you?' I can't figure this guy out, he's so grown up and serious and so like a lost child too.

He hesitates for a moment but seems to relent. He's already given so much away, maybe it's a case of in for a penny... 'I'm thirty-one.'

'So you were...' I can do this. Concentrate. Elliot waits for me. 'Nine? When your school took you to Paris?'

'That's right.'

I don't know which competing feeling wins out; sympathy for little homesick Elliot or amazement that I got that simple bit of mental arithmetic right first time.

'And here's me thinking our school trips to Melrose Abbey and Robert Smail's Printing Works were awesome,' I say. Actually, they were. Seeing a nineteenth-century printing press at work was kind of mind-blowing for ten-year-old me, and definitely a formative experience in my love of old books, but still, *Paris*!

Elliot's not stopping, and he's turned to face me a little, addressing this all to me. 'My favourite was Livraria Lello in Portugal. I spent the entire day there a couple of summers back. Have you seen it?'

Course I haven't. 'Haven't even heard of that one.'

'It looks like a wedding cake from the outside and a gothic cathedral inside. It's all stained glass ceilings and winding staircases and wall to wall treasures. I bought a cigar in the café there, don't even smoke, but in my head I'd become Ernest Hemingway or something.' He laughs lightly, and I love the way the amber in his eyes flashes.

'You were alone there too?'

'*Uh*, no, I went with my ex.' Just like that, the magic of listening to Elliot speak and the light in his eyes ends and I see him retreat again. 'Sorry, I was talking too much.' I get the impression he means he's *said* too much.

'No, you were talking just the right amount. I liked it.'

His eyes search my face and I can't work out if he's trying to suss out whether he can trust me with his stories or whether he can trust himself not to spill any more of them, but I can tell what he concludes when he stands up and slaps his hands to his thighs, and says, 'Sea's coming in.'

I pack away my disappointment, trying to keep the mood light. 'That's a shame. I've wanted to paddle in the sea all day long.'

'Good idea,' Elliot says, and he reaches his hand down to pull me up.

'Oh, right,' I mumble, trying not to think how his big hand makes mine look tiny in comparison. I let him lift me, but still stumble a little, which is dangerous when I'm right on the precipice.

A few moments later and he's led the way along the harbour wall. There's a string of white bulbs glowing into the twilight and a big lantern behind us that serves as a kind of mini lighthouse for boats searching for the harbour mouth. The lantern must have burst into light at some point as we ate but I couldn't tell you when. I'd been distracted.

As we pass the pub, sea shanties and chatter spill out. 'Lively for a Monday night,' Elliot says. 'Hold on, I'll be back in a sec,' and he nips into the bar.

I dump our chip wrappers and cans in the bin by the door, glad of a quiet moment to collect myself because he'd gripped my hand for the tiniest fraction of a second too long after I got to my feet, and I'm sure we had a moment where I was looking up into his face and he was peering down at me with narrowed, intent eyes. That or because he wasn't wearing his specs, his eyes were adjusting to my proximity in the dull light… or maybe he had a stray hair in his eye? Yes, that's likely what it was. Anyway, my hand's still sort of tingling. 'Oh no,' I mutter to myself. 'That's not good.'

'What isn't? Don't you like beer?' I spin around to see Elliot with a frothy pint in each hand and a grin on his face. 'I figured we've earned these.'

'Well *you* have. I didn't do anything heroic today.'

He laughs, a little abashed, as he hands a glass over.

'You're an actual doctor of something lifesaving. What can I do? Prescribe you a poem? Suture you with a sonnet?'

'Words are just as important as medicine, for healing,' he says, eyes dark again, and he takes a drink of beer before changing the subject again – something, I'm noticing, he's rather good at doing. 'Right, paddling! Come on.'

It isn't easy making our way over the beach; I stumble a few times over the big pebbles that make up the shore. I resent spilling nearly a third of my beer and decide to drink what's left as fast as I can with one foot on the edge of a small boat that's stranded far up the beach. 'To prevent spillage,' I say. 'Cheers.' Elliot joins me, raising his glass to mine and then draining it with a big gulp.

It's hard to make out the rusting chains leading from the little boats all the way to the sea wall from where they're moored, but we take our time scrambling over them in the dark on our way to the water's edge.

'What were they called?' I say, as we leave the pebbly bit of the beach behind us and hit the wet sand and I immediately untie my Converse. 'The dogs your parents gave you?'

'Oh,' Elliot laughs before he answers. 'A pug called Andrew, and a shih tzu called Selina.'

'*Uhh*, ok-ay.'

'What! I was just a kid! Actually, Selina was an au pair my parents hired when I was in pre-prep school. I had the biggest crush on her. She left when I was seven, broke my heart.'

'So you named your dog after her.'

'Never forgot her.'

'And Andrew?'

'I just thought that was a really cool name for a puppy.' He's smiling fondly at his own childhood innocence and it makes me smile too.

We're just a few metres from the waves. They're rougher than I thought they'd be and splashing cold spray into the air. 'You don't have any pets now?'

'Not exactly.'

'What does that mean?'

'I have some animals. My parents are looking after them, I think.'

'You think? Don't you know?'

'They are, they're looking after them.'

I've turned my trousers up by this point and am wading into the cold water. My skin tingles at the chilly sensation. It's rather wonderful really. The reflected lights from the sea wall and the pub break up, rippling and shimmering on the surface of the gentle waves. 'You can't *not* come in for a paddle. Get in here.'

I'm pretty sure he rolls his eyes, although it's hard to see in this light, but he still throws off his shoes and joins me up to my knees in the chilly surf.

'So this is the wide Atlantic then?' I say, goofily.

'Next stop Newfoundland. Granted, you might run into a few Scilly Islands on the way.'

'Sounds nice. I've never been anywhere apart from here,' I admit. 'Except for in books; I've been twice around the globe and half way across the galaxy in books.'

'Thank goodness for books,' he says.

'Right? I think our little bookshop came along at just the right time for me, Elliot.'

'You said *our* bookshop. Does this mean you're getting used to having me around?'

'I don't have much choice, do I?' I hope he can see me smirking.

'Charming!'

'You know it's true. Anyway, I'm glad you were here today. I don't think I'd have braved examining Aldous by myself. In fact, I doubt I'd even have thought of it, and who knows what could have happened to him if you hadn't suspected something was up.'

Elliot's looking down to his feet under the dark water. 'The bookshop came along at just the right time for me too. Thank you for letting me stay.'

'No problem,' I tell him. I lift my face to look at him and his dark hair is a glossy, metallic blue under the scant harbour lights, strands lifting in the breeze around his face. He must see me goggling at him because he looks up at the sky suddenly, remarks on how there's no moon tonight, and shifts a little further away. Why that wounds me, I don't know. He told me he'd keep his distance, and I'd insisted upon it too, so I'm getting what I wanted.

I make my way to dry land again, pins and needles tingling in my chilled feet. 'I should probably call it a night,' I say. 'I have cupcakes to make in the morning.'

—

Later, as he drags the mattress down the spiral stairs, this time knocking a ceiling light so it swings perilously in its fitting, I can't bring myself to look at him, and I pretend to brush the sand from my feet and make a fuss about how it's getting everywhere, and we say our usual awkward goodnights.

While I brush my teeth and get into my jammies I can't help but let my mind wander all over the place.

Maybe it's the sea air? They say it changes you, don't they? Makes you hungry for fried fish and helps you sleep deeply at night. Maybe it also makes you ever so slightly fancy big, nerdy, high-achieving, muscly holiday-crashers who you don't know the first thing about and who have it in their power to save helpless creatures' lives and... No. No, I'm not doing this.

There's eleven days of my Clove Lore escape left and I'm here to enjoy it, drama free, like Willy Russell's Shirley Valentine running off to Greece. Oh no, that's a bad example. She ends up in bed with that sly geezer, doesn't she? No, I'm more like Bathsheba Everdene in *Far from the Madding Crowd* when she's running her farm: self-reliant, business-like, out to prove herself. Of course she ends up trapped in a mad love triangle, doesn't she?

I give up. I'm going to bed, but just before I let myself drift off, I can't help reaching for my phone, switching it to silent and searching for Elliot's YouTube channel. What was it called? Something adorably nerdy? *Dr Elliot's Day?*

'This channel has been removed by the maker,' the app tells me. Bit weird. Why would he do that? I guess it saves me the shame of stalkerishly watching him operate on small furry animals for the next hour, which is absolutely the kind of thing I know I'd end up doing.

I hear Elliot downstairs climbing into his makeshift bed and saying to the empty shop 'Goodnight Aldous, little mate,' in a low, solemn voice, and I throw myself under the covers with a groan.

Chapter Sixteen

Tuesday morning started with discovering Gran's card on the shop doormat with two ten pound notes inside and the words, 'To be spent on something frivolous.'

It's not my thirtieth until the end of September but it took me back to birthdays when I was little, while making me despair at Gran's trust in the postal system. I immediately decided against telling her how risky sending cash through the mail is. She'd only say, 'You got it, didn't you?' I've already sent one of the bookshop postcards straight back to say thank you.

Elliot was gone by the time I'd butter-iced this morning's cupcakes, off to check on Aldous at the vet's with Jowan, and I've managed both the shop and the café by myself all morning. Not that I was rushed off my feet. It's drizzled steadily since dawn and there's only a tiny sliver of blue sky peering out behind clouds now that it's noon. The rain must be keeping the visitors away from Clove Lore today. I bet those cobbles are deathly slippery.

Elliot's been back for ten minutes bringing the good news that Aldous is doing really well, although he's refusing to eat the plain rice Anjali's been offering him.

'You should have offered him one of my scones,' I tell him as he gets into his apron to take over at the café counter.

'I'm afraid Aldous's days as a connoisseur of baked goods are over. No more scones and cheese sarnies. It's rice and shredded chicken for the foreseeable for him.'

'Chicken soup's probably all right, isn't it?' I say.

'*Hmm*, I can't see why not, as long as it's salt-free. Jowan told me the daft mutt's been on a can of cream of chicken soup every day for the past two and a half years down at the Siren.'

'The little guy's had a whole village of enablers all this time,' I say. 'Indulging him nearly killed him.'

'He's grieving though,' Elliot says, and I see his fondness for the stinky mutt written all over his face.

Just as Elliot is leaving me to my own devices for the afternoon, the shop bell rings out and a familiar-looking woman appears, white-haired and rosy-cheeked, a stubby pencil behind one ear, and literally half Elliot's height.

'Hello, me dears. I've brought a little treat from the ice-cream cottage,' she announces, handing over two small tubs. 'Clotted cream vanilla; my best seller.'

'Thank you! Mrs… Crocombe?' I ask, gleefully taking the tub. It's ages since I had ice cream.

'We're practically neighbours; my shop's only Down-along,' she says, her eyes darting between me and Elliot.

'I've seen it,' Elliot says, taking his tub and, as I predicted, starting to eat immediately, even before he's finished thanking her, with big wolfish gulps. I can't help smiling at the sight of him working on the tiny tub. He's what Gran would call approvingly, 'a good eater'. It's kind of endearing.

I snap right out of that line of thought when I realise Mrs Crocombe's eyes are upon me and she's wearing a salacious sort of triumphant grin.

'Are you, *um*, one of the volunteers who help out the bookshop charity trust?' I say, hoping to keep our visitor's mind off her plans to repopulate the village school in the space of one summer.

'In a way,' she replies. 'I offer Jowan's tenants the use of the washer-dryer in the back room of the ice-cream cottage. Here's a key. It'll let you in the back door. Laundry room's separated from my flat above by a locked door so you'll be quite alone. Powder and softener's on top of the machine. Feel free to use it any time.'

'That's very generous of you, thank you,' Elliot puts in, now that he's finished his ice cream. I've still only had two bites.

'It *is* a generous offer. I was beginning to worry I'd have to go on an emergency shopping trip for clean pants any day now.' Why did I say that out loud? Mrs Crocombe's giving me a look that tells me she's not sure she wants my DNA in her future vision of Clove Lore.

'Have you always lived in the village?' Elliot asks, saving me from mentally kicking myself much longer.

Mrs C.'s eyes light up and she takes a few steps closer towards Elliot. He's clearly a lot more promising a candidate for prodigious parenthood than I am. 'All my life, born and raised. You know, Jowan was telling me about Aldous and your trip to Anjali's practice. Nice girl, isn't she?' This is said *very* deliberately. She's fixed on him like a pointer on a hare and won't be distracted; not even Izaak stumbling into the shop and coming to stand by me at the counter puts her off. I smile my welcome at him.

'She is,' Elliot says, totally unaware that Mrs Crocombe's half way to having the pair of them married off already. 'She was very proficient. An excellent surgeon.'

'She's single, you know,' Mrs C. reaches into the pocket on the front of her apron, checks something's there – I'd be willing to bet it's her book of eligible villagers – and, satisfied, withdraws her hand once more. 'Lovely family. They live a little way along the headland, you know?'

'In the school catchment area, then,' I whisper to Izaak, and he stifles a laugh.

'Single, are you?' she asks Elliot, not missing a beat, and I admit, I look searchingly at Elliot too, and so does Izaak. All three of us are hanging on his next words and he isn't even aware of the fact.

'*Umm*, yes?' Elliot says, and I see him retreating into himself once more, just like he did when Minty was giving him the third degree. 'I think that was the bell in the café,' he says.

'No it wasn't,' cries Mrs Crocombe, quick as a flash, her eyes still fixed on Elliot.

'Pretty sure it was,' Elliot calls over his shoulder as he clomps away across the shop, knocking a box set of Marjorie Blackmans and our entire Roald Dahl collection off a display table, and he's gone, crouching to get through the little door connecting the shop and café.

'He can move fast for such a tall guy,' says Izaak.

'And so broad about the shoulders,' Mrs Crocombe puts in, rather dreamily, drawing her notebook from her pocket. She mutters something to herself, along the lines of 'He'll do very well,' and turns to leave. I thank her again for fixing my laundry predicament and for the ice cream, and she's gone, but not before looking between me and Izaak, hopefully at first, before seeming to think again and shaking her head dismissively.

'I think you and I were almost set up there,' I say to Izaak, when she's out of sight.

'*Hmm?*' Izaak doesn't seem to register what I'm saying and is now wandering amongst the shelves.

'Is there something you're after, Izaak?'

'I'm looking for a book.'

'Any one in particular?' I say, clapping my hands, ready for my first sale of the day.

'It's orange.' He says this with a nod of finality, like I should know instantly what he's on about.

'O-kay, anything else? Title? Author? Date?'

'Yes, it's got a date. That's right.'

'Right. So it's orange and it's got a date. *A Clockwork Orange?*' I say, taking a stab in the dark.

'No, read that, wasn't a fan. This one's got the big screens and the thingies that listen, you know? In your house. And, *uh*, there's these pair meeting in secret, and they go to the countryside, but they get caught. You know the one?'

'*Umm*, not really,' I say.

'*Nineteen Eighty-Four!*' comes Elliot's voice from the café.

'That's the one!' Izaak calls back.

'Are you hiding out in there, listening to us?' I shout back towards the café door.

'Big Brother is always listening,' says Elliot's grinning disembodied head, appearing around the café doorframe before it disappears again. His hair had hung down in a mussed, swishy curtain of black which makes me stare after him for a while, long after he's out of sight.

Izaak clears his throat, amused. 'So have you got it then?'

We spend a long time searching for a copy but fail to turn one up. 'Sorry, Izaak, one of these days I'll have the book you're after. Can't I interest you in an *Animal Farm*, we've two copies of that, or *The Road to Wigan Pier*?'

'Oh, I don't think so,' he says. 'Not to worry. I'll get one on the internet.'

I make a note to myself to ask Jowan if we can order books in from wholesalers. That way I can send Izaak away happy one of these days.

—

I'm glad I decided to take a break from the shop this afternoon. I left Elliot to cash up and raced Up-along at ten to five.

The sight of the visitors' centre shops yesterday as we hurried Aldous to the vet has been burned on my retina, and Gran's notes are similarly burning a hole in my pocket. I'm on holiday, I should be allowed to buy myself a little souvenir, and Gran gave me strict instructions to spend it on something nice, and I know she'd be annoyed if I told her I'd bought more books with it.

By 'frivolous' Gran means nothing practical or educational; a proper treat. If *she* were here she'd probably splurge it all on clotted cream fudge, but I have a better idea.

I'd clocked the little clothes shop last night when the taxi dropped off Elliot and me – and our fish suppers – after our vet adventure. It was all locked up by then, of course, but I spotted the colourful clothes behind the window grille, thinking I'd detected the tell-tale signs of a hippy clothes store, the kind of place you might find Himalayan knits and llama keychains. And I was right.

I tried on a few things, shopping right outside of my comfort zone, because this stuff isn't really 'me', and then the shop assistant said she had Just The Thing.

As soon as I tried on the midnight-blue, ankle-length strappy dress with a braided tie-waist in the incense-scented changing room, I knew I had to buy it. The best thing was, Gran's money covered it, just. The girl cut the tags off there and then, and so now, I'm floating back down the damp cobbles in flowy cotton, comfy in my Converse, with my old clothes in a carrier bag that reads 'Astral Breeks – Alternative Clothing and Surf Shop'.

The drizzle's stopped and the view of the blue summer horizon and gulls gliding by is truly breath-taking. I tell myself to loiter a bit and enjoy it but my feet are listening instead to a quieter voice at the back of my brain saying I should rush back to the shop and show Elliot this dress – the same irrational, nagging voice that told me back there in the changing room to fix my hair and put some lip gloss on before seeing him.

I reach the shop door and take a deep breath, not quite knowing what I'm supposed to do next. Do a twirl for him, maybe, like I'd do for Gran if she were here? Obviously not. That would be needy and… well, odd. I'll just get on with my evening and keep out of his way like we planned.

Elliot's nowhere to be seen anyway. I check upstairs. Nothing. Maybe he's gone to see Aldous again? Or he's with Anjali, the lovely vet from a Mrs Crocombe-Approved family.

He's already cashed up and the money box is back under my bed, so I head to the café to eat any of this morning's remaining cupcakes all by myself over the sink.

Halfway across the shop floor I hear the music, something delicate and jazzy coming from the café. I lower my head to get through the little door and there's Elliot jumping to attention, looking surprised.

'*Aww*, you're here already. I'm not quite finished,' he says, before standing aside to reveal the little table set for two. He's unpacking a big wicker hamper and inspecting each item before laying it on the café counter. And he's changed his clothes. Black pants and a shirt, open at the neck, and sleeves rolled up, the thin white cotton under as much stress from his arm muscles as I am right now.

'What's all this?' I say, stuck against the doorframe, my feet not wanting to move.

'Jowan dropped it off, to say thank you for saving Aldous. Look, it's all Devonshire produce. There's cheese, bread, loads of deli stuff. I don't know *what* these are.' He turns to me and holds out a plastic tub containing something wrapped in some kind of leaves, but as he does so, he freezes, just for a second.

'You weren't wearing that when you went out.' His eyes scan down my body and when they reach the floor he seems to jolt out of his thoughts suddenly. He turns back to the hamper, rummaging again, eyes narrowed with renewed concentration. 'You look beautiful. Is that new?' he says, failing to convince me he's examining the label on a bottle of wine.

I ramble for a while, telling him about the shop I found and he listens in silence. 'Let's open this,' he says when I'm done, but not before throwing a sidelong glance at my dress again while I pretend I'm absorbed in straightening the cutlery at the little table.

'I'll get the glasses,' I say, making my way through the shop and into the little kitchen which we haven't cooked in yet, not even once since we arrived.

I imagine myself for a second, my hair wrapped up in a towel maybe, and Elliot in a robe, standing at the little hob making bacon and eggs for two. I shake away the domestic daydream and grab the only two glasses there are, mismatched vintage tumblers, from the little yellow cabinet, and make my way back through to the café and to Elliot.

It's exactly this kind of homely fantasy that got me into so much trouble with Mack, I remind myself – the man who, it turned out, was actually a stranger to me. Just like Elliot.

I ask myself, what do I even know about my fellow bookseller, really? But the answer gets away from me when I dip back into the café and find Elliot has drawn the lace curtains a little and is lighting two tall white candles in silver holders between our place settings.

'There… were candles in the hamper?' I ask. I don't know what I'll do if he says the romantic lighting was all his idea. Actually, I do know. I'll die here on the spot.

'Yeah, is that usual with hampers?' he says, quirking a brow.

'*Umm*, not really.' I put the glasses down and immediately pour the wine, strawberry-jam red and smelling utterly gluggable. 'This was nice of Jowan,' I say, standing over the now candlelit table, side by side with Elliot.

Elliot doesn't look at me when he answers. 'I think he was feeling decidedly guilty about letting Aldous have his own way all this time. Maybe now he's realised his lenience was actually neglect.'

The music emanating from Elliot's phone on the counter switches to something deep and soulful with a Motown vibe. We both freeze, looking at all the food laid out so invitingly, but neither of us sit.

'Should I open the curtains again?' Elliot says, as though suddenly unsure of himself.

I tell him its fine and force his wine into his hand. Maybe if we drink up it'll make this a little less strange.

'Cheers,' I say, before diving into my tumbler. Surprisingly, Elliot doesn't neck it, like everything else I've seen him taste so far. I watch him over the rim of my glass. He's savouring a mouthful, swallowing slowly, closing his eyes.

After that, I can't concentrate on much. I feel as though my eyes are somehow fixed to his mouth by an invisible electrified wire, and from there it connects to the pit of my stomach.

Daniel's words of yesterday dance through my head as Elliot suggests we sit down to eat, and I think maybe my friend is right, I *could* have a holiday romance. Why not? I've already treated myself to something frivolous today. I could do it again.

But that thought doesn't quite land correctly. It feels like a misfire, especially when Elliot tops up my glass and leans over all the lovely food and asks, 'What should we try first?'

He's capable of acting like a normal human being. I need to as well. 'The obvious answer is the bread and cheese,' I quip, 'closely followed by anything else with carbs.' I'm giving away my nervousness, I'm sure of it.

I try to be sensible and focus on our meal. We fill our plates with crumbly white cheddar, chutney, pâté, and great hunks of bread torn from a rustic sourdough loaf. There are greenhouse tomatoes too, and olives and sweet peppers in herby oils.

'I could live off stuff like this,' I tell Elliot, who smiles back, his hands hovering over his cutlery, again taking it slowly, like he's here to savour everything this time.

No sooner do I have a mouthful of food than Elliot asks me a question. 'Did Mrs Crocombe say anything to you, after I'd left?'

'*Mmmm*… nope,' I force myself to swallow, shaking my head and digging into the potato salad and the little pancake things topped with salmon and frilly dill fronds. 'She disappeared sharpish, like a woman on a mission.'

'That's what worries me. I think her and Minty are in cahoots. I just… I don't like being talked about.' Elliot pushes some baby leaves around his plate.

'I think that's unavoidable around here. For the past four days I've felt as though *we* were the most interesting stories in the shop, for the locals, I mean.'

'*Hmm*,' Elliot doesn't smile at this. In fact he looks pretty miffed.

I take a deep breath before I say what's on my mind. 'Look, if I tell you something, do you promise not to run off and hide every time you see the volunteers?'

He meets my eyes, startled and staring. 'Oh no, what?'

I laugh. 'It's nothing, it's silly really. You'll find it funny.' I can't say for sure he'll find it funny but I want him to relax and stop worrying about the village tattletales. I'm from a town just big enough to generate some pretty low-key scandal and small enough for gossip about it to spread fast, so maybe I'm more used to this kind of thing than Elliot is. He did say he grew up in the countryside though, didn't he? He must know how this kind of thing works? 'The thing is,' I say, feeling my cheeks colouring a little in spite of myself. 'Mrs

Crocombe has a long-running village sweepstake on single people coupling up, and I... I think we're in her book.'

'Oh, is that all?' His shoulders visibly sink with relief.

'Why, what did you think was going on?'

'Nothing.' Elliot eats again with renewed interest in his plate, but still he's chewing slowly, contented.

'You don't mind them betting on you?'

He shrugs. It says, *I can think of worse things.*

'Who do you think Mrs Crocombe's money's on?' I push, wishing I had some kind of filter between my brain and my mouth.

'No idea,' Elliot replies.

I *could* say what I'm thinking, that she wants to see Elliot and Anjali together but I'm leaving Anjali out of this. It's not fair to talk about her when she's not here. 'Who do you reckon Izaak's money's on?' I say instead.

'Definitely you and him,' Elliot says, and this time he does laugh, but it's gentle. I don't mind him teasing me, not when his amber irises are sparkling in the candlelight and directed intently at me.

'Who do you think Jowan's betting on?' I say, feeling increasingly warm and hazy from the wine.

Elliot nods at the candles. 'Us, I'm guessing.'

We both smile down at our plates for a while. After that, things seem easier. Ella Fitzgerald is singing about the summertime fish jumping and the cotton being high, and I feel myself relaxing at last, for the first time since I encountered Elliot on Saturday night, in fact.

I'm sure his eyes are on my mouth as we talk and drink. That doesn't stop me looking twice to check, and yes, his eyes keep falling, fixing on my lips, and I've seen him getting lost and his own lips parting a little as he looks.

When it happens again, I smile and he jolts a little, blinking, and our eyes meet and I am certain we both feel the shift between us. I let myself sink deeper into the warm, relaxed atmosphere, even though a tiny, frightened part of me is half-heartedly looking for a way out.

Elliot's asking me a lot of questions and I'm happy to answer every one. I tell him about my parents and the Facetime we had earlier (at last, I caught them at home) when Mum showed me round the new house, dodging cardboard boxes and looking happy but tired.

I talk about their holiday plans. I think he's looking at me a little quizzically at one point and it makes me self-conscious, like I'm talking too much, like I only have my parents' lives to talk about and no real experiences of my own to share. I talk on, trying to drown out my worries that I've no anecdotes of my own because I've done so little with my life so far.

We've finished eating and the wine bottle's somehow empty, and when did it get dark outside? That's when I throw his questions back to him. 'Tell me about where you're from. Tell me about being at uni, and doing a doctorate.'

'What exactly do you want to know?' he says, laying his cutlery down and cradling his glass close to his face in both hands.

'I want to know everything about you,' I say, and it's true. I really do.

Elliot's eyes leave mine for a moment and it feels like winter coming, I'd been so warm under his gaze. He gets up, reaches for his phone on the counter and skips a few songs.

'Or, we could stop talking?' he says.

I draw my neck back, trying to work out what he means.

'We could… dance?'

I think I see the little flash of inspiration pass over his eyes when he blurts these words. It makes me laugh, it's so unexpected.

I don't let myself think about how something feels a tiny bit off, as though I'd been meaning to say something but it slipped my mind, or maybe I'd been waiting to hear something? But, it's gone now, whatever it was. Elliot's reaching his hand out to me, standing there in the middle of the candlelit café. Marvin Gaye's singing satin-sheets soul now, and even if I could find the strength to refuse Elliot, no one alive can refuse Marvin.

I'm on my feet and stepping close to Elliot. We're holding hands with elbows bent like we're ten-year-olds at a disco and for a moment I don't really know what I'm supposed to do next. I have a vague notion of the Hokey Cokey and the choreography to 'Tragedy' by

Steps (who doesn't?) but I have the good sense to know it's just *not* the occasion for either of those.

I'm searching my brain for dance moves, *any* moves, when Elliot draws me closer with a hand placed firmly on the small of my back. I instinctively slip my arm around his back too and he changes his grip on my hand, bringing it to his chest and holding it there tucked up inside his grasp, and somehow we both know to start to sway.

I'm just going to breathe through this.

Dancing with Elliot, my head inching closer to his pecs, his head bowed over me and his mouth so close to my temple… it's a lot to process.

The track changes, Billy Paul starts singing about 'Me and Mrs Jones' and Elliot's palm spreads flat across the base of my spine. I feel him inhale sharply close to my ear through clenched teeth and I know I really am in trouble, and I let my head drop onto his chest.

I thought people only heard other people's hearts beating in books, but against the soft fabric of Elliot's shirt and the hardness of his body beneath, I hear it and feel it, and it is pounding.

'Is this still OK?' he says, and his voice rumbles deeply through his chest wall and the whole thing makes me a bit swoony.

I close my eyes and I nod, just the once. Yes, this is definitely still OK.

I hear my brain excitedly whispering something about how I'm *just* like Scarlett O'Hara when she comes out of mourning and dances with Captain Butler in her black crepe dress in *Gone with the Wind*, and why haven't I read that book recently, it's so darn good?

We're hardly moving at all now, and the whole world seems to slow around us as Elliot draws his knuckles lightly up my back, over my dress, until he reaches skin and he turns his hand so I feel the soft, searching sensation of fingertips trailing upwards following the undulations to the top of my spine, achingly slow, coming to rest against the nape of my neck where all my nerves prickle and fizz like a bonfire night sky.

I pull my head from his chest, letting him cup my face and I drowsily open my eyes long enough to see him bring his mouth

138

down, and as his lips press lightly against my cheekbone just below my eye, I lean my body closer into his. After a slow moment our mouths touch at last and his breathing hitches and that's all the sign I need to let my hands travel wherever they want to along his body.

This is kissing. This is what it's supposed to be like – like it is in books – but this isn't a book, it's happening to *me*.

Elliot lifts me onto the counter like there's nothing easier and I wrap my legs around him, pulling him close, letting the world outside dissolve away entirely until there is only the wine racing in our bloodstreams, the tattoos on Elliot's shoulders as I push his shirt off, and the sound of my name on his lips moaned against my throat.

Chapter Seventeen

We spend the next three days like this (when we aren't working in our shop or café) and in all that time Elliot never once drags his mattress down onto the bookshop floor at night.

We've barely set foot outside the shop and Elliot's forgone his morning run to stay here with me each morning instead. Watching him doing core crunches on the bedroom floor, one hundred reps every morning, is probably one of the nicest sights I've ever beheld.

Oh, and that tattoo? It's a fox bursting through red flames and trailing black stars and swirls in its wake all across his shoulders, up his spine to his hairline and over the backs of his upper arms. Perfect.

The one thing we *haven't* really done much of is talking, so I was thrilled this morning, a bright and sea-breezy Saturday dawn, when we managed this exchange before going our separate ways for the day – him to the bookshop, me to my early morning spot by the ovens:

'I'm getting up now,' I said.

'Should I look away?' Elliot replied, sleepy and half-smiling under the sheets.

'Bit late for that.' I slipped out from under the covers, totally naked, and unhurriedly made for the door. Elliot sat up a little in bed to watch me.

'*Aww*, hell,' he said in a low voice, clutching his hand to his bare chest.

I panicked immediately and flew back to his side on the bed. 'Oh my God, what is it? Are you all right?'

'It's just, it's just…'

'What? You're worrying me!'

'It's just we might have a problem here with, like, how much I'm attracted to you.'

'Shut up,' I cried, smacking his arm, and the muscle didn't yield at all.

'I'm not kidding. You're so beautiful and I'm just so…'

'Stop being daft,' I warned, hoping he'd never stop.

His eyes trailed over me and it made my skin prickle like it did the first time we undressed after our café picnic and Marvin Gaye.

'It's not my fault,' he said, mournfully. 'It's these eyes of mine. They can't help it. But every time I look at you it actually physically hurts, right in here.' He jabbed a finger between his pecs, making me laugh. I made a show of pretending to push him away when he reached his arms around me. 'I don't know what to tell you, Jude. It's a problem.' He tilted his head to kiss me before breaking off. 'Listen, I've got an idea. *Maybe* my eyes will get tired of you if they just stare at you for, say… the next fifty years or so? And one day they'll be like, OK, *meh*, I'm over it.'

Pushing Elliot onto his back, I clambered on top of him, only the cotton sheet between us. 'I don't like the sound of that.'

'The fifty years bit?'

'The *meh, I'm over it* bit.'

'Hey, take pity on me and my poor heart! I can't feel like this *forever*,' he smiled slyly.

'Well, all right, better start your fifty years of looking right now then, get it over with as quickly as we can.'

'Good plan.' He trailed a fingertip up my arm and the sparks it sent through my nervous system made me limp and I folded, bringing my face close to his. 'I'm gonna get tired of those eyes first, probably,' he continued, low and deep. He kissed both my eyelids in turn and each warm press of his lips felt like a promise. 'And your lips…' He trailed his mouth to mine, languidly claiming it. 'I look forward to the day I can finally say I'm done wanting to look at them… can't come soon enough.'

With our mouths together I heard his breathing accelerate. I kissed him hard until he moaned into my mouth. He turned us both over and at the same time somehow shifted us down the bed and I don't even know how it all happened next, but I couldn't kiss him deep enough, or get enough of his touch and the sweep of his tongue, or the sound of his cries, and another Clove Lore summer dawn slipped away from us.

'Thank God, only forty-nine years, three hundred and sixty-four days left of this torture,' he said as, later, we lay in each other's arms, knowing I was late to turn on the ovens and mix the scones.

'Not long now,' I told him, and we smiled because everything was perfect.

For three days, as soon as the 'Closed' sign was turned in the afternoons, we made our way upstairs and we kissed away the whole night. We've fed ourselves pretty much exclusively on the remnants from the hamper and on the morning's leftover baking and – as in, ahem, other areas of my life – my confidence in the café kitchen is growing.

I've tried rock cakes, sweet bread rolls to be eaten split with jam or chocolate spread, and cherry scones for a twist on a classic, all taken from Grandad's recipe book and all snapped up by café customers.

Jowan brings down the extra ingredients I need from the visitors' centre shop if I text him a shopping list, and since Aldous is still refusing to eat anything other than chicken broth he's got to stay at Anjali's surgery for a little longer.

Mrs Crocombe hasn't popped in again since she put the fear of God into Elliot on Tuesday with all her prying and matchmaking, and Izaak's only been in once enquiring if we had a copy of 'that one with all the chocolate, you know, Frenchy chocolate?', and Elliot and I had both said at the same time, 'You mean *Chocolat*?' And we'd been so pleased to crack his riddle so easily and then so disappointed to realise I'd sold the only copy we had to a holidaymaker from New Zealand a few days before.

I tried not to think of the time slipping by and how a week had already passed and it won't be too long until I have to return to Marygreen, alone. Mum and Dad fly off to begin their cruise this morning, Saturday, leaving my bedroom waiting for me in their new house with my boxes still to be unpacked. The very thought makes me ache for my lovely bookshop and Elliot's arms, makes me wish this was permanent. So I choose not to think about it, for now.

My insistence on needing a self-sufficient summer of solitude was, it turned out, nonsense. This was exactly what I needed, and I don't ever want it to end.

Chapter Eighteen

On Saturday afternoon, moments after the photo of Mum and Dad excitedly raising coffee cups to the camera in the airport lounge pings up on my phone, making me smile and sigh at the same time, Minty breezes briskly into the shop. Everything she does is brisk, I'm learning. She's followed by a stolid, stocky little man. Both of them are in matching tweeds and quilted green body warmers, but while Minty is all natural blonde and horsey, a true thoroughbred of the old English country house variety, the man is definitely redder about the face and more menacing-looking, like a countryfied bodyguard.

Minty's made a beeline for our stationery selection. 'I'm looking for invitations. Have you any?'

'What's it for?' I say. 'There's a few birthday invites and some wedding acceptance cards.' I'm quite proud of the way I've got a handle on our stock. It's only taken a week but I'm completely at home now.

'It's for the estate's fox and field day. These won't do at all. Never mind.' She looks like she minds very much. 'I'll have them made up online. Bovis, can you see to them, have them emailed straight to the VIPs?' This is addressed to the tweedy bruiser, who nods and makes a note on a pad.

Minty introduces us. 'This is my estate manager. The place couldn't run without him.'

Bovis doesn't return my smile, but I get a curt nod from him.

'A fox and field day?' I say.

'Oh yes, annual tradition, going back generations,' tolls Minty. 'Dashed expensive to organise but country ways must be upheld, even if we have made a few changes here and there over the years. I'm

144

sure you must have heard of it? We've been on *Countryfile* twice, you know? Ben Fogle said it was the highlight of his filming calendar.'

I raise my eyebrows in what, I hope, looks like a 'wow! I'm impressed' kind of a gesture, cut short by Minty's sudden change in tone.

'Bovis spent five minutes putting your scattered litter back in bin bags out on the square, you know?'

'Did he? I didn't realise it was scattered anywhere!' I gulp.

Bovis just looks at me, giving off *if your name's not on the list, you're not coming in* doorman vibes. 'Jowan mentioned the gulls, and I definitely covered the rubbish with the blankets like he told me to.'

'Gulls are one thing. What you've had there is a fox,' Minty interjects, and Bovis nods his head sagely.

'Really? That's lovely!' This is greeted by Minty's wide-eyed incredulous expression that tells me I *would* think that, being a clueless townie. 'I've never seen a fox before,' I tell her.

'Scavengers. They live off cold chips and food scraps.'

'Oh!' I say, not wanting to court Minty's disapproval any further by telling her I really hope I spot one before my holiday ends.

I'm relieved when the phone rings, breaking into the conversation – if a little surprised. Nobody's phoned the shop since our arrival last Saturday. I'm saying, 'Excuse me a sec' to Minty and mentally rehearsing how I'll answer (*Hello, Borrow-a-Bookshop, Jude speaking*, poshest voice, will do nicely), when Elliot's broad form appears from nowhere and he snatches the phone from its charging station and stomps into the little kitchen with it. His hair obscured most of his face but I caught a wildness in his eyes that startled me.

'That man…' Minty whispers, peering after Elliot. 'I didn't catch his name?'

'Elliot,' I say.

'His surname?'

Well, this is embarrassing. Did he ever tell me his surname? I *think* I've asked, but did he ever answer? 'I… *uh*… can't quite recall at the moment, Minty, sorry.' Nope. No name's coming to mind, and considering I know plenty of other *far* more intimate stuff about him,

I'm horrified enough that I blush. He knows *my* name, I'm sure of it. I'll ask him when he comes back.

'Do you know where he's from?' Minty's eyes crinkle, she's squinting after Elliot so hard. 'I'm sure I recognise him. From a country family, is he?'

'You'll have to ask him that. He lives in Cambridge, I think, but I've no idea where his family are from. Dad's in agriculture, he said.'

'*Hmm*, well.' Minty says it like she's not sure she whether she believes me but she drops the subject, thankfully. 'Jowan tells me you're doing all the baking? For the café? He remarked that your scones were really rather decent.'

Decent? Is that posh for delicious? Or is she sniping? I can't tell. She's smiling though, or at least trying to.

'Do you take commissions?' she adds.

I'm guessing the surprise shows on my face yet again because she's started speaking louder and more slowly. It's pretty offensive.

'Commissions? Do you bake to order?'

'*Umm*, I've never been asked. I only do the cakes for the café.'

'I'd pay you. Bovis, write a cheque. Or do you prefer cash?'

'I'm not allowed to take money. All profits are to go into the till.'

'This wouldn't be shop business, would it? You'd be working for me.'

'Oh!'

I definitely need some cash, and quick, to get me through the rest of my stay, so I tell her yes, I do take commissions, before she changes her mind, and after a few minutes I've received my orders, fired at me like a drill sergeant with a new army recruit.

I note down her instructions and she checks I know what I've to do before turning to her companion. 'Come along, Bovis,' she commands him, as though talking to a loyal hound. 'Bring the bakes to Izaak's booth by the estate entrance on Friday morning. Gates open at ten to visitors but you can come at nine-thirty. Toodle-pip, lots to do. The hunt won't organise itself.' And off they go, leaving me mulling over Minty's last words.

Hunt? I thought she said it was a fox and field day, or something? Wouldn't be surprised if they hunted newcomers to the village, frisking them to see if they're marriage material. They're all as bonkers as Mrs Crocombe round here.

Only when the shop door is firmly shut again does Elliot emerge from the kitchen, returning the phone, and I forget all about the possibility of being inveigled in some kind of hunt. 'Wrong number,' he tells me, and turns for the café again.

'Elliot?'

'*Hmm?*' He spins to look at me, a little reluctantly, I think.

'What's your second name?'

'*Uh…*' His eyes dart around the shop as though looking for a covert to dive into to escape the question.

'You do know your own surname, right?'

'Of course, it's *uh*, Desvaux.'

I'd have remembered that name if he'd mentioned it before. He looks a little defeated, as though he's disappointed in himself for telling me, or maybe he looks torn somehow. Definitely regretful.

'*Woo*, fancy!' I say, childishly, hoping he'll smile and stop being so evasive. He *doesn't* smile and his eyes are big and round like he's choking or something. 'Minty was wondering if you were from a country family she might be acquainted with, like this is *Pride and Prejudice* and you were once introduced at the Meryton ball.' I want him to laugh so badly, drop his shoulders and come to the counter to kiss me, but he just stands there frozen, his jaw grinding, not seeing the funny side of Minty's snobbery at all.

'I'd better get back to the café,' he says, leaving me alone wondering how I could have spent the last few days sharing a bed with someone whose full name I didn't even know. I'm starting to wonder what else I don't know about him.

My eyes fall to the phone on its cradle. The phone I wasn't supposed to pick up, *dammit*. I promised I'd leave the calls to him. It seemed so important to him when we made our 'rules' last weekend, but we've broken so many of them by now, I didn't think it would matter anymore. 'Sorry,' I shout out after him, but he's gone already.

The rest of the afternoon is quiet, or should I say disquieted? I can't shake off the memory of the way Elliot scurried away to talk with whoever was on the phone. He was gone for quite a few minutes if it really *was* a wrong number, although he might have been hiding from Minty, waiting for her to leave?

I can't help it. The anxious part of me – the part with the long memory that's smart enough to bear grudges – is trying to tell me something. I've seen someone behave like this before. The spectre of Mack and my humiliation is back, haunting my beautiful bookshop and making me doubt myself, making me doubt Elliot, until I'm not sure what to think.

That's it. Tonight we're talking. I want to know every little detail about this guy, starting with why he's here all by himself, why he hasn't called or texted anyone since he arrived – not that I've seen, anyway. Doesn't he have loved ones missing him? And why does he shrink whenever anyone asks him about his personal life?

Somehow I have a feeling that Elliot, who is so expressive and intuitive when we're in bed together, won't be quite so open and careful of my feelings when I start quizzing him.

Chapter Nineteen

The rest of the day has dragged. I've sold a Jean Rhys, a Stephen King, a book of Dolly Parton lyrics, and a volume on Copernican economics, all to a married couple on holiday for the week, but those only came to fifteen quid. I seriously wonder whether the holiday let money is the only thing keeping this bookshop going.

Just as I'm turning the sign on the door at five o'clock, I spot Anjali outside on the steps, and she's grinning. I let her in, followed by Aldous on a lead. At least, I *think* it's Aldous.

'*Wow!* Somebody's had a makeover.'

'We had to shave his tummy for the operation so I figured while he was unconscious I might as well give him his quarterly haircut. Grooming's not my area, to be honest,' she says.

He does look a little odd, like a hastily shorn sheep, and he's surprisingly pink and skinny under all that matted fur but he looks clean and tidy for a change, and he's wearing a new collar. 'How did you get him on a lead?'

'We've been helping him practise his lead work at the surgery, taking him for short walks to aid his recovery. I know he's used to roaming wherever he likes, but he'd do better walking with his owner from now on.'

I bend down to scratch him. He doesn't seem very interested in the attention, but at least he lets me touch him. 'See, Aldous, you *are* a real dog!'

Anjali hands over a big bag of dog food and tells me Jowan's paid for it. 'Give him one scoop every morning, mixed with water. If he doesn't eat it, leave it in his bowl until he does. He's stubborn and holds out for something better, but this Bedlington has eaten his last scone, I'm afraid.' Her eyes dance around the shop. 'No Elliot today?'

'Oh, uh, no. He closed the café at four and went out for a run,' I tell her.

He runs to clear his head. He told me that on our first night together when we ate at the Siren, but he hasn't wanted to run recently, not since we got closer. I thought it might mean something, like maybe he was feeling less restless when he was with me, but since the phone call and Minty's visit this afternoon I guess he suddenly felt the need to seek out some freedom again? I hide all this from Anjali, of course.

'What a pity I've missed him,' she says, then recoils wide-eyed. 'I mean… I don't mean I *miss* him, miss him. Oh dear! But… Jude, do you mind me asking? You're not… dating, are you? I mean, you both arrived here separately, right?'

I wonder if Mrs Crocombe's popped over to Anjali's parents' place for a chat, otherwise how would she know about us arriving alone? Unless Elliot got chatty during Aldous's surgery? I can see how that might have been a bonding experience for the two vets.

'Ah, well…' I hesitate. Are we dating? I'm not sure we are. We kind of skipped right to the other stuff, the stuff you do after lots of dates and sharing of anecdotes and sweet words. 'We're not *not* together,' I say weakly. 'It's… it's a bit complicated… too early to say what this is.' Or maybe it's already too late, and we're not really anything at all? I can't get my head around today's sudden change in atmosphere.

She looks so horrified I want to give her a hug and tell her not to panic and that it's fine, but that would probably scare her even more.

'Sorry, I shouldn't have said anything,' she cringes. 'I'd better get back to the surgery. Will you give Aldous some clean towels to sleep on until his stitches are completely healed?'

Anjali's hurrying out the door. I wish she'd stay. We could have a cup of tea and chat like girlfriends, but maybe that would be weird since it's no secret she likes Elliot now. I don't have much experience with girlfriends so I'm not a hundred per cent sure what's normal in these situations. Probably not this embarrassing scene. I can see her wincing as she tries to get out the door as fast as she can.

'See you, then,' I call after her. 'And thank you, for everything you've done for Aldous.'

'My pleasure. See you at the fox and field day on Friday?'

'I haven't been invited to it,' I call out, making her pause inside the doorframe.

'Invited? No, don't worry about that. Everyone in Clove Lore will be there. We've had it on our calendars for a year, and only the dignitaries get proper invites. The gates open at ten to the villagers, OK?'

'I've got to pop by the estate around nine-thirty, I'm dropping something off for Minty,' I say. 'To be honest though, Anjali, I'm not really sure if it's something I'd enjoy.'

Anjali's pulling a face like I'm talking nonsense – something I'm growing used to round here – when the phone rings for the second time today.

'I'll leave you to get that,' she says, and bolts.

Aldous ignores Anjali's departure and stands frozen on the rug waiting for someone to take his lead off, but I'm staring at the phone. I promised Elliot I'd let him pick up, but he's not here, is he? It's probably Jowan anyway, checking his dog's home safely.

'Hello, Borrow-a-Bookshop?'

'Good evening, may I speak with Elliot Desvaux?'

This has to be Elliot's dad. Posh, formal, a bit stiff. The curious streak I'm developing about Elliot's home life takes over and the questions queue up. Has he mentioned me, by any chance? Do he and Mrs Desvaux have any plans to visit Clove Lore again soon? Though I don't even know if his parents are still together, come to think of it, so that might be rude.

I scramble for a sensible reply and manage, 'He's not here at the moment. This is Jude Crawley, his… colleague in the bookshop. Can I pass on a message?'

'This is Dennis Alleyn at the CPS. Please ask him to return my call urgently.'

That's disappointing. I thought I'd fast-tracked to meeting the parents, just like we fast-tracked everything else.

Mr Alleyn spells out his surname and I write his message down on the notepad. 'CPS?' I echo.

'Crown Prosecution Service.'

This jolts me. 'Do you mind me asking what this is about?'

'I'm sorry, that information is confidential. But he needs to ring me immediately, do you understand?'

'OK. Got it,' I say, and the line goes dead.

—

Elliot stays away all of Saturday evening and when he finally gets home just after nine he makes straight for the shower. By then, I'm in my PJs with the duvet pulled up to my neck. I didn't really know what else to do with myself but tried to concentrate on reading the Vera Lancing book for Monday night's meeting at the Siren, while eating toast and drinking tea, waiting for him, and then I gave up waiting.

'Sorry I'm late, I couldn't stop running,' he says, emerging from the bathroom, a towel around his waist. He sits on the end of my bed raking his fingers through his damp hair before resting his head in his hands.

'You ran for five hours?' I say, and not in an especially kind way. In fact, he'll be left in no doubt that I'm fuming.

'Kind of,' he says, evasively.

'And did Dennis manage to get you on your mobile?'

I see him freeze at my words before he turns to me with a searching look. 'Yeah, he did. Did he say anything to you?'

'No, he told me he needed to talk to you, and that it was confidential. It frightened me a bit, if I'm honest, Elliot.'

He looks away again and I hear him exhale as he rubs a hand over his face. 'I'm so tired after that run. Should I take the mattress down now?'

'*What?* No! You're going to sit there and tell me what all this is about.'

'I can't.' His voice is so firm, all of its playfulness and warmth that I'd basked in gone.

'But you can tell me anything,' I plead, and I hate the way it sounds. I see myself standing at Mack's door with my toothbrush in my hand and him turning me away. It's happening again, only this feels worse because I understand that it's happening this time.

Elliot's face is grave and immobile. 'Not this, I can't.'

I sit up now as the anger hits me. 'You *can't* tell me this, and you *won't* tell me about your family or your work. You won't tell me *anything*! What are you, Elliot? Are you a spy or something? A criminal investigator? Are you under cover? For God's sake, tell me. Is this witness protection or something?'

I know I'm clutching at straws, but anything's better than the more likely possibilities circulating round my brain now: the possibility that he doesn't trust me enough to tell me who he really is, or the possibility that I shouldn't trust him and that the few scrappy details I think I know about him are all lies. 'Are you going through a messy divorce? A legal dispute?' I say, hoping it's something simple like that. I could cope with that. It wouldn't be a problem, and it shouldn't be a problem for him to let me know either.

'No,' he protests. 'I'm sorry Jude, I can't tell you any more than I already have.' At least he has the decency to look pained.

'After everything that's happened between us this last week? You *still* can't tell me?'

He shifts across the bed and takes my hand. 'I want to tell you. I wish I could,' he says, his voice deep and insistent. His hand trails up my arm and into the nook between my neck and shoulder and I let him cup my face, absorbing the warmth, trying to imprint the feeling in my brain, knowing I'm going to miss this so much. 'My life isn't my own right now. I should never... I should never have come here when I knew there was an innocent person—'

'Innocent? Elliot? Are you... are you some kind of criminal?'

He pulls his hand away and I already know that's the last time he'll ever touch me.

'I'm not a criminal,' he says, standing now, dragging the mattress from the bed, his eyes dark like I've never seen them before. It's worse than alarming. It shocks me. I'm hurt. Wounded, even.

'Elliot!' I don't want to call after him, but I do it anyway, and I hear myself in the quiet of the bedroom. I sound pathetic.

He leaves me alone for the night, and I don't know what to do to make him come back and talk, not if he's refusing to let me in. It's utterly frustrating. I call him every name I can think of under my breath, and I scold myself too for convincing myself I was falling for him so easily, but I don't lock the bedroom door. It stays open. I sit upright at the head of my bed for hours, motionless, trying to work out what's gone wrong.

Seven days ago we were total strangers, a few days later and we're kissing and telling each other stories about our childhoods and we're flirting — at least, I thought we were, maybe it was all unrequited?

Was I so overwhelmed that someone like that, someone so stunning, someone who really looks after themselves, could also want to look after me? Is my self-esteem really that low? And then, *bam*, I'm locked out of what felt like the best thing that ever happened to me?

I just don't understand what went wrong, at least, not until I overhear Elliot's voice carrying up the stairs hours later, just before midnight.

He's down in the shop having a one-sided conversation. I tiptoe to the door and strain my ears to listen in. He must think I'm asleep. Otherwise, he wouldn't be doing this. He couldn't be that callous. Unless, of course, this is the real him talking, and he's already forgotten about the silly woman he seduced on holiday.

He's saying, 'For the hundredth time, I'm sorry. I didn't mean to hurt you. If you'd been there that night, you'd understand. I never meant to get involved, then suddenly I was in too deep and admittedly I'd had a few beers — and I know that doesn't excuse anything...'

There's silence for a moment. My chest aches from recognising how earnest his voice is. He means this. It's hurting him.

He speaks again. 'I know. I know how humiliating it must be for you, but if you could try to see it from my side. I just want to come home. I miss you… Hello? Hello?'

Silence again. They've obviously hung up. I hear Elliot crumble. He's sobbing.

So now I know. He's just another cheater. I don't even have the energy – or the pride – to confront him.

Now I do flip the little hook on my door and I lock myself away once more.

Chapter Twenty

Sunday morning brings the inevitable silence. I'm up just after dawn and in the café's kitchen before Elliot and Aldous (who I was surprised to see curled up on the mattress at Elliot's feet) are awake. I crept past them on my way into the café and they didn't stir. Maybe Elliot had difficulty getting to sleep last night. A guilty conscience will do that to a person. If he's capable of such a thing.

It's cool this morning even though summer's still here. The ovens warm the little cooking cubby hole as I mix chocolate brownies (page thirty-two of Grandad's book) and my usual scone recipe, enough for twenty-four of each.

I boil the café kettle in anticipation of the brownies coming out of the oven and take a steaming, milky tea and a gooey, oven-hot slice of brownie out onto the café doorstep to eat.

I'm going to have my breakfast surrounded by the summer morning dew and watch the early bees buzzing drowsily on the drooping pink flower spikes spilling over the wall of the cottage garden opposite.

The chocolate is gooey and stretches like cheesy pizza on a TV advert, and even though it scalds my tongue a little, it's good, maybe even the best thing I've baked here in Clove Lore.

The sun's already making its way lazily up over the buildings and I can feel its warmth spreading over the village, chasing away the chill.

I haven't paid enough attention to this kind of thing on this holiday, I tell myself. I was supposed to be observing life, working out where I fit in with the grand scheme of things. I was supposed to be escaping, communing with the world, working out who I am, and who I might become. Tall order, I know, but I'd hoped to at least get started.

Instead, I've spent a week looking at Elliot Desvaux, if that's his real name, with love-heart eyes. I've squandered a whole week of what might be the only opportunity life ever throws at me for independent escape.

Have I explored Clove Lore? No. Have I made the most of my beautiful, *beautiful* shop and my café? I really haven't. Where are all the friends I was going to make? And at what point during all this was I working on myself? I just… wasn't. I was too busy projecting all my hopes and wishes onto a man I don't know.

Here's what he's told me so far, the grand total of my combined knowledge about this person:

1. He's a child of neglectful, posh parents. That I can believe.

2. He was surrounded by books and au pairs from a young age and was sent off to pre-prep school and boarding school like the Little Lord Fauntleroy I fantasised him as being.

3. He loves dogs. Loves all animals in fact. That's definitely genuine.

4. He really looks after himself. In fact all he does is look after number one. He carb loads, he skives work to exercise or to shower, and he takes what he wants, and he conceals things.

5. All the time he *seems* like he's sharing aspects of himself, but he isn't. He's just tricking people. Making them feel important and interesting and valued, and beautiful. And because of all that I gave him what he wanted. I didn't put up an ounce of resistance.

6. Girls go wild for him. Me. Anjali. Mrs Crocombe. Me. Especially me.

7. Jowan and Minty were unsure of him from the start. I should have taken this as a big fat warning sign. When people who've been around the block a bit have a gut reaction to someone like that, instantly mistrusting them, well, there's something in that.

157

8. The scar. There's a freshly healed scar across his brow. Close up it looks like threads of silver silk, and he closes his eyes when it's kissed, and I won't ever be able to forget the sound of his breathing when I… No. That's enough of that.

Anyway, that's what I've learned about Elliot, and here's what I've learned about myself: I'm still just as gullible and easy to distract from my ambitions as I ever was. In spite of everything Mack did to me. In spite of all my resolutions.

I'm demolishing the brownie without even tasting it now, and I'm angry, with myself mainly.

So much for my holiday romance, and the little flutterings of hope that this could actually be something more. *Live your life*, I'd told myself. Spoil yourself for a change. Indulge your whims. Chase your dreams. But all I've done is let myself get side-tracked, again. I've spoiled my bookselling dream. Jude the bloody obscure. A lost cause if ever there was one.

By the time the chocolate and the caffeine hit my bloodstream, I've messaged Daniel and Gran on my phone. Daniel's got a day off today after his interview for the senior staff nurse position yesterday. I texted him last night to ask how it went but he didn't reply. He's probably knackered and sleeping off the stress, so I don't bombard him with too much *woe is me* moaning, only a quick update, but I do let Gran in on more of the gory details. I know she'll read it straight away; she's an early bird.

> I met this guy at the bookshop. And I liked him. But it turns out he's married or something, and he's just here to lie low for a while. I overheard him phoning someone, telling them he wanted to go back home to them. He was begging forgiveness for humiliating them, saying he was drunk when 'it' happened. What am I supposed to do now, Gran?

Sure enough, a message pings straight back, all the way from her New Start in the Borders to sleepy Clove Lore.

> You keep your head held high and you carry on.

> Six more days is a long time to be stuck with him though. I don't leave here until Saturday.

> Maybe there are other surprises in store for you that will take your mind off him.

She's added some emojis, which is adorable, but I'm not really sure she knows how to use them. There's a sunshine and a love heart, an aubergine, two peaches (I really hope she doesn't know what they mean) and a beach umbrella on a desert island. It makes me smile anyway.

> How could I not see it, Gran? I'm such a good reader, why can't I read people better? I've read all the books on infidelity and bad men and over-trusting women umpteen times.

I run through them in my head now while Gran types her reply. Elena Ferrante's *The Days of Abandonment*; Mr Rochester with his poor wife locked up in the attic while he gets it on with Jane Eyre, and just about every romantic comedy I ever picked up. *Ugh*, a parade of literary cheaters and the women they destroyed crowds my head. Why didn't I see it when it was happening to me, yet again? My phone pings.

Because those are books and this is real life. You don't learn from reading, you learn from making mistakes. Some mistakes are at least a lot of fun while you're making them and you'll find you make them ten times over, but you'll learn in time, when you grow surer of yourself. Tell me you at least enjoyed being with him?

I did. I was happy.

Well then, could that be enough?

I just stare at the words wondering if what I shared with Elliot really could be enough to live off with no regrets. Could I put it all behind me and move on and not be sorry – it was, after all, kind of beautiful. Gran must get fed up waiting for me to reply because another message pops up.

Do you want it to be more?

'Not possible,' I say to myself, but I won't write that. Gran might worry, so I message her back and tell her I'm feeling better already and wish her luck at her New Start Village Secret Poker Society game tonight. Her reply is characteristically upbeat.

Don't care much for poker but lots of us ladies and
some of the chaps are hoping to get on a table with Avi.
He only moved in on Tuesday. He's rather good-looking,
even if he overdoes the Brylcreem a bit. I'm trying to
tempt him into joining me for a private crochet lesson
and cocktails in my room one afternoon!

I'm not sure how to reply to this other than wishing her luck and
sending her some kisses, and I stand up, drain my tea cup and tell
myself I have to get a grip on my bookshop holiday before it's over.
I've a week left; I need to throw myself into Clove Lore life, even
though something deep inside my chest is aching today and my hands
are unsteady. I put it down to the lack of sleep. See? I can lie to myself
just as easily as men are able to lie to me.

–

One thing's going right at least. There's a cheque in my pocket for
sixty pounds and a commission to turn into reality. I stand at the
café counter and scribble the ingredients I'll need for Minty's custom
order onto a napkin.

Brown sugar, ground ginger, more icing sugar – lots of it, nutmeg,
big tins of treacle. Better get more butter. What else?

I'm almost fully absorbed in the task when Elliot stirs on the shop
floor. I hear him grunt himself awake, then the rustle of bedding,
followed by the hurried dragging of the mattress up the stairs, and all
the time he's muttering under his breath.

When he presents himself to me in the café, he looks worn and
sunken-eyed, and ethereally pale beneath his long black hair. His
morning stubble makes him look wild and rough.

I take a deep breath and face him. 'Are you going to talk to me
about what's going on?'

This is generous of me, I think. He can come clean, apologise and
we can move on. I can't guarantee I won't throw a bag of flour over
him, but still, I'm being the mature one here.

He looks at the floor. 'I'm sorry, Jude. I told you, I can't.'

I'm winded by how much those words feel like a punch in the gut. 'Well then,' I say, my voice wobbling. 'I can't talk to you anymore. I can't even look at you.' I make my way past him towards the shop. There are tears stinging my eyes but he's not getting to see them.

Elliot just nods, forlorn but accepting. 'I'll get the cash box, start the shop till for you,' he says.

'No don't. I can sort it myself,' I call over my shoulder. I made myself vulnerable before, telling him about my messy relationship with figures, but my stubborn pride won't stand for his heroics anymore. I've got a head on my shoulders and I'm going to use it. I retrieve the cash box from under my bed and text Jowan with my shopping list for Minty's commission, and so another day in my bookshop begins.

It's beautifully sunny outside, completely at odds with the storms inside me. I prop the door open to let in the sea air and I try to smile as I dust shelves and tidy the stock. I make myself a cup of tea in the little kitchen, and then another one, and try to ignore the sound of Elliot serving customers in the café.

This is fine. I've always been so good at this, carrying on, regardless of my feelings. I can smile my way through anything, like all those times Mack slighted me and I refused to acknowledge it, and all the times as a teenager and in my twenties when invitations had come for parties and nights out and I'd had to refuse them. I'd smiled through mopping the bakery floor and wiping the fine flour dust off the windows and scrubbing the ovens out every single day. I've done it for years. I can keep this up for as long as is necessary.

I decide to tackle the display of spy thrillers on the table nearest the door which the last occupants left for me. It's looking a bit thin now since a few of them have sold. I'm gathering fresh stories of espionage from the shelves to replenish it and trying to come up with an idea for what I'll leave on the table on my last day. No point consulting Elliot. I've very much reverted to the 'my shop, my rules' way of thinking.

What kind of display could I do? What do I want to leave as my legacy? Definitely not love stories. *Ugh!* Maybe a display of self-help books? I browse the shelves for suitable titles. *Men are From Mars: Women are from Venus*; *Emotionally Manipulative Males and the Women Who Love Them: Breaking the Cycle*; *Help, My Man's a Shady Scumbag*.

OK, I made that last one up. On second thoughts, I don't think I'm in the best frame of mind for thinking about the display, or indeed about my departure from Clove Lore.

There's a steady stream of tourist customers all morning to keep me from thinking too hard about the predicament I'm in. I'm extra attentive to them and wishing I'd put my mind to bookselling like this last week too. I'm finding I'm actually good at it, even though I have to check and double check every price I type into the till and I recount every penny I hand over in change.

At around twelve I hear the sound of a woman laughing gaily outside mixed with the hearty chuckle of a baby properly belly-laughing. It's a lovely, distracting noise and I walk to the door to see its source and there's a woman and a man making their way across the square with their kids. They look like a family in a catalogue for the kind of seasidey, Breton-stripy clothing I can't afford. She's blonde and tanned and carrying the laughing baby in a carrier on her front, and he's striding along in pink shorts and shiny hair with a toddler up on his shoulders.

'Hello!' the woman calls out and I realise they're coming into the shop. The mum hugs me – which surprises me – and I get an inadvertent whiff of the baby's blonde curly head and it does something really unexpected in my ovaries which leaves me a bit numb and struggling to smile. What the hell's all that about?

'We're the Burntislands,' she says. 'I'm Monica and this is 'bastian.' She indicates the smiling baby in the carrier.

'Good to meet you, I'm Fabian,' the daddy says next.

'And that's Barney,' both of the parents chime at exactly the same time. There follows a lot of them laughing and saying 'Jinx', and I introduce myself, feeling besieged and bewildered and not really sure why because this family seem lovely.

'We've brought you a little something. Hope you like pasties?' Monica says, handing over two paper bags. 'Is your partner here today?'

For a second I don't compute. 'Elliot? He's in the café.'

'I'll take his through,' Fabian says jovially – I'm starting to hear a South African accent – and off he goes, taking little Barney in his wake.

'The Burntislands? You're the couple who met here at the shop aren't you?' I say, thinking of Mrs Crocombe and how this couple's chance meeting had fuelled the old matchmaker's desire to fill her village with families just like Monica's.

'That's right! You already know about us?'

'Izaak told me. You were single when you came to the bookshop?'

'That's right. Fabian was on a gap year after his business Masters and I was just finishing my teacher training. I'm a part-time classroom assistant at the local school now and I bake my own pasties to sell up at the visitors' centre. Fabian works from home. He's in securities trading.'

'Wow,' I say, not really sure what that means, and still feeling all kinds of unwelcome emotions. I think one of them is jealousy and that's really not like me, so I tamp it down.

'I hear you're in a similar situation?' Monica's unstrapping the baby from his carrier and placing him on the floor. It turns out he can toddle and off he wobbles across the shop, smiling and gurgling to himself.

Monica doesn't see how panicked I am, but, luckily, she drops the subject when her son distracts her. 'Aww, look, 'bastian's heading straight for Aldous. They really love each other, those two.'

Aldous is of course asleep on his bundle of fresh towels on the windowsill. I'd given him a chair to make the climb easier and the baby is already clambering up onto the seat, reaching for the dog.

I launch into the story of Aldous's surgery and how he's still recovering and Monica hastily rescues the poor mutt from any unwanted toddler attention. By the time the excitement is over, her husband's come back. Giving her a kiss, he stands with an arm thrown casually around her shoulders. I watch Monica lean her head onto his forearm and think how they really do look right together.

'What a lovely family you've got,' I remark as I ring up the copy of *Guess How Much I Love You* that little Barney's picked out. You know, the one with the hares who love each other to the moon and back?

'Thanks, we think so,' Monica chirrups and they get ready to leave.

'Thanks for bringing lunch,' I call out, indicating the pasty bag. Monica leaves me her number and tells me to call her any time.

I hear them in the square talking in low voices about me – or rather about me and Elliot – and I watch them turn Up-along, presumably going back to their idyllic family home on the headland.

I stand for a long time by the door comparing myself to Monica, so happy and centred with her adoring husband. The bookshop has housed all kinds of love stories over the years. Monica and Fabian, Jowan and Isolda, me and Elliot. I sigh. One of those couples is very much not like the others.

I get on with some shelf tidying and eventually Elliot emerges from the café, having closed up for the day. He hands me the day's takings in a banking bag, eyeing me cautiously.

He's eaten his pasty, I can see a few tell-tale crumbs on his black shirt. I don't know what to say to him, but my mind turns traitor yet again and for a fraction of a second I picture Elliot with a baby carrier strapped across his chest and the sweet curve of a baby's head resting on his shoulder, with dark fluffy hair like a chick in a nest and chubby little fingers clasping at a strand of Elliot's long hair. I really hate my imagination sometimes.

'Do you want me to help out in here?' he says, peering at me so intently I look away.

'I don't want anything. I'm fine on my own.'

It hurts to say the words, and it hurts to see him flinching at them, but he backs away awkwardly, nodding again, accepting this is how things are, how he made them.

—

He's just left, out on another run, I'm guessing.

I'm not going to close the shop tonight, not until late. If curious locals drop by wondering what's going on, I'll tell them I'm trialling late night Sunday opening for holidaymakers out for a stroll after dinner. There's nothing in the guest book about having to close before a certain time.

And so I sit in my shop all evening. I eat the Burntislands' pasty (it's delicious and definitely tastes homemade) and I do what I came here to do. I'm a bookseller by the sea, I tell myself. I'm having a really great adventure. I sell a Jenny Colgan hardback and a copy of the first Jack Reacher book, which brings in another tenner.

Elliot doesn't come back to the shop until after dark, and I don't ask him where he's been and he doesn't tell me.

I read *Persuasion* in bed – my faithful copy brought from home – and I tell myself that at least I know now what to expect from the coming days.

It hurts. Not like the humiliation Mack brought me; this is a different kind of pain I've never felt before, something right in my chest like heartburn, but so much worse. There's the feeling of having a hangover too, except it wasn't booze I over-indulged in, it was the lovely warmth of Elliot's smile, and his hands, and his words. They've left me dazed and groggy and sick, in that desperate morning-after space where you wonder if there's nothing else for it but another sip to take the edge off. But there's no more where that came from. So I'll lie in my little bed and tell myself I'm lucky to be here and maybe he'll be out of my bloodstream by tomorrow. I'll try to sleep him off.

Chapter Twenty-One

> What kind of business hours are you keeping, Jude?
> This is no way to run a bookshop.

I squint at my phone, eyes blurry from a long restless night and a lot of pages turned waiting for Anne Elliot's happy ever after to soothe me. I don't understand Daniel's message until I see the time and realise it's just after nine. I've slept in and haven't baked a thing this morning. I'm pulling on underwear before it hits me.

> How do you know the shop's not open yet?

That's when I hear the knocking pattern on the shop door, loud and jaunty, much too long and a bit annoying. I drag my new blue dress on, the one that turned Elliot's head, and I fly down the stairs, only to see Elliot clomping his way from the café across the shop to unlock the door, and there, with his face and hands pressed comically to the glass like a Dickensian urchin in knock-off Balenciaga is Daniel. I'm not aware I'm screaming hysterically until I see Elliot flinching.

I shove past Elliot and haul the door open. 'You're here? You're really here!' and we're both screaming and jumping up and down on the doorstep and hugging so hard one of us could be in danger of passing out.

When Daniel finally puts me down I feel my joy giving way and I know I'm close to tears. 'Why are you here?' I cry, my eyes welling.

'I'm on my way to Mum and Dad's holiday home at Land's End. I've got a few days off and I wanted to give them the good news in person.'

'You got the promotion?' That's it, I'm ugly-sobbing now. 'I'm so happy for you.'

'You *seem* happy.' Daniel's appraising me, bemused, and then his eyes drag upwards. I don't need to turn around to know that Elliot's still glowering behind me because Daniel's eyes say everything.

My friend looks at me, wordlessly conveys how incredibly bleeding hot Elliot is, then his quirking eyebrows do the work of telling me he's detected that something's gone horribly wrong with my holiday, and then the awkward silence in the shop betrays literally everything else.

'Ah,' Daniel says, and he steps around me to introduce himself to Elliot who's just standing there bewildered.

As the pair of them shake hands, Daniel buzzing with intrigue and Elliot stiff and confused, I notice for the first time that Elliot's black baggy pants and scoop neck T-shirt (the one that offers tantalising hints of hidden tattoos and shamelessly flaunts his neck muscles) are covered in flour, or maybe it's icing sugar. His hair's tied back and he's got a black baseball cap pulled down to his brows, and he's wearing the menacing straight-mouthed stare he had when I was first getting to know him. It's the cautious, self-protective look of a man hiding himself away from the world, warning others to stay away.

There's more white powder on his cheek and the tip of his nose. The sight of it sends a pang of longing straight to my core.

'You're baking?' I say, so stiff and severe Daniel turns back and shoots me a look of amazement. *Yes*, my eyes tell Daniel, *this is the new hardened me.*

Elliot replies, level and dry. 'You were asleep and I didn't want to wake you, not when you've been so… busy lately, so I got up and made some scones, like you showed me. Turned out OK, too.' A grim smile curls his perfect lips. 'Then I tried some fairy cakes.' He shrugs and concedes, 'They don't look so good.'

Another glance from Daniel. It says, *He is The Cutest! Don't be angry with this enormous baker guy.*

I shake my head. I have to get out of here. This is too much. That's when I remember I have a date tonight – with the Siren's Tail Sleuthing Club. I'll break that to Daniel later. He won't mind; there'll be beer and sandwiches.

'Elliot,' I tell him firmly. 'I'm taking the day off.'

—

'You're just going to leave the poor guy to run the place all by himself?' Daniel is panting behind me as I stride Up-along past the holidaymakers with their coolbags and beach towels heading for the shore.

'Yep,' I say, head held high, facing the blue sky. 'Are you really staying all night?'

'I got the last double room at the Siren, with breakfast. You said in your text you think he's seeing someone else?'

I stop dead, and Daniel catches up to me. If I spill it all now, we have a chance of enjoying ourselves today. 'Yeah, he is. I didn't know a thing about it until I caught him talking to his missus about wanting to get back to the family home. He's probably got kids for all I know. He refused to explain when I confronted him. Can you believe it? The gall of the guy. Actually, you know what? I *did* know about it. All the red lights were there from the start. He was grumpy and secretive, he won't let me answer the shop phone...'

'*Tsss!*' Daniel hisses through gritted teeth. 'Jude, that's a dead giveaway.'

I ignore the knowing, weary tone in his voice that's saying, *you let yourself be played again, Jude?*

'And there's some sort of legal case he's involved in, but I don't know what. He wouldn't tell me anything about the last few years of his life, just that he's taking a break from work. I've no idea why he came here to Clove Lore, or why he couldn't stick around wherever he came from to fix whatever mess he's in.'

I see Elliot in my mind's eye talking so earnestly to me that night we went to the Siren, telling me the bookshop had come along at exactly the right time for him, how it saved him like it was saving me. I sniff a wry laugh at the memory, anger bubbling up at how easily I let myself fall for it, how willing I was to be blindsided. I take a deep breath and carry on. 'He told me some sob stories about his childhood, but nothing else... but, I liked him, in spite of all the warnings.'

'I can see how that could happen, Jude. I mean, look around. It's beautiful here, and you're far from home, and he's...' Daniel's squinting, searching for the right words, 'He's basically an Adonis in gym pants.'

I don't want to hear Elliot being praised, but yes, Daniel's right. I want to say *you should have seen him in that white shirt the night we first kissed*, but I don't. And I don't tell him about the stupid, romantic part of me that hoped we could be more than a holiday fling – the bit that's absorbed too many novels about moody, chivalrous, aloof men who meet their match and find themselves letting down their guard and smiling at the heroine, asking if they might stay behind after church to ask them a very particular question... *Ugh*, my gullible, sentimental brain!

I don't need to tell Daniel I was imagining the Hallmark movie version of me and Elliot holding hands and walking through crunchy leaves and sipping frothy coffees with chocolate sprinkles in the shape of love-hearts together this autumn. Daniel already knows all this without me having to confess it. He knows me too well. It's comforting and excruciating at the same time.

'Come on, let's keep climbing,' I say, hiking on up the cobbled slope. After more than a week here I'm getting used to the steep path, but Daniel's struggling behind me, even though he works out most days and must be a hundred times fitter than me.

'Can you slow down? I'm getting altitude sickness!' he shouts after me. 'Where are we going anyway?'

'There,' I say, triumphantly pointing at the sign ahead of us.

'Donkeys?' he reads, scrunching up his nose.

After an hour of scritching the heads and ears of sweet velvet-nosed donkeys in the stable yard by the visitors' centre I was definitely feeling brighter. Even Daniel was enjoying himself, once he'd got over the oddball quaintness of Clove Lore and the smell from the mucking-out wheelbarrow in the corner of the cobbled yard.

We'd learned all the donkey's names and picked out our favourites (I liked Clive, an elderly knock-kneed gent, tiny and sleepy; Daniel favoured Moira, a wiry old girl who nibbled at sightseers' backpacks and handbag straps as we moved amongst the animals). We dropped cash donations into the big bucket and discovered the stable was owned by the estate and that none of the donkeys worked anymore. They live here as a tourist attraction and to maintain a sense of the old days, when the lime kiln on the seafront fired and the herring catch was hauled Up-along in great baskets and the animals transported goods and materials of all kinds up and down the slope.

Leaving the stables, having scrubbed our hands for at least ten minutes, I told Daniel all about Minty, the fox and field event this Friday, and my baking commission, and he said Minty sounded fabulous.

Then we swung by the tourist shops and I bought us each an ice cream from the little convenience store to celebrate his promotion and we scoffed them as we wandered back down to the seafront, the slippery descent and the speed the ice creams were melting in the midday sun making it tricky to talk much.

Once at the harbour I followed him inside the Siren as he checked in to his room and unpacked. I asked him if I could stay the night with him and he said, 'Well, obviously.'

Then we made the excellent decision to order sandwiches and cocktails and found Finan and Bella's speciality was Devonshire cider mimosas (too delicious to stop at only the one) before we headed out along the beach in search of the waterfall that I'd read about online back in Marygreen, and that's where we're off to now.

The beach is beautiful in the afternoon sunshine and the sea is a bright swirling green-blue like an artist dipped his brush into the water to clean it, and it's so calm today.

Daniel remembered to bring sun lotion, thankfully. He's looking delectable in long shorts, a pale blue shirt, a few days' stubble, and some new sunglasses I haven't seen before. He won't wear a sunhat because of his perfect hair so I help him lotion the tips of his ears which are turning an adorable pink in the heat.

I slip my arm in his as we stumble over the pebbly beach heading away from the harbour following the towering rock face to our right. He tells me my new dress is 'very you', and I know exactly what he's implying. He's telling me that I seem to be finding myself at last. I definitely felt like I *was*, but then... *Ugh*, I don't want to think about Elliot anymore.

'Do you get a pay rise with the promotion?' I ask, kicking the risk of any more conversation about my failed attempts at self-development into the long grass.

'I do,' he smiles proudly. 'But I still have to deal with all the usual nonsense, only now I'll have even more paperwork.'

'Some of the new recruits still struggling to fit in?' He knows I mean Ekon, his cookie-gifting nemesis.

Daniel blows out a deep sigh. 'Yeah, you could say that. I don't know what to do with half of them, but Ekon is definitely the trickiest.'

'What's he done this week?'

'Nothing. I haven't seen him since he gave me the cookie.'

'Did you eat it?'

He gives me a *What do you think? Of course I did!* look.

'And did you say thank you? Maybe it was a peace offering?'

'You don't know him.' Daniel's shaking his head, keeping an eye on his tread as we pass out of the sun and into the shade of the cliffs. 'He's always got a smart-arse answer for everything. Oh, that smirk, I could... I could...' he falters, and we stop. 'He's just so annoying, you know?'

'What are you saying? Is he bullying you? Intimidating you? What?'

'No, it's not like that. It's like… he knows I have to be professional, that my job's important to me, and there's a lot of responsibility on my shoulders, and he's… testing me.'

A glance at my friend tells me this really is troubling him; he's forlorn about it. 'Why would he do that?'

'To see if I'll let my reserve slip? To see how much he can get away with? To see if I… like him?' He says this like it's a revelation only just coming to him.

This slows our pace. 'Are you having some kind of Ekon epiphany, Daniel?' I try not to grin when his face is so stricken. 'Hey, it's OK.'

As I'm putting my arm around his shoulders, I detect the sound of water rushing somewhere ahead of us. We follow along the foot of the rock face and find ourselves in an indent with the waterfall directly ahead of us. It must be forty feet high, if not more, and the water's showering down, hitting the beach and seemingly disappearing into some hidden chasm below. The rocks on either side of the falls are verdant with life, trailing leaves, moss and algae. It's like the entrance to a giant's cave in a fairy tale.

Neither of us remark about the waterfall, we just come to a stop in front of it, our eyes trained on the falling wonder, our ears tuning in to the hushing rush of its music.

That's when I realise Daniel's eyes are full of tears and he's mortified about it.

'Daniel?' I admit I'm alarmed; he's always the one with his life together.

'I don't know what's wrong with me! Why am I crying over this guy?'

'It's OK to cry,' I soothe. 'Gran says tears are a sign that something special's happening.'

Out of nowhere he laughs and his eyes shine through the tears. 'Is something happening? I have no clue.'

'Why don't you call him?'

'Really?'

'Yes, why not? Call him now. Thank him for the cookie and ask him if there's anything he wants to say to you, something he can't say at work, and that's why he's acting out?'

Daniel gulps. 'But he's such an annoying little prick.'

'Is he, though?' I say, smiling. 'Or is he under your skin because you like him and you've been denying it, quite rightly trying to maintain your authority?'

'Don't.'

'Don't what?' I say, all innocence.

'Don't say this is just like so-and-so in some awful melodrama you once read and that we're destined for each other…'

'Me?' I interrupt, hand on my chest, mock-horrified. That *does* sound like me. The old me. 'Look, those books have clearly taught me nothing. What I *do* know is, you've been talking about Ekon non-stop for weeks. I haven't seen you this animated about anyone since, well…' I let the word 'me' float away unvoiced, but he knows what I'm saying. I reach into his shirt pocket and hand him his phone. 'Have you got a signal out here?'

He looks at the phone, smiling and confounded at the same time, but he takes it. 'What? *Ring* him? I never ring anybody. Not a text? I should text, right? What do you think? Oh God!'

'Breathe. Just breathe. I think you should ring him. You can pick up a lot from the tone of someone's voice that you just don't get in a text.'

'And you'll be OK waiting here?'

'I'll be communing with nature. Me and my waterfall,' I say. We smile nauseatingly at each other the way we always do, and he does a nervous sort of wriggle dance, then walks off along the beach, phone to his ear.

The waterfall sings to me and for a few moments I just breathe in the salty sea air, fresh and warm, and I listen to the gulls up on the cliff and the waves over pebbles behind me. The sun's beating down on my shoulders but there's a summer breeze cooling me too.

This is nice, I tell myself. This is the kind of golden moment I came here for, if only I didn't have this heavy rock in my chest, dragging me down.

Daniel's up on the sea wall now, still absorbed in his phone call, I can just make out that he's smiling, head down, scuffing and kicking his slip-ons absent-mindedly on the stones beneath his feet while he talks.

My mind flits to Elliot alone in the shop and in spite of my self-righteous anger I feel guilty for leaving him to fend for himself. What if he's run off his feet? Can he handle the shop and café on a sunny day like today? It'll be getting lots of footfall, I bet. But my best friend's here, and dammit, I've earned a bit of respite from the horrible tension of being stuck in the same building as Elliot.

No, Elliot can get on with things alone for a while. It'll be back to business soon enough once Daniel leaves for Land's End in the morning.

After a few moments Daniel's back, and he's doing a coy kind of pout behind his dark sunglasses.

'So?' I say.

'We're meeting for coffee next week, and not in the staff canteen either. We're going *out* out, on Saturday.'

I frighten a nearby seagull with the little squawk of happiness I make, and we hug, and Daniel can't contain the smile that's making his cheeks glow. I haven't seen him like this for years.

'I asked why he always acts out so much around me and he said, "can't you tell?" He said he's liked me for weeks and I've missed every signal.'

Another bout of delirious squawking from me. So what if it's juvenile? This is the kind of grade A romance the old me would get high on. I'll make an exception in Daniel's case because he really does deserve some romance in his life. I grasp his arm and we turn back for Up-along. I need to pick up my overnight stuff if I'm sleeping at the Siren tonight.

We walk side by side, heads tipped together.

'So, a date, huh?' I say. 'With Ekon the hot nurse. Tell me you're not going to work out *all* week long for it?'

'Oh, you know I am.'

The sun is already making its mid-afternoon descent over Clove Lore when we burst through the doors of the bookshop, laughing and conspiratorial, happy and relaxed.

Chapter Twenty-Two

The shop is devoid of visitors and I can hear Elliot clomping from the café to greet us.

'Oh, I thought you were customers,' he says, rubbing his hands on the apron that's folded in half around his waist, showing his inky blue shirt, open at the collar, the sleeves rolled up.

He must have changed out of the floury clothes at some point this morning. The baseball cap's gone too and his hair's tied back messily. My heart hurts at the sight of him and I'm suddenly aware the temperature in the shop is notably chilly compared to the sunny street.

'I, *um*, I'm just grabbing my stuff. We're staying at the Siren tonight,' I say, hiking my thumb in the direction of the spiral stairs.

'*Uh-huh*,' Elliot says quietly, nodding.

'I'll get us some water,' Daniel announces, a little too loudly, and makes a hasty exit for the shop kitchen.

'Will you be back tomorrow?' Elliot asks me.

'In the morning. I'll have to bake.'

'Of course.' Elliot nods, lifting a hand to the back of his neck where it stays and we just look at each other stupidly, stuck to the floor, immobilised with the heaviness of whatever this feeling is. Sadness, mainly, on my part.

I don't know what Elliot's thinking but he's looking panicked, and shifty too. I see his eyes flit to the little kitchen at the sound of Daniel running the tap.

'Was everything all right while I was away?' I say.

'Oh, sure. The bookshop was busy before lunch, then it went quiet. I sold some scones.' His eyebrows rise showing a flash of pride that quickly fades. 'None of the fairy cakes went though. They might have to go in the bin.'

'Right.' I laugh weakly before reminding myself why I'm here, and I turn for the stairs. Elliot doesn't move and I'm aware of him watching me as I bound up the spiral.

Once I've grabbed the things I need for a night at the Siren and Daniel's joined me at the top of the stairs where we both silently down a glass of water, we make our way back out into the sunshine. The shop's empty as we leave. Elliot's back in the café, and I don't feel the need to tell him we're going.

'Jude!' The sound of my name called, deep and alarmed, from the shop doorway, makes me freeze in the middle of the little square by the palm tree, and I turn slowly on the heel of my Converse. Daniel bows out without a word, squeezing my arm encouragingly, before making his way onto the sloping street and leaving me to face Elliot alone.

'Jude,' he repeats, bounding down the shop steps and coming to stand in front of me. His chest's heaving like he's been on a long run and I momentarily drop my eyes at the sight of his Adam's apple bobbing as he swallows hard.

'Yes?' I say, eyes fixed down at the ground, hoping I'm coming across as unmoved and stony, when really I'm telling my hands to stay jammed by my sides in case they reach for him.

When I glance up, wondering what the silence is about, I see Elliot's mouth moving but there's no sound coming out, and his brow furrows in frustration.

'What is it, Elliot? Daniel's waiting for me.' There it is again, the feeling of wanting to cry right here in front of him. This man's made me the happiest I've ever been, and the saddest too. How can he not know that?

I watch Elliot's eyes flash as the words come to him, then a moment's hesitation strikes, before he swallows again and bites his lip, angry and frustrated. *As if* he has the right to be either of those things.

'Jude… I… I will never not be thinking about you.' There's desperation and resignation in his voice, and he jams his fists into his pockets and hangs his head. I'm winded by the force of the exclamation, but the words don't help me feel any better.

Silence eats up all the feelings in my chest. All I can do is nod. I can't do this right now, whatever *this* is. We can talk tomorrow, if that's what he's trying to tell me he wants to do.

I turn away, hiding the tears in my eyes, and I find Daniel waiting for me in the shade of the passageway that leads to Down-along. He comes for me, slipping his hand around mine, like a dad collecting his little girl from school, and I let him lead me away.

'Let's go to the bar,' he says calmly.

As we're about to disappear from Elliot's sight I glance back, feeling apologetic somehow, only to see Elliot staring hard at me, his jaw tight and his amber eyes pained.

Chapter Twenty-Three

Daniel and me are the first to arrive at the Siren for the book club. Bella is laying out two big platters of sandwiches on the pushed-together tables with chairs set out all around them off to one side of the bar.

'Sorry I haven't read the book,' Daniel tells her, and she twinkles back at him, saying it doesn't matter, half the group wouldn't have either.

'Where is everyone?' Finan asks his wife as he brings over the jug of beer and the tray of glasses. 'Minty's normally the first one here.'

'She's sent her apologies, and someone to deputise for her,' Bella tells him, just as the door pushes open and Bovis skulks in.

'Who's that?' Daniel whispers to me.

'Minty's henchman,' I tell him, and we smirk at each other. 'Doesn't look too pleased about being sent in her place. Bet he's here in case Minty misses any gossip.'

Bovis drops a five-pound note into an empty crystal bowl at the centre of the table and I realise we're all expected to do the same, so I follow suit, paying for Daniel and myself.

Bovis refuses a drink and takes a seat at the bar, just as the two men I'd seen when I first arrived come in. They're not in their yellow waders and wellies tonight but are brushed up in short-sleeved shirts and jeans and smelling conspicuously of competing brands of aftershave. They pour themselves beers and Finan introduces them.

'This is Monty and Tom Bickleigh. You'll have seen their fishing boat in the harbour.'

The brothers are so alike they could be twins. They pull up chairs on either side of Daniel and me and stretch their legs out before them as if they're exhausted.

'Long day?' Daniel asks Monty on his left.

'Out on the water by five this morning, as usual,' he replies, before taking a long drink of beer.

'Good catch was it?' I ask, struggling to know what else to say to a fisherman. I've never met one before.

'Paltry,' Tom tells me. 'It's getting harder to make a living off the boats. Some days I'm glad Dad's not here to see the catch coming in.'

'It's their father's boat,' Finan explains, as he busies himself laying out napkins and bowls of crisps.

'Passed away ten summers back,' Monty adds. 'My family have been fishermen here for three generations, and we'll be the last.'

The two brothers give each other matter-of-fact looks before sinking the dregs of their pints. I refill their glasses straight away as I have a feeling they're here for the beer and not the books.

Mrs Crocombe is the next to arrive, closely followed by her daughter and Monica Burntisland. Mrs C. has her eye on Daniel the second she comes in and she manoeuvres herself round the table and pulls a chair into the space between Tom the fisherman and me, making Tom tut and shift over.

Daniel's texting Ekon again, absorbed in their conversation, so he doesn't notice when Mrs C. throws her Vera Lancing paperback onto the table, leans towards me and conspicuously whispers, 'Who's that, then?'

'Sorry?' I say.

'That lad? Haven't seen him around. What's he doing here?' Mrs C.'s throwing daggers at Daniel who's grinning at his phone.

'Oh, that's Daniel, from back home. He's come to see me. We're staying at the Siren together tonight.' I'm smiling at the sight of him so happy, and not caring a jot if Mrs C. thinks it's because I'm his besotted girlfriend.

'Oh, bother! I've lost a tenner because of you.'

'*Eh?*' I squint.

'I had a tenner on you and Elliot being together by the end of your stay, maybe even staying put in the village for a while after, but that's out the window now you've brought your Daniel.'

'Me and Elliot? I thought you liked Anjali as a match for Elliot?'

'I did. But then I saw the way he was looking at you,' Mrs Crocombe says testily. I can only blink at her. 'It was clear to see the man was head over heels for you.'

I gulp and keep my eyes on my beer glass. I was enjoying goading the old matchmaker a second ago, but it's not funny anymore. 'I'd return all the bets on a bookshop romance involving either of us, Mrs C., if I were you. Nobody's coming out of this a winner.'

I watch the ice-cream selling, one-woman marriage bureau give me up as the lost cause that I am, and she smiles forlornly with a nod, though it's not without a hint of sympathy too. 'Oh well, can't win them all, eh?' She sighs and reaches for a sandwich. 'No sign of Jowan tonight?' She scans the room, asking nobody in particular.

Bella takes a seat at the table. 'He's late, maybe we should make a start without him?' And that's how the meeting is called to order.

Bovis turns in his chair at the bar to observe us but doesn't show any signs of wanting to participate. Mrs Crocombe's daughter and Monica Burntisland, who I'm realising are colleagues at the primary school and clearly know each other well, reluctantly join the group at the table. They've bought a bottle of sauvignon between them and are swigging from large glasses and talking about teething troubles and nits and how Fabian really should speak to his mother about not staying for an entire month every August, it really is too wearing.

Neither of the young mums have their books with them. It's clear they're not here for literary enlightenment. They're escaping the demands of parenting and being a wife for a few hours. They're both in shades of red lipstick but don't seem to have brushed their hair and they've each grabbed a bowl of crisps and set to work on them without stopping talking once.

It strikes me that the perfect Burntislands are just the same as everyone else, in spite of their Instagram-ready appearance and their perfect-looking family life. They're just as chaotic and clueless as the rest of us. The same goes for Mrs C.'s daughter, the head teacher, who under the bar lights looks tired and relieved to be anywhere but home or school.

Izaak runs in late and pulls up a chair, silently holding up his copy of the book and showing me the cover with a bared-teeth excited grin.

Once everyone settles down, we make a toast to the Sleuthing Club and Finan says Daniel and I are very welcome tonight, and then we all decide to start at the beginning and talk about the book's plot.

The Heart that Shattered is a twisty, complicated psychological study with a grisly murder, a missing weapon, at least three plausible suspects, and a rather steamy burgeoning romance between the serious-minded Glaswegian investigating officer, Sergeant Beltane McClure, and the reticent, grave young police cadet, Emma Lindisfarne.

Bella wants to talk about the love story first, but Finan cuts in saying it was a 'pointless distraction from the main story – the murder investigation.'

'I couldn't disagree more,' Bella retorts, making her husband smile indulgently.

'Here we go,' Tom the fisherman throws in dryly. 'They're always like this.'

'I don't know what you mean,' says Bella.

'I have to agree with Bella,' Izaak interrupts. 'I think the love story was the most successful part of the whole book. It made me care about stuffy old Beltane McClure. Without it he's just a grumpy git.' The music of Izaak's delicate accent makes this all the funnier and everyone laughs, except Finan, who shakes his head, and Tom and Monty who just shrug at one another.

The brothers are clearly more interested in the two women sitting at the bar in their summer dresses sipping pink wine than they are in anything we have to say. I see Tom nod his head in their direction, and Monty nods back and the pair grumble their excuses and off they prowl, smiling salaciously at the women, who seem delighted to be approached by the two rugged, storm-beaten young fishermen.

This piques Mrs C.'s interest, who in an instant has reached for her betting book and asked Finan, 'Who are those girls?'

'Visitors in room five and six. They're leaving tomorrow.'

'Aww, pity.' The old matchmaker's shoulders slump in disappointment, and I'm sure I see her daughter rolling her eyes at her mum, making Monica laugh beside her.

'As I was saying,' Bella remarks loudly, like a woman used to steering a rowdy crowd back to the subject in hand. 'Falling in love brings out a side of McClure the reader hasn't seen before, it's necessary to develop his character, otherwise the series might stagnate. This is what, the fifth McClure murder book?'

Izaak tells her she's right, he's read them all.

'Rubbish,' Finan says firmly. 'It's unrealistic. A man like that can't fall in love. He's a closed book, desensitised by his military training and by the violence he's seen in his career, not to mention his sad childhood.'

'Seeing him soften and open up to Emma read as very natural to me,' Mrs C. says. 'People change when they fall in love, you know?'

'But he left her in the end,' Finan argues. 'Didn't change all that much, did he?'

'He left her for her own good,' Bella chimes in, holding the book to her chest, and I'm sure I see Finan's eyes sink to his wife's neckline and stay there for a moment. 'Because he loved her, and it's tragic because she'll never understand that. He felt unworthy of her love, and he didn't want to put her at risk, not when he's got a price on his head from all those gang lords!'

'So romantic, and so sad,' Mrs C. adds, dreamy-eyed.

'What do you think, Jude?' Finan asks me and I have trouble articulating the things circulating in my brain but eventually I find my voice. 'Well, to be honest, I thought the love story was inane.'

Daniel's eyes snap from his phone to mine as though he can't believe what he's hearing. 'What? *You* didn't like the romantic bits?'

'That's right.' I know it's out of character for me, siding with the cold logic of Finan and Beltane McClure, and eschewing the romance and sentimentality favoured by Mrs C., Bella and Izaak, but there it is. 'There's nothing noble about leading a woman on, making her feel loved and wanted, making her think she's breaking through his tough exterior and seeing the softness beneath, then dumping her *for her own good*. What rubbish! And the poor woman never finds out why he's left her. She's stuck thinking it's her fault. He's not some self-sacrificing hero for giving her up; he's just heartless and stony.'

Daniel raises his eyebrows and lifts his glass to his mouth as if to say, 'You've changed,' and I shrug at him because I know I have.

'Emma had her suspicions about McClure from the start though, didn't she?' Izaak says. 'She tried to resist him.'

'People should always follow their gut instinct, especially in a crime novel. Instinct never lies,' Finan says resolutely, and we all nod our agreement, except Izaak.

'But people lie all the time, and that can confuse our instincts, can't it?' he says.

'If someone's dodgy, they're always dodgy. End of,' Finan says.

'Depends what they're lying about,' says Bella. 'People lie for all sorts of reasons, some of them noble reasons, like McClure does.'

'That's true,' Daniel says, drawing everyone's attention. 'People put up walls and hide their true selves all the time, because they're afraid.'

Everyone around the table seems impressed with this and they all nod sagely and mumble their agreement, especially Izaak who's saying, 'True, true.'

'What's McClure afraid of?' I ask.

'His past catching up with him, the woman he loves being harmed,' Finan says.

'Getting hurt, being vulnerable,' Bella counters.

'The truth is rarely pure and never simple,' says Mrs C.'s daughter, and everyone is amazed she's stopped drinking her wine and whispering about her home life with Monica. 'What?' she protests, laughing at all of us. 'Oscar Wilde said that.'

Everyone *woos* at her and we break into laughter and the discussion moves on from the need for romance even in the grittiest of real-life scenarios, and the virtues of breaking a loved one's heart to protect everyone involved and to keep dangerous secrets.

Now they're chatting about the novel's red herrings and the lost murder weapon but I'm letting my eyes glaze a bit and looking at my glass, thinking about Elliot.

The last words he said to me earlier seem to ring in my ears all the more loudly in the din of the busy pub, and I lower my head in case I cry right here surrounded by these people, some of whom are beginning to feel like friends. *I will never not be thinking about you*, he said.

'Same,' I tell the bottom of my beer glass before I reach for a sandwich, and try to focus on book club.

At the end, once the discussion has descended into slightly drunken chatter and the book has been long since forgotten, just as Finan said it would, and Izaak has gone home, Daniel gives me a hug, which doesn't go unnoticed by Mrs C. who is getting ready to leave but having trouble with her cardigan sleeves after half a glass of beer.

'I see you,' he says to me.

'What?' I'm nicely tipsy and full of bread and ready to sleep after a relaxed and (almost) enjoyable evening.

'Looking glum, missing Elliot.'

'I'm not missing him, I'm fine. Better to be disappointed now than to go back to Marygreen thinking he's…' I recall Mrs C.'s words earlier, and wince. 'Head over heels for me. This way I can go home and launch myself into my new life unhindered and with no distractions. You know? To the amazing career I'll suddenly stumble upon with all my wisdom and life experience to help me.' I give a wry and slightly boozy laugh at this, but Daniel's frowning.

'You have a lot more going for you than you know. First of all, you know about commitment and patience and loyalty, all those years looking after your gran.'

'*Hmph*,' I grump.

'And you have your degree, and your special award! Don't forget about that. It means you did better than all the rest. Employers will be lining up to interview you, Jude, you'll see.'

I'm not at all convinced and I can't hide it.

'At least, give yourself a chance, OK? Don't write off your future just yet. You'll find the thing you want to do and the place you want to be. These things just take time. OK?' He jostles his arm around my shoulder until I agree. 'And maybe you should give Elliot a chance while you're at it.'

'You're kidding!' I say gathering up my belongings, ready to climb the stairs to Daniel's room, hoping he packed his cucumber facemasks and some chocolate bars.

'You're the one that told me to call Ekon. What if I hadn't? *Hmm?* Things might have rumbled on at work like they have for weeks before the whole thing petered out and I'd be none the wiser that he liked me.'

I give Daniel a level look. 'It's not the same situation at all.'

'Just talk to him again, OK? Try to get his side of the story?'

'Oh… OK then,' I sigh, really exhausted now.

'Besides, if I hadn't given Ekon a chance, would I be getting messages like this?' Daniel proudly holds up his phone and there on the screen is a gorgeous stranger, his nurse's scrubs hanging on the door handle behind him, posing topless in his bathroom mirror and pulling a sort of *come get me* face.

'Jesus, Daniel!'

'Oh, sorry. I meant this one.' He flicks to the next image, biting his lip with embarrassment, not to mention salacious pride, and there is Ekon again, on a sofa, his grey hoodie covering his sexily shaved head, smiling shyly at the camera and holding up a crossed finger and thumb in a heart shape, looking every inch like the cute, attentive boyfriend Daniel deserves.

I'm glad for Daniel but have to admit there's an ache in my chest at the thought of the cosy, domestic moments Elliot and I shared this week and how I wish I could get back there, in the little bubble that was us.

'Come on, let's get some sleep. You can try again tomorrow,' Daniel says guiding me away. As we're saying goodnight to the stragglers from Sleuthing Club, the pub door opens.

'You missed it,' Finan calls out to a harried-looking Jowan, who's standing inside the doorframe with Aldous coming to a stop on his lead. The dog's little tail, normally a sad curl between his legs, is now kinked like a horizontal question mark behind him, and he's looking every bit like a regular pet pooch, apart from the untidy tramlines and gouges from Anjali's inexpert grooming.

Jowan doesn't say anything but strides over the room towards me. I tipsily offer Aldous a scratch behind the ears which he moodily accepts with an *if you really must* air, but Jowan wants me to stand up straight and listen.

'Jude? I don't mean to worry you, but I collected the cash from the shop and café this evening to take to the bank and it was just under eighty pounds short according to the till records. Elliot isn't there, neither are his belongings, and the shop was locked up – not that I'm accusing anyone of anything but… any idea what's happened there?'

I gape at Jowan, utterly lost for words. Bovis, Minty's estate manager, who has overheard the entire thing, exchanges pointed looks with Jowan before reaching into his pocket for his phone and silently leaving the bar.

Chapter Twenty-Four

'It's my fault, it has to be,' I say, close to sobbing, standing over the open till the next morning, a bright and mild Tuesday, the twenty-fourth of August. Daniel left an hour ago to catch his train for Land's End, and Jowan met me at the bookshop.

'What do you mean?' Jowan says, his mouth crumpling beneath his neat sandy whiskers.

'I don't really tell people, and I was never diagnosed or anything – I don't even know how I'd go about getting a diagnosis – but I've always struggled with numbers and money, and that sort of thing. And I've read about dyscalculia online and always thought some of the signs sounded exactly like me and my experiences.'

He's not saying anything and he's not looking at me like I've lost my mind, so I carry on. 'And I can never work out my share of the bill in a café if we're going Dutch, and I can't really get to grips with percentages, and what the hell even *are* fractions and long division? I never got any maths qualifications at school...' My shoulders slump. 'But I've never made such a big mistake before.'

'Nobody's blaming you,' Jowan's saying. 'And anyone can make a mistake counting out change.'

'Seventy-eight quid, Jowan? That's too much to just hand over and not notice. And look, I wrote down the price of every book I sold...'

'I know, I know. Don't panic. It's not the money that's the problem so much as the fact that Elliot disappeared at the same time as the money. It doesn't look all that good for him, you see?'

He's right, of course. It wouldn't take Agatha Christie to put two and two together and make Elliot a criminal. But somehow that feels like utterly the wrong conclusion.

'Elliot, a thief? He can't be.'

'That's what they all say,' Minty butts in. The news must be all round Clove Lore by now because she came bounding through the door a moment ago like a hound chasing down a vixen. 'You can't stray two foot from a murderer or a kidnapper but you'll find a neighbour or an old school friend only too willing to insist upon what a nice, unassuming person they were, and how they simply can't believe it.'

She's got a point. 'So what do we do now?' I say.

'I don't think we need to involve the police, not until we're sure of what's happened,' says Jowan, his eyes crinkling in a kind, sympathetic smile. It's a smile that tells me he has an inkling of what's been going on between me and Elliot. I don't mention the call from the CPS last week. That would definitely have Jowan dialling 999, even with all his kindness and understanding.

'He might only have gone for a run?' I say, desperately, but who takes all their clothes in a backpack and goes for an overnight run? 'Or… maybe he's with Anjali? They did spend some time together last week after Aldous's operation?' The very idea makes my stomach hurt. 'He could walk through that door any second.'

'That's right, we have to give people the benefit of the doubt, don't we?' he says.

'Pfft!' Minty scoffs. 'What about that pair who stole those valuable first editions the day they checked out? Remember them? You never saw hide nor hair of that money, and would you involve the authorities? No, you would not!'

Jowan nods, but he's giving Minty pretty short shrift this morning. 'We don't know about people's personal circumstances. Maybe they needed the money? Maybe they thought they'd paid for them, but they'd forgotten to?'

Another tut from Minty who's got a fiery look in her eyes that says Jowan's utterly soft and soppy and she'd happily set her dogs on Elliot's tracks and smoke him out of hiding for them to rip him apart.

'Could a volunteer have taken it in return for helping out?' I say, feebly, running through the options.

There's Mrs Crocombe and her laundry expenses, or Izaak and his… what exactly does he do to help out? Come to think of it, he hasn't been in the shop for days.

Jowan shakes his head. 'No, if any expenses are incurred helping our booksellers, the charity covers it. It wouldn't come from the till. It's more of a bartering system than a cash-based type of thing round here. Izaak keeps an occasional eye on the bookshop guests for me in return for some of my home brew and some bits and bobs from my veg patch. Minty brings books to the shop in return for help with the Christmas harbour light display, that sort of thing.'

I sigh in resignation. That's all my ideas for getting Elliot off the hook used up.

'I'll take over at the café today, Jude,' Jowan says, softly. 'If you feel up to running the shop?'

I agree and thank him, glancing at the till, its drawer gaping open at me, only a few pound coins and some coppers left of the float now that Jowan's cleared away the remaining notes – the ones that haven't mysteriously disappeared.

We'd taken the drawer apart in case the cash had been shoved behind it somehow but there was nothing to be found and I'd scoured the shop floor and behind the desk in case somehow it had been dropped, but there was no sign of the missing money.

Elliot's rich, or at least he's posh and comes from a rich family, and he's got a good job – or he did have, I'm still not sure what happened there – and he's got some pretty serious qualifications. Why would he need to steal? It doesn't add up.

I can't shake the guilty feeling that it was my error to blame, or a series of errors since I started cashing up alone. Could I have routinely undercharged customers? Or handed back twenties when I thought they were tens? I hate to think it, but that all sounds chronically like me.

Minty bustles off after reminding me about my baking commission for Friday – as if I could forget – and Jowan seems to put the disappointment of the missing money behind him and I hear him chatting happily with customers and locals all day long in the café.

He rustles up some flapjacks that seem to sell well. I serve in the shop, cautiously counting and re-counting every penny of change and checking that I've typed the prices into the till correctly to the extent that customers are left gawping and smirking at the nervous, shaky-handed bookseller sweating behind the till.

The day passes and Elliot doesn't come back, even though I jolt my head to the door every time the bell rings and I check my phone for missed messages even when it's in my pocket and I'd know instantly if he had got in touch. My heart sinks a little more with every passing hour. Wherever he is and whatever he's up to, this just goes to show I didn't know him at all.

–

I don't find the note until I go to bed. It's under my pillow. I sit on Elliot's mattress to read it. He'd neatly tucked in all the bedsheets and smoothed down the covers as though he'd never been here.

> *Jude, I'm so sorry I have to leave. I don't know if I'll be able to come back to Clove Lore before our tenancy ends on Saturday, but if I can, even if it's just for a second, to say goodbye to you properly, I will.*
>
> *I'm sorry I spoiled things. I should never have come to the bookshop. That was selfish of me. I shouldn't have got you involved in my mess. It was very hard to resist you and in the end, I couldn't. I'm sorry.*
>
> *I hope you can salvage the rest of your holiday and enjoy it. My mobile number's on the back if you need anything.*
>
> *E.*

Chapter Twenty-Five

I love the smell of gingerbread biscuits in the morning. Their aroma is wafting around the little café from the overloaded cooling racks on the counter telling me this is definitely a good batch with just enough ground ginger to lend them a fiery warmth.

Grandad's recipe book told me exactly what to do, but I've improvised a little too, adding some cinnamon and all spice, guesstimating the amounts, adding a sprinkle at a time to the fragrant, dark mixture in the bowl – all golden syrup, black treacle and soft brown sugar – and hoping I'd be able to tell when I'd got it just right.

It was surprisingly easy to roll and cut into shapes once it had chilled for a while – thank goodness the special cutters I ordered online arrived in time – now all I have to do is ice these bad boys and I'm done.

I'm not opening the café or the shop this morning. If the locals are to be believed all of Clove Lore and most of the morning's sightseers will be up at the big house for Minty's fox and field day. To be honest I'm glad I won't be alone in the shop on my last full day in the village. I'd hate to get all maudlin and mopey. I've done enough of that on this holiday.

There's been no word from Elliot, though I haven't tried to contact him either, so I just had to carry on with the baking and bookselling by myself. The whole village seems to be kept busy with the run up to Minty's event. Maybe she's roped everyone in to the planning?

I've missed Izaak and his cryptic book requests and had hoped I'd finally be able to furnish him with exactly the title he wanted but as Mrs C. said, you can't win them all.

Even Minty's stayed away since Tuesday morning and hasn't been around to make me feel self-conscious and silly. At the very least she'd have been company.

Mrs Crocombe's left me alone as well. I suppose she's lost interest in me now she knows I won't be winning any of the locals any money or churning out babies to fill her daughter's school.

Even Aldous is hardly ever here now that his near-death experience has transformed him into a regular dog and jolted the villagers out of their tendency to feel sorry for the solemn little mourner and indulge his doggy whims.

I spotted Jowan out walking Aldous on his lead yesterday. Jowan was talking to him the whole time and he was smiling too, and Aldous was actually wagging his tail at the sound of his master's voice. It was so nice to see. Both of them looked brighter, actually.

I'd gone to the shelves and lifted down Isolda's John Donne and re-read the lines Jowan shared with me the week before, '*his hand shall bind up all our scattered leaves again*'. It seems that the scattered leaves that made up what was left of the little holy trinity of Jowan, Isolda and their little dog, have stitched themselves together somehow. The operation was the shock they both needed to remember that life goes on, even when it hurts.

Now that Aldous is busy re-learning how to bask in Jowan's loving care, I took the opportunity to nip round to the laundry room at the back of the ice-cream cottage last night and wash all of his manky blankets and Isolda's old jumpers and they're all nicely folded and waiting for him on his windowsill if he ever comes back to sleep at the shop, which somehow I don't think he ever will. It's a sad day when even a housebound, toothless dog doesn't want to hang out at home with me anymore.

Home. That's dangerous thinking. Even with all the confusion and turmoil I've come to think of this lovely little shop as my own, and the knowledge that I'm leaving tomorrow morning is just… well, I can't think about it. I'll cry if I do.

I haven't settled on my book display idea either. Once that's done, it really *will* mean I'm leaving. I'm only just getting used to Clove

Lore and its quirks and its routines. Knowing I won't ever be here again hurts my heart.

Last night, at five, after a long quiet Thursday in the shop, I cashed up – thirty-one pounds and twenty-five pence daily profit, counted three times and checked against till records, thank you very much – and I walked down to the harbour.

It had obviously been a beautiful summer's day but, as usual, confined to the shop and café, I'd missed the hubbub around town with all the day-visitors crowding out the pub and lining the sea walls, eating fish and chips or picnic lunches, dangling a line to catch a crab or just sunning themselves watching the beach scenes and the traffic of the fishing boats; things I wish I'd had more opportunity to do during my holiday.

Anyway, I bought a pasty and a pale ale at the pub and wandered along to the end of the sea wall, quiet now most of the visitors had left, and watched the sun begin to set. I tried to read a little, but in the end the sight of the sky changing colour and the clouds rolling in, low and fluffy, held my gaze and I'd stared out at the scene, trying to convince myself I was simply glad to have met Elliot and shared a little bit of magic with him.

I even smiled thinking of his awkwardness, clomping through the shop, knocking things over, always having to mind his head under every beam and doorframe, and I'd had to bite my lip when my brain reminded me of the contrast between that great clumsy Elliot and the tender, passionate, intense Elliot who I'd come to know in more intimate moments, the Elliot with his deft mind and gentle hands. He was different then, more relaxed, safer, maybe? As though the invisible thing he was afraid of wasn't chasing him anymore and he could switch his focus only to me.

As the sun was almost melted into the horizon I heard footsteps behind me on the sea wall and turning, my heart in my mouth, I saw Anjali and tried not to show her what I'd been hoping, that she was Elliot coming back to me.

'I've been looking for you,' she said smilingly.

'I was just saying my goodbyes to Clove Lore. I'm leaving on Saturday morning,' I told her, then I offered to nip along to the Siren to buy her a drink.

'I'm fine, thanks, but can I sit for a sec?' She pointed to the spot beside me, which I immediately patted.

'Of course. How have you been?' I said.

'Good, thank you. I just wanted to say goodbye. I wish we'd been able to spend more time together.'

'Me too,' I say, thinking there are so many things I wish I'd done more of here. 'We should have had lunch or something.'

'Next time you visit,' she said, and I didn't want to say there wouldn't be a next time, so I smiled and agreed.

'I wondered if you'd seen this,' she said, pulling a book from her bag. 'Mrs C. told me Elliot left suddenly and that there was some problem with the shop takings.' Anjali was biting her lip, waiting for my reaction as I took the text book from her hands.

'*Into the Wild: Adventures in Veterinary Care*, by Elliot Desvaux?' I said, reading the title. There was a picture on the front of what were unmistakably Elliot's hands holding a tiny kitten and feeding it milk through a plastic syringe. I turned the book in my hands, feeling a lump rise in my throat.

'I thought you should see it,' Anjali continued. 'You might be finding yourself wondering who he is, and this might help answer some of your questions.'

I nodded and she told me the book was mine to keep.

'Really?' I said, astonished. When I opened the hard, glossy cover I saw the book was signed and dedicated to Anjali.

'Oh,' she laughed, 'I asked him to sign it the other day when he came to check on Aldous. He was a bit of a hero of mine when I was a student.'

I smiled and ran my fingertips over Elliot's signature in sweeping black Sharpie; his name was written large and somehow delicately too.

There was a dedication printed on the second page. It read, '*For Mum and Dad, I hope this book makes you proud.*' How could they not be proud of him, I wondered. '*Wow*,' I said, flipping through the pages, wishing the answers to all my questions about him really were somehow in here amongst the diagrams, charts, descriptions of surgical procedures and diagnostic advice.

'I know what the village thinks of him,' Anjali said, 'that he stole some money and ran away, but I don't believe it.'

'I don't either,' I told her.

'He's a good person, I'm sure of it,' she added. 'I was gutted when his YouTube channel disappeared. It was so helpful in the clinic, for training up the new staff, and you know, it was just kind of nice to look at him too,' she conceded with an awkward laugh.

I laughed too. I had to agree with her there.

'Do you know what happened to him? Why he deleted the channel? Why he ended up here?' I pushed.

Anjali shook her head. 'I always figure if people want to keep a secret from you then it's their secret to keep, isn't it? You can't pry it out of them. They need to be willing to share.'

I nodded, wanting to cry, wishing Elliot had been willing to share with me.

'Anyway, I thought it was important to let you know how I see things, just in case you're… regretting anything,' said Anjali, and we both looked out over the harbour mouth to sea and fell silent for a moment. 'Hah, look!' she said suddenly, pointing to something sticking out of the water.

At first I thought it was someone swimming, their head popping up over the gentle waves, but the round shape turned on its side to reveal it was actually flat before sinking again beneath the surface and re-emerging once more. 'What is it?' I said.

'Sunfish. They float on their sides and stick their fins out of the water, worshipping the sun.'

'Wow,' I said, noticing there were two of them – no, three – all flapping and turning as the light died, as though saying goodbye to the sun for another day.

'They're jellivores, you know?' Anjali's voice crackled with delight.

'Huh?' I'm really intrigued now.

'They come to these waters every summer to eat jellyfish.' Her eyes sparkled and I thought how surely no one who loves nature and devotes themselves to understanding and caring for creatures can be a bad person.

We smiled and watched the flipping fins in silence before Anjali got to her feet, saying she'd better get home. I stood too and hugged her, thanking her for the book, and for the little injection of faith she'd given me.

'Come back one day, OK?' she said, her hand on my arm.

'I will,' I lied.

'And tell Elliot I said goodbye when you see him.'

I sniffed a laugh and rolled my eyes at that, hoping she'd laugh too. '*Hmm*, all right then.'

'Do you know what that book taught me, Jude?' Anjali nodded to Elliot's textbook in my arms. 'What being a vet has taught me? You have to keep believing that the majority of people are intrinsically good, even when all the evidence is there to suggest they're not and that we're just a big trash fire scarring a planet and hurting everything. At first it was hard for me to see it. For every owner of a pampered, beautifully groomed and well exercised pony or puppy, there's a person who beats their animals, or leaves them to be cold, or hungry, or afraid.

'At the start of my career, I'd see the rescues coming in to the surgery, barely clinging on to life, and I'd be angry and spiteful and I'd start to wonder if humans were actually bloody awful things if they could hurt innocent animals and not mind it one bit.

'Elliot says the same thing happened to him, in that book. But he wrote something that changed my mind. He said that he learned to count all the helpers too – all the volunteers and the vets and the charity workers and the carers and the activists – who give up their time to look after creatures that can't look after themselves, and I realised there are millions of us, just doing our best to be kind. It helped me a lot, stopped me becoming bitter and hateful. We have to believe in the best of people, and remember there are more of us, more helpers, than there are the other kind. Don't give up on Elliot yet. He's one of us.'

She hugged me again and I wiped the tears from my face before she left me alone on the sea wall where I slumped back down and watched the sunfish waving their fins at the Clove Lore sunset, trying to think well of Elliot and keep my trust in his goodness, and that was how I spent my second last night in the village.

Now here I am with less than twenty-four hours of my holiday left, my commission for Minty almost finished. I snap off a bit of gingerbread biscuit and absently dip it straight into the orange-coloured icing I've somehow mixed up to a nice consistency whilst absorbed in my thoughts, and I taste it. The fire of the ginger brings me round and it's so good I polish off the whole cookie with a mug of tea.

This will have to sustain me today. I've got all these spicy shapes to ice before setting off for the hunt. I won't stay long at the estate, there's no point. I've no interest in seeing wildlife being chased by hounds or whatever obscure countryside spectacle Minty's got planned and I've still got to pack my case and lug everything downhill to Diane who is still, I hope, safely waiting for me in the car park behind the Siren. I'll set off for Marygreen at first light tomorrow. The end of my adventure.

I seem to have had so many endings and so few beginnings in my life, so many avenues cut off to me, and my current situation makes the autumn ahead impossible to picture clearly. Maybe there'll be a job at the retail park for me, or maybe New Start Village are looking for staff. That way I could go back to caring for Gran and I'd see her every day, though I know she's really busy and probably wouldn't have much time for hanging out with me. It would be something at least.

I sigh and reach for the piping bag. 'Sixty cookies to ice,' I gee myself up, ignoring the voice in my head repeating Elliot's words, saying he'll come back if he can, even if it's just for one second, to say goodbye to me. With the last little bit of hope I have left I listen for his footsteps as I work.

Chapter Twenty-Six

It's almost nine and as I'm getting ready for the long trudge uphill to Minty's estate the shop phone rings, and I race to answer it, still praying that it's Elliot. I'm greeted by Izaak's beautiful accent.

'Jude? I need a book.'

'Ah, okay,' I say bracing myself for what's to come. What vague description will he give this time? Does he want the one with the thingy, you know? That big thingy and that man with the whatdoyoucallit?

'Are you still there?' he calls to me.

'Sorry, Izaak, what can I get you?'

'A book of poems… and love songs too.'

'That's it?' I draw my neck back, surprised.

'Yep. Something romantic. Do you have anything?'

'I've got just the thing,' I tell him, delightedly.

Within moments, I'm marching Up-along, clutching three big Tupperware tubs full of iced gingerbread shapes and, balanced on top, a mid-century copy of *Palgraves Golden Treasury of English Songs and Lyrics* bound in berry-red leather with fine gold embossing on the title. It was twenty-three pounds – but it's in great condition. It took up a sizable chunk of the money Minty gave me for the cookies, but it'll be my farewell gift to Izaak.

I'm so glad I finally stocked something he asked for. The rest of my commission I'll give to Jowan when I repay the shop's missing cash. It's weighed on my mind since Monday night when I learned it (and Elliot) was gone and I won't be happy until it's settled up and I know for sure Jowan isn't out of pocket.

It doesn't matter anymore how that money disappeared. I've worked hard, really tried my best with the shop money, and it's been right every night since Elliot left me to it, so I know I *can* do it, if I'm very, very slow and methodical. There's no reason why I couldn't work in another shop back in Marygreen.

I think I've proven myself if not exactly gifted, at least quietly competent when it comes to figures, with a lot of checking and care – and maybe I will still make the occasional mistake, because nobody's perfect, and that's good enough for me. I did all this by myself and it was OK in the end.

I follow the signs to the estate entrance – through the visitors' centre, across the car park out towards the main road and along a grassy path through woodland – and I take my time as I walk. The birds are singing in the trees all around me and the sun is bright and already hot in spite of the breeze up here at the top of the village.

Everywhere there are signs of the impending big event. Boards leaning against fence posts directing cars to the visitors' parking, coloured bunting strung along the hedges, and in the distance across a wide lawn there's a great white marquee, refreshment stands and tables all set out ready for the crowds later today.

It all looks rather civilised and I'm having a hard time reconciling the beautiful scene with what I *think* is to happen here later today. I'll be long gone before the hunt begins. The whole idea of people on horseback shouting Tally-ho or whatever it is they do feels so far from my upbringing back home I know for sure I won't fit in, and as I give it more and more thought, I'm sure I won't want to.

A caterers' van rolls past me as I make my way onto the lawn. The big house in the distance is grand and imposing in its prominent position overlooking the Atlantic.

Clove Lore is out of sight from up here, hidden down in its steep valley, clinging to the rocks, hoping not too many people discover its secrets but that enough of them find their way here to keep the place afloat.

On my way I pass by Izaak's caretaker's booth and I spot him leaning by its open door, paying very close attention to a tall man with glasses and thick, curly blond hair. As I get closer I see they're lost in conversation and not quite holding hands, but letting their fingertips touch in an easy, intimate way.

'Sorry to interrupt, here's the book you asked for,' I call out when I get closer and I can't help beaming with happiness to see Izaak's flushed pink cheeks and the slightly dazed loved-up look these two are sharing.

'Jude! Come and meet Leonid.'

I shake hands with the blue-eyed stranger who has the most adorably gappy front teeth, and I stand expectantly, trying not to rock on my heels with anticipation. 'And Leonid is… visiting?'

'He's my boyfriend,' Izaak beams back.

'You are Jude with the books?' Leonid asks and I can hear *Dr Zhivago* and Tolstoy in the melody of his accent.

'She is,' Izaak tells him, and I'm surprised to find Leonid delivering an effusive double kiss on my cheeks which makes me grip the gingerbread tubs tightly while Izaak makes a protective grab for them.

'Put those down… ah, what a nice edition,' Izaak says, spotting the book as he sets the cookies safely upon the ledge beneath the open booth window.

'Love songs and poems,' I grin, looking expectantly between them. Leonid's looking at the book with wide eyes too.

'Thank you, Jude,' Leonid says. 'Izaak, you don't have to buy me more books now I'm here.'

'All the books you were requesting? They were for Leonid?' I say.

Leonid answers first. 'We have been apart for a long time, and at night we read to each other over Skype. Izaak in English or Russian, and I would read in Polish. That way we improve our language skills and we don't get so lonely.' Leonid accepts the *Treasury* from Izaak and they exchange soft smiles.

'You've known each other for a long time?' I'm fizzing with happiness, thinking how romantic this all sounds and how quiet Izaak had been about Leonid's existence – mind you, I never asked him if he was seeing anyone.

Izaak tells the story. 'We met when Leonid visited Clove Lore with his university colleagues – they were touring the gardens of the south west and came here to see the camellias – and we spent a few days together here before he had to leave. That was two years ago, we haven't met in person since.'

'Until now,' I say, most definitely misty-eyed again.

Leonid takes over. 'I flew in on Wednesday. I am a botanist in Russia, but I lost my job when I stood in a protest outside my university one day. I always try to be discreet but that day I couldn't help myself. I picked up a flag and shouted with my students. The police came. I wasn't arrested but the university authorities found out and somehow my landlord heard too.' Leonid smiles grimly.

I already know what kind of protest he means before Izaak clarifies it was an LGBT rights demonstration of only ten or so brave students. I'm winded by the thought of their selflessness and vulnerability, and by the steadfast look behind both men's eyes.

'Leonid's been trying to get a work visa for a long time so he can join me here,' Izaak adds.

'A long time,' Leonid echoes and the pair gaze at each other once more.

'Thank God for Minty,' Izaak adds.

'Minty? What's she got to do with it?' I say.

'She asked about the books I was buying – my old favourites from when I was learning English as a teenager, by the way – books I wanted to share with Leonid. I told her about Leonid's situation and she worked hard to create a job for him here. It took a long time and we had to wait for the paperwork but… meet the estate's new camellia specialist. He can stay permanently as long as he's at the estate.'

'Minty did this?' I say again, flummoxed. '*Minty?*' Somehow I can't imagine her stepping in to help these two reunite. They laugh at my incredulity.

'You'd be surprised how kind she can be,' Izaak smiles. 'She's a true romantic, unlike Mrs Crocombe. I didn't tell her about us. The villagers can lose all their bets about me too. Serves them right for making assumptions.'

Smiling, I shake my head in amazement. 'So you're staying, for good?'

'Hopefully,' Leonid nods, reaching an arm around Izaak's waist and it's only now I see the tentativeness and the newness of their bond. It makes me smile and it makes my heart crack a little at the sight of them, together again after months of patient waiting.

I've been missing Elliot for less than a week but it strikes me, if somehow it *could* all come right in the end, like Leonid and Izaak, I too would wait years for him. What a pity he clearly didn't feel the same way. I try not to sigh in front of them.

'*Are* you a camellia expert?' I say. My voice is strained but I'm trying to keep smiling.

'I will be,' Leonid replies, and the pair lean their heads together contentedly, still smiling down at me.

That's when I remember what I'm supposed to be doing and I start flustering, grabbing the Tupperware tubs again.

'Oh my goodness, *Minty*! I have to get these cookies to her.' I lift the lid on the top box and quickly offer the lovers a gingerbread.

'You can leave these with me, I'll deliver them to the big house right away,' Izaak says, taking them back, and it's dawning on me that now I've delivered my commission, my holiday's almost over.

The moment's cut short by Mrs Crocombe bustling across the field 'coo-eeing' at us. She's out of her ice-cream shop apron and in a floral sundress, and she's with her daughter, and a man, presumably her son-in-law, and three curly haired, very excited children, all dressed in their summery best and looking forward to the hunt.

'Have you heard the news?' Mrs C. shouts out, long before she reaches the booth.

'I was just about to tell her,' Izaak calls back and I watch her increase her speed so she can be the one to deliver the gossip.

'They've had 'em, you know?' She's out of breath as she reaches us.

'Who?' I'm drawing a complete blank.

'The ones that have been going round the shops, the distraction thieves! They've stolen from Borrow-a-Bookshop, Astral Breeks, the fudge concession, and half a dozen other places between here and Truro. Police nabbed them last night at Launceston.'

'The bookshop money? So it *was* stolen?'

'Yes! Keep up!' snaps Mrs Crocombe. 'A youngish couple too, a man and a woman. They're professionals. She keeps you talking, asks for stock in hard to reach places or out the back and while you're busy, *whoosh*, he's got his hand in the till. Career criminals, the police said. It's in the paper this morning.'

She hands over the rolled newspaper from under her arm and, sure enough, it's front page news. I'm struck by the thought that not even one ounce of my being is wincing hoping I'm not about to see a photograph of Elliot and some mystery woman being cuffed and dragged into a police van.

The couple in the picture, taken from CCTV footage, are strangers to me. I don't recognise them at all. If they *were* in the shop it must have been on a day when I wasn't around. That's when the guilty feeling hits me as I remember the day I skived off down to the waterfall and then to the Siren with Daniel. Elliot must have been too busy to notice the thieves at work. If I'd been there none of this would have happened.

'Somebody needs to tell Elliot,' I say, turning away, dazed and reeling. There's no signal up here for my phone and my feet are already carrying me back towards the village where network coverage is better. Izaak calls out behind me, telling me to make sure I come back to say goodbye later, and I catch the fading sounds of Mrs Crocombe suspiciously asking who Izaak's new friend is. I wish I could be there to watch as he explains and the nosey old matchmaker has to concede to even more lost bets.

I'm holding my phone at arm's length, searching for a signal as I go, the crowds of happy holidaymakers and locals streaming past me as I walk against the tide. Anjali was right. Everyone seems to be going to the fox and field event. Just as I reach the visitors' centre car park, my phone rings. When I answer, a voice that makes my stomach flip asks, 'Where are you?'

'Elliot! I'm up at the big house.' I find myself rambling. 'The estate hunt starts in a few minutes and I was delivering the cookies Minty ordered. What are you doing? Where on earth are you?'

'I'm at the bookshop.' His voice is grave and desperate. 'I need to see you…'

My heart's racing and my pace quickening. He's here! He came back. Down the line I hear the sound of him locking the shop door and his boots clomping as he marches, presumably, towards me. 'Hold on, did you say a hunt? What kind of hunt?' he asks.

I think of my batches of gingerbread biscuits, Minty's commission, sweet little foxes iced in orange and white, sixty pairs of black beady eyes behind individual cellophane wrappers. 'Fox, I guess,' with a shrug. I'm about to say, 'Fox hunting's banned, though, so it can't be that, surely?' but Elliot's hung up.

What the hell? 'Elliot?' I keep the phone to my ear, calling out to no one at all. What's he doing now? I don't understand anything this guy does anymore. What I do know is that I'm running.

I clear the crowds entering Minty's estate and I race across the visitors' centre car park, where there are only a few stragglers unloading their kids and picnic baskets and making their way to the event.

I'm not even trying to remember when the last time I ran was or paying too much attention to my heart pounding and my lungs straining; all I'm thinking about is Elliot, and where he is, and why he's here, and what he'll do when we meet again.

I know what I *want* to happen.

I want him to open his arms and gather me up into the kind of hug that lifts you off the ground and I want to hear him apologise and explain where he's been and what exactly the heck is going on with him and all his secrecy, and I'll kiss him and there'll be an end to this feeling of having been abandoned and not understanding why.

I'm dizzy at the thought of it, or maybe it's the lack of oxygen reaching my brain as I run. I'll be sweaty and red-faced when I see him and I don't even care.

I make the turn onto Down-along, and to stop myself careering headfirst down the slope, straight past the bookshop and into the sea, I have to walk, slow and steady, gripping the garden railings and gates as I plod, trying to catch my breath.

Clove Lore seems even more magical for being utterly abandoned. Not one person is walking the streets or sitting in their tiny front gardens, and all I can hear are the gulls calling from the rooftops and the waves down below me, and my heart's making my eardrums pound a loud rhythm too, and over all that, and getting louder, comes the sound of boots.

The approaching noise stops me in my tracks and I find myself frozen on the cobbles, gulping and flushed and not knowing what to do with myself. All my inhibitions want me to take cover and hide, let Elliot march past me unseen so I can't be hurt again, but my heart won't let me.

First I see black hair flowing as he runs up the slope, then the stern set of his brows, taut jaw and straight mouth. All I can do is watch him approach. I'm stuck here, wide-eyed and feeling like a child, unsure of myself, shy and bewildered all at once.

He's all in black of course, with the poise of a boxer and a ballet dancer etched into his movements, those thighs powering him up the hill, his amber eyes trained on me. He's not smiling, and neither, I realise, am I.

The closer he gets the less I can do. The ball is firmly in his court because I've suddenly lost control of all my cognitive and emotional faculties. He'll have to do the talking. Yet, as he reaches me, it's clear from the determined look on his face he's not stopping to talk, in fact he's going to run straight past me.

'Come with me,' he growls as he passes and I see him reach for my hand. Instinctively I take hold of him and he practically drags me back up the hill. 'Can you run?' His voice is deep and husky – and sexy enough – to somehow trigger my legs into running again, and so we stride up the hill together, going God knows where.

That's when I see the little streak of beige by Elliot's feet. Aldous, running full pelt, his tongue lolling out of his open, panting mouth, and he looks absolutely delighted and very much like a real dog, paws clawing at the stones, his back undulating like a greyhound in full pursuit. He must have sneaked back to the shop for a snooze after all.

Every now and then Aldous looks up into Elliot's face as if asking whether Elliot's pleased with him and whether he's a good boy or not. I can see now I'm not the only one who'd grown grateful for Elliot's presence and had missed him when he disappeared. I supposed that's what happens when someone saves your life. So we run all the way Up-along, the three of us, though Elliot's the only one amongst us who knows why.

'Elliot! What are you doing?' I cry as we make it to flat ground at last and break into a sprint past the tourist concessions at the top of the village. The sight of the surfy clothes shop sparks a memory and I try to tell Elliot through gasped breaths – I really am absolutely knackered now and Elliot's pace is not letting up – about the robbers.

'It's OK about the money,' I pant. 'You know it was stolen, right? By the… (deep gasp) distraction… (rushed exhale)… thieves.'

We've crossed the car park now and the estate entrance is in sight. Elliot doesn't even glance at me on hearing the words. I'm lagging behind now, even though he's still clasping my hand.

'What money?' is all he says, and a strained laugh erupts from my chest.

I've been so worried about something he wasn't even aware of, and whatever his dark secret is, the thing that made him bolt, I'm still none the wiser. We're on completely different pages, and I think we have been from the start.

There's nobody in Izaak's booth as we pass. He must be down at the hunt with Leonid already.

'Elliot, please can we just slow down!'

A tannoy sparks into life somewhere over by the big house and a voice carries on the still summer morning air. 'Welcome to the Clove Lore estate fox and field day and annual hunting party.' It's Minty; there's no mistaking her upper-class tones. A ripple of applause is broadcast over the PA system too.

'There'll be no hunt in Clove Lore today, not if I can help it,' Elliot shouts, his pace quickening.

He drops my hand and I watch him sprint ahead, across the wide, beautifully manicured lawns and past the marquee, and Aldous finds the energy from somewhere to carry on, skipping along by his side, letting out a sharp yap of excitement every now and then.

There's no sign of the crowds so everyone must be congregating over on the other side of the house by now. I run, trying to keep up, but there's a stitch in my side.

'Elliot, stop, what are you up to?' My cries are futile; he's not going to stop.

Minty's announcements continue and I force myself to run in Elliot's wake, my legs turning to jelly as I reach the very limits of my endurance. Elliot leaps over a low hedge and rounds the side of the big house, passing into its shadow then disappearing from my view.

'It gives me great pleasure to continue my family's traditions by hosting this great event once more,' Minty proclaims. 'Please enjoy the hunt – while staying *off* the planted areas of the gardens, if you don't mind! Keep a close eye on your little ones, and please join me in the countdown to releasing the foxes.'

'Oh my God!' I scream. I'm almost at the house now and I can hear the excited countdown, loud and jolly, a few hundred voices united, 'Five, four, three…'

Elliot's right; we have to stop this hunt. What kind of weirdo wicker-man kind of community rips foxes apart in front of kids in broad daylight? I can hear dogs barking; one of them is definitely Aldous's high-pitched yip.

'…Two, one,' the crowd cheer.

I clear the side of the big house and turn left following the sounds and am immediately halted by the great crowd, their backs to me, some with toddlers raised on shoulders, all crying out happily, '*Release the foxes!*'

I push my way through the gathering, not caring that it's rude and I'm sweating all over these bonkers, blood-thirsty barbarians.

I hear Elliot shouting before I see him. '*STOP! There will be no illegal hunt on this land today!*' He's right in the middle of the knot garden, his arms stretched up towards Minty who's standing on a white balcony, much like Evita but in a waxed gilet, and she's only just noticed Elliot the interloper.

The shock contorts her face, but it's too late; the crowds are cheering for the foxes, and some of the people standing closest to Elliot are jeering and laughing and dogs on leads are yapping all around us. Aldous is nowhere to be seen.

All at once every window on the upper floor of the big house springs open and uniformed staff in red hunting jackets and black velvet hats lean out and start pelting the gathered crowd with... well, *what are they?*

My question's answered as I finally get within touching distance of Elliot and see his expression turn from horrified outrage and stoic dynamism to utter confusion as a big stuffed animal bonks him on the head.

'*They're toy foxes, you lumbering idiot!*' Minty shouts into her microphone, just as three red-faced, stocky men in camouflage hunting gear wrestle Elliot to the ground.

There are stuffed cubs and vixens falling all around us, landing in bushes and scattered across the parterre, and a great swathe of little kids stumble around trying to grab at the plushies before their siblings and friends can.

'Oh!' I hear Elliot say as he realises his horrible, embarrassing error, just a second before Bovis, Minty's neckless estate manager, lies across Elliot's shoulders, shouting, '*Got 'im!*'

The crowds are laughing and clapping delightedly, most of them oblivious to Elliot's failed heroics, and my own laugh hitches a little in my throat as I watch Aldous emerge from the rumpus of delighted kids all searching for a toy of their own, as more stuffed animals rain down on the gardens from above, and the devoted, scruffy little Bedlington sits delightedly beside the man he owes his life to, proudly presenting the struggling, confounded, and decidedly flattened-looking Elliot with a cuddly toy fox.

Chapter Twenty-Seven

'I don't expect much from the likes of you, Elliot Desvaux, but *you*!' Minty turns accusingly to me, and I shrink under the weight of her disapproval. 'What do you think you were doing, spoiling my hunt?'

'I… I…' How do I explain I was just following Elliot and I had no idea what kind of stunt he was going to pull? 'I think it was all just a big misunderstanding,' I shrug. 'Can you let him go now, please?' I plead.

Bovis and his tweedy friends are still holding Elliot's arms behind his back. They've marched us to the edge of Minty's estate and it's quite clear we're being ejected. The whole event had all looked quite nice and innocent once I'd taken the time to peer around me at the candyfloss stalls, and the ice-cream van and the very obvious family atmosphere Minty had worked so hard to cultivate. I can see why Ben Fogle enjoyed the hunt so much now. I'd rather like to stay and watch the kids eating my gingerbread cookies, which had been arranged so beautifully on the refreshments stand by the entrance to the marquee.

'I'm sorry,' Elliot says, his brows knitted, as he struggles against the hands binding him. 'Jude mentioned there was a hunt and I just… snapped. I assumed it was an organised hunt with hounds.'

'After the ban?' says Minty. 'On *my* estate? At ten in the morning? On a summer's day? With half the tourists in the county watching?'

'I know, I didn't think. But even with the Hunting Act wildlife is still being killed all over the place…'

'Not 'ere it's not!' Bovis cuts in menacingly from somewhere behind Elliot. I can't actually see him.

Minty takes over, her voice very serious and cross. 'We haven't hunted at Clove Lore for over forty years. My father was a wonderful huntsman, kept fifteen couple hounds at one time. But the expense was too much for the estate, and we couldn't afford the boarding, or keep up with the roading for that matter.'

'Roading?' I say.

She looks at me, incredulous as usual. 'The exercising and training.'

I silently mouth, 'Oh, right,' and let her carry on.

'I wanted to do something to maintain the tradition of bringing guests onto the land, and I wanted to raise some money for the estate, so years ago now, Jowan and I cooked up the idea for the fox hunt and a family fun day.'

'It really is a lovely idea,' I say, regretting it immediately when Minty raises a dramatic brow at the interruption.

'It's important to encourage young people onto the land. I don't want the gardens to close, too. It's bad enough living in three small rooms in one wing of the house with the rest of my family home redeveloped into umpteen apartments and turned over to strangers.' She looks pained at the admission. 'With the ticket sales for the annual fox and field day and the general admission charges for garden visits all year round there's a chance we can stay open for many years to come and, more importantly, I can keep the estate staff and their loved ones here.'

'That's very admirable,' Elliot says, and Minty's eyes snap to his.

'I *know* who you are, Elliot Desvaux.' Minty rounds on him, looking up into his face fiercely. 'I know what you *did*.'

'Wait just a minute…' Elliot's voice is stern and level. He's shaking his head in frustration.

'Minty, he didn't rob the shop!' I butt in. 'It was in the paper today. It was a pair of crooks on a crime spree tour of holiday spots.'

'I know that, I saw the newspaper,' snaps Minty. 'Are you going to tell her, or shall I?' she asks Elliot.

'What does she mean, Elliot?' I ask, suddenly afraid. I lift Aldous into my arms and the mutt and I look between Minty and Elliot in confusion.

Elliot huffs out an angry breath and finally manages to shake off the grasp of Bovis and his mates.

'*I'll* tell her,' he storms, and the look on his face is fearsome with his fury.

'I have to get back to the hunt.' Minty turns to me. 'The quartet will be striking up soon, and there's the magician to introduce, though your friend here has already provided *quite* enough entertainment already.'

Elliot huffs again and as he rakes his hair back I catch a glimpse of the silvery scar once more.

'Shall I call Jowan and ask him to accompany you both back to the shop, make sure there's no more funny business?' Minty asks me.

'I'll be OK,' I tell her, and she nods sharply. 'But you can take Aldous back to Jowan. I think he sneaked into the shop earlier.'

Minty takes Aldous from my arms and turns on her heel but before she goes she calls back, 'Oh, and your gingerbread foxes were marvellous. You are a very fine baker. Thank you.'

'You're welcome,' I tell her, not letting the strangeness of this morning's events deflect from the feeling of pride this gives me.

She smiles thinly, throws Elliot one last withering look, and leaves us. Her minions follow after her.

Elliot has the strangest look on his face – and quite a lot of gravel and dirt from having his cheek squashed into the paving stones for so long. His eyes are shining as he looks at me, and he's actually smiling, or trying to repress a smile and it's not working.

'I've missed you,' he blurts, and I bite the inside of my cheek, feeling myself shrink a little. I can't tell him I've missed him too, not yet. Not until I know his secrets.

'You have a lot of explaining to do,' I tell him, coolly. 'And I won't settle for any of your nonsense about not being able to tell me. You can, and you will.'

Chapter Twenty-Eight

I lock the door and turn the sign so it reads 'Closed'.

'Come on,' I tell Elliot, making my way to the little kitchen at the back of the bookshop.

Elliot hasn't said a thing all the way Down-along, and I used the walk to prepare myself for whatever it is he's going to tell me. I can't get the anger in Minty's voice out of my head. What is it that she knows about Elliot? The incendiary thing he couldn't tell me before now?

'Sit,' I say, and like an obedient puppy, Elliot pulls out a chair. I make us both sweet tea. 'Ready?' I present Elliot with his mug and sit down at the little table.

He nods, sips his tea, then clears his throat. He's struggling with this. 'It's hard to know where to start,' he says.

'Start at the beginning,' I urge, and so he does, and as he speaks I watch his eyes darken as he sinks back into the memories of recent months and I finally come to understand the weight of the secret he kept from me, and I can't help but cry.

—

'Before I start, you need to know it was an accident, OK? I didn't mean any harm,' he begins, ominously, and I take a deep breath and try not to show that I'm shaking. Elliot steels himself with a deep breath and slow exhale too.

'So... it was last Christmas. My parents always host the entire family – they come from all over the surrounding counties and some come up from London. It's always a big affair and it's best not to

214

upset Mum by staying away, so I left Cambridge and headed across the counties to get home. My, *uh*... girlfriend was with me.'

I try not to start at the words but Elliot must see my eyes widen because he quickly blurts, 'my ex-girlfriend! We, *uh*, we shared a flat together in Cambridge. She's a biologist. I was lecturing on a veterinary degree programme at one of the colleges and working at a very smart practice nearby. It was a life, you know? A steady life. Maybe it wasn't perfect, but it looked OK from the outside, and it made my parents proud, so...' He shrugs resignedly. 'Anyway, as much as I enjoy seeing my family on Christmas day, it's a lot, you know?'

I don't know, but I nod. Our Christmases were always so small and cosy at Marygreen, just Mum, Dad, Gran and me, with Daniel and his parents just next door, and there was always so much lovely baking. Mum's mince pies, Dad's Christmas pudding and the biggest Christmas cake I ever saw – the centre of our bakery's window display all December long and our family festive treat.

Elliot's Christmases sound like a far bigger social occasion than anything I've ever known. We're from different worlds, just like Mack and I were. Unaware that I'm sinking deeper into despair at how radically dissimilar our backgrounds are and how, as a consequence, we must be utterly unsuited to each other, Elliot talks on.

'Antonia – that's my ex's name – she had to leave to go to her parents' cocktail thing, like she does every Christmas day after lunch, and so I'd always escape in the afternoon and walk across the fields to the Broom and Antler. There's always farmers and vets in there who I've known all my life, and sure enough, there were old friends at the bar that night too, and there was live music, and the fires were lit... It was so good.' He smiles warmly at the memory. 'You'd like it there,' he adds suddenly, glancing at me, then back to his hands clasping his mug.

I'm still reeling from the words 'like she did every year', and the revelation that Elliot's been in a long-term relationship until recently. The glow in his amber eyes fades as I watch his mind working through the memories.

'That was the last normal day of my life,' he says. 'The last time I was in control of it, anyway.' He blows out a heavy breath.

I reach for his hand as his chest hollows and his shoulders slump but he doesn't take my hand in his own, he only looks at it warily as though he's afraid I might snatch it back once I've heard what he has to say, and he carries on.

'I don't remember much about the walk back to my parents' that night. I'd had quite a few pints and then the landlady had brought out the mulled cider, and I'm sure I drank something that was flaming and blue that one of the young farmers paid for, and...' he shrugs. 'I don't really remember, but it's a long way across country back to my parents' place where I was staying for the rest of the holiday, and I always cut through the fields to get to the pub. It's a good hour, hour and a quarter's walk. I know those fields and footpaths like the back of my hand; I spent so much of my childhood out wandering, spotting wildlife, looking for birds and insects...'

I wait for him to come round from the memories of his childhood that he's getting lost in. He almost looks happy, but his expression quickly clouds again. 'It must have been long after midnight. The moon wasn't quite full but there was enough moonlight not to need a torch and there were so many stars... I guess I was just staggering home, like I'd done a thousand times, a bit worse for wear, but still...'

He sinks into silence, reliving the cold, dark trudge across country alone. I watch him silently, not wanting to interrupt, not now when he's finally sharing his burden. I'm too afraid to speak, anyway. What is he about to tell me? Something that's so bad Minty's got wind of it all the way out here in Devon?

Suddenly, Elliot seems to flinch at his memories and his eyes flicker, dark and wild. 'I was almost home when I heard a noise from far behind me, a couple of fields off, and I knew what it was straight away. Horses. It sounded like thirty or forty of them thumping over the frosted stubble fields, and the night was so quiet. The birds scattered from all the bushes and everything that could run and hide did, except for me.

'The dogs reached me first. I suppose I threw them off the scent they were tracking, and suddenly I was surrounded by them. They were circling and sniffing, totally confused to find me interrupting their trail, but then they picked it up again and in an instant they were off, heads up and alert, rushing into a corner of the field.'

'A fox hunt?' I spit out, and Elliot talks on.

'I could hear the horses approaching fast and I realised they were likely to come leaping over the hedges and on top of me, so I ran, trying to get clear of the field, and then… It happened so fast – it sobered me right up, I can tell you.

'I ended up in the same corner of the field as the dogs, under a big oak. It was pitch black in there but I knew if I leaned myself against the oak's trunk I couldn't be crushed by the horses, and that's when I saw it. The vixen, or just a glimpse of her brush, rather. She was limping, her tongue out, exhausted. The hounds chased her into a covert and they were howling mad, digging away with their paws, and one by one the horses flooded into the field too and they were upon me in an instant. I fell backwards into a ditch beside the oak and I just lay there, dazed and… just watching it all happen.

'One of the men climbed down from his horse. He wasn't in hunting scarlet. This guy was all in camo, but he was with the hunt all right, a terrier man. He had a shovel in his hands. I saw the lights from vehicles that seemed to have arrived from nowhere – five or six of them out on the road in the distance – and there were people talking on phones, and guys recording everything on camera, and great hunting lamps being brought over right to where I was lying. I'm not surprised nobody spotted me at all. Someone called the dogs off the covert, but there were five or six of them that wouldn't stop scraping at the bank, trying to get to the vixen. The place was in chaos. Then I heard the shouts from across the field – like a fight breaking out and someone swearing and there was shouting into a radio, something about "bloody sabs".' Elliot looks at me to see if I'm following. 'Saboteurs.'

'It sounds dangerous,' I say, almost in a whisper. My voice has left me.

'It felt it too. The atmosphere was so charged, and the voices so aggressive. I didn't know what to do, but when I saw that man coming closer with his shovel ready to dig out the fox I just stood up, like, automatically, and before I knew it, I was shouting at him to get back, to call off the dogs, to leave the fox alone.

'The huntsmen all got back on their horses – I don't know, I guess they thought I was a saboteur too, and these other blokes came at me, a bunch of heavies, the kind that are used to intimidate saboteurs, and they're filming me and swearing and telling me to get out the field, and one of them was holding what I'm pretty sure was a metal bar. So, I backed away, with my hands up, telling them I was just a bloke walking home from the pub, but I was a vet too and I knew hunting was banned and what they were doing wasn't legal.

'I reached for my phone, trying to film them, and all the time I was walking backwards, trying not to look too threatening – which is kind of hard when you look like this – and I heard the snort of a horse behind me, and something struck my face, really smarting and cutting, like a whip, and I stumbled. After that, it was a mess.

'I fell against the horse, and it reared and kicked, and then there was a huntsman on the ground, and there was so much blood coming from his head. I don't know how but his helmet was off, and he was only a young lad really. I tried to help him, but the whole time this guy was filming me and most of the riders on horseback cleared off and the dogs ran with them. An ambulance came, I don't know, it felt like hours after, and the police came too.

'I remember there were sabs trying to get me into a car, but I couldn't leave the guy bleeding on the ground. I may only be a vet but I know how to staunch a bleeding wound, and then there were hands on me and I was in the back of a police car being arrested for GBH.' He exhales, and his shoulders fall further. 'And I couldn't say for sure it wasn't my fault that he fell, so I didn't.'

'Oh my God, Elliot!' I cry, but he isn't stopping his tale now.

'He was in hospital unconscious for days and even when they let me leave the station I wasn't allowed to visit him or find out how he was doing. The police told me to expect a trial and that I wasn't allowed to leave the country, and… that's when the phone calls started at my parents' place. I still don't know who it was, telling me I was a murderer and that I'd pay for it, that they'd kill me. I was beside myself.

'It was still the Christmas holidays and Antonia was with her family and I was stuck at my parents' place miles from my flat and my work. Their place seemed like the safest option to stay put and it was near the police station.

'Anyway, it was in the papers and splashed all over the countryside press; a few young huntsmen out exercising their horses on Christmas day, one of them violently knocked from his horse by a drunk vet mistakenly thinking there was an illegal hunt taking place, and now fighting for his life. You see, they'd almost all dispersed by the time the police arrived; there was no evidence of the hunt to be found anywhere.' Elliot smiles wryly, his eyes glazed.

'What about the saboteurs? Couldn't they help you in court?' I ask.

'They tried, but with no proof, it was their word against the huntsmen, and the judge didn't seem all that inclined to listen to a bunch of activists, some of whom had long records of breaching the peace or trespassing, all while trying to stop illegal hunting, of course.

'Anyway, I only found out the lad was going to live when I was called to court. The relief, you know!' He dissolves into sobbing tears that shake his frame. 'I thought I'd killed him. For days, I thought he was dead.'

I fall onto my knees at Elliot's feet and clasp his hands in mine and he lets me do it. 'What happened next?'

'The case was pretty big, and *uh*… I told you my dad's in agriculture? That's not strictly true, I'm sorry. He owns a lot of land in my home county, *uh*, family land, going back generations. He's very well connected with all the hunts across the surrounding counties too, going back years, so his friends were furious with him, and with me, and it caused him a lot of shame and embarrassment.

'Mum's a local councillor and she had to face difficult public meetings with people wanting to know about her hooligan son. Then the vet's practice where I worked were getting calls too, asking that I be struck off for attacking a horse and causing a man to fall – that's what their barristers said I did – and it was reported like that in all the papers, but I swear, Jude, I'd never, *ever* harm an innocent animal.'

'I know that. I never for a second thought you would.' I squeeze his hands tightly.

'My practice manager said it would be better if I laid low until the case was over – and like everyone else, they assumed I'd end up in prison – so they relieved me of my job. And so did my college. They have a certain reputation to keep up, and there were complaints from students and their families. Even my YouTube channel was deluged with death threats and the most awful comments you've ever seen, accusing me of all sorts, and I had to take that down too. I felt besieged, and like my whole life and all my achievements were being erased. The case lasted months, and all the time I stuck to my version of events, pleading that I was just in the wrong place at the wrong time.'

'Which you were,' I interrupt.

'Except they had a video,' Elliot says abruptly, tears still wet on his face. 'They showed it in court one day and it changed the whole course of the trial. In the dark and from the angle it was shot, it really did look like I lunged at the horse and caused the rider to fall.' His tone changes from despair to bitterness. 'After they showed it in court, my parents didn't want me in the house. Dad said he couldn't look at me anymore, and Mum… well, she didn't say anything at all.' Elliot swallows hard. 'Then there was Antonia. She'd been supportive up until that point, in her own way, I guess, but when the tide seemed to turn against me in court she just took off. My stuff was in bin bags by the door of our flat when I got back there, and I was, to all intents, homeless.

'I had some pretty decent savings so I've been living off those, staying in a hotel near the court. Everything was adjourned for a few weeks while the lawyers scrabbled for better evidence, and that's when Jowan called me.' His eyes meet mine guiltily. 'I knew I was supposed to stay put, and I knew I'd be sharing the bookshop with another person, but I honestly thought I could keep myself to myself, stay in my room and out of trouble for a fortnight, working during the day to take my mind off things and getting away from myself and anyone who knew me. I didn't realise how close you and I would be here… how close we'd become. And all the time, I was telling myself to keep my distance from you, and keep the truth from you, and I loved the way you looked at me, like I wasn't a monster, like I was my old self.'

Elliot takes my hands in his and places them onto my lap where he leaves them, like he's already accepted that I won't want him touching me again, like I'm going to cast him aside too.

'Minty, she knew,' he says, grimly. 'I could tell from the first moment we met she recognised me from the pictures in the country magazines, but she couldn't place me, at first. She was looking at me like everyone else I knew back home – the way the jurors had, the way my parents do – she looked at me like I was a threat… a criminal. I kept hoping she wouldn't work it out and that I could stay here and just enjoy my break before I went back and… well, it was unrealistic to expect I could get away with that. And the phone kept ringing and every time it did I was terrified that this was it, that there was some new evidence uncovered that would send me down for sure.'

'That's why the CPS called here?' I ask.

'Uh-huh, they were keeping me up to date with the case, making sure I wasn't doing a runner. Eventually, on the day your friend came to visit you here, I got word I had to go back to court. There were police waiting for me at Truro to escort me, and I went. You were at the book club. I didn't have time to say goodbye to you. I had to pack up and leave. Didn't even have time to cash up.'

'I thought you'd had enough of me, or that maybe you were… jealous of Daniel and you'd stormed off.' I cringe at my self-centred stupidity. 'Here you were dealing with all that, and I was running around thinking…' Suddenly, it hits me, and my words falter, and I want to curl into a ball of embarrassment. 'I overheard you talking on the phone.'

'*Huh?*'

'That night, you were talking to *your parents*? Asking if you could go home. Begging forgiveness.'

'Oh.'

'I thought you were talking to your wife or something.'

I'm so glad when Elliot laughs. 'Wife? There's no wife. As if I'd go falling in love with you if I was married.'

'*What!*' I spring up onto my knees, then retreat back into the chair. 'What did you say?'

'Oh, shit, I'm sorry.' Elliot is cowed and his eyes dart around, his voice turning staccato. 'I shouldn't have said that. I've been trying so hard *not* to say it all this time, because I've no right to. I came here and messed everything up for you, even though you *told* me you were here to recover and to have fun, and I stomped all over your dream holiday in my size elevens, spoiling everything. So I tried to withdraw, leave you in peace, but it was too late, we'd gone so far, and I'd really come to... know you. But I had this whole secret life to hide. I knew if you ever found out, you'd look at me the way Antonia did. You'd hate me too.'

'I don't hate you. I never hated you.'

'Even when someone loves you it's easy for them to become convinced you're bad. Look at my parents. They won't see me. And now the case is over, I don't know if I want to see them.'

'The case is over?' I yelp.

Elliot heaves a sigh. 'It is now.' His voice tightens. 'I can hardly believe it, but it is. I was rushed into court on Tuesday morning and there was this recording, filmed by one of the saboteurs. I hadn't even known she was there that night. She must have been in the dark somewhere trying to save my skin. There was film of me being whipped across the cheek by one of the riders and pushed by one of their heavies, stumbling backwards onto the horse and making it throw its rider. The whole court heard me saying I was just trying to walk home from the pub and that I didn't want any trouble. They could see I had my hands up, holding my phone out, trying to get away. I had to stay there for three days while the jury came to a decision.'

'Why did it take so long to find the film?'

'They'd taken it. Someone in the hunt had grabbed the sab's camera *and* my phone. It must have happened in all the scuffles after I fell, I suppose. I don't remember. The camera and the recordings were recovered when police got a tip-off and searched a barn belonging to one of the huntsmen's grooms. I was cleared of all charges last night.'

When Elliot breaks down in front of me, he makes the sound of a man who has been besieged from all sides, keening with relief and pain. There's trauma in it, and sadness for everything he's lost, and he hunches over his knees, howling like an injured animal.

I fly to him and throw my arms over him, running my hands in soothing circles over his heaving back.

He should have told me from the start. I'd have listened... maybe? Or maybe I'd have called the police too, right at the beginning when I wanted him out of here? I might have judged him and cast him away from me, like all his friends and family have, like Antonia has, and I'd never have made the discovery that this man might be just about the best thing that has ever happened to me.

'It's over,' I whisper. 'It's over now. It's OK. You're safe.'

As I hold him, I think of the look in his eyes as he ran onto Minty's property this afternoon mistakenly thinking innocent animals were going to be killed, and at the same time not thinking at all, blinded by emotion and the instinct to protect vulnerable creatures from harm.

'Elliot?' I say, slipping once more down onto the floor by his feet. He raises his head, his hair falling in sleek black whips over his cheekbones, framing his amber eyes. 'What would you do if you could go back? If it was midnight on Christmas day and you'd stumbled into a hunt and there was a vixen being dug out of their covert to be thrown to the hounds? What would you do?'

Elliot's face is sad and grave. 'I know what I wouldn't do. I wouldn't hide or back away this time, not for one second. I'd fight tooth and nail to stop them. Even after all this. *Especially* after all this. It's changed me. I'm so angry now. I'm not done fighting these people.'

He hangs his head, and I cry at his feet.

Chapter Twenty-Nine

After a long time, I don't know how long, Elliot stands and lifts me to my feet. I'm still amazed by his strength when my own body feels tired and weak and my legs are tingling with pins and needles. His hands rub circles round my shoulders and he holds me at arm's length.

'You're not angry with me?'

I shake my head. 'Nope.'

'You're not afraid of me? Or ashamed?'

'Not a bit.'

'So what do we do now?'

I glance through the doorway into our little bookshop and only one thought strikes me. 'We open our shop for one last afternoon, even if everyone is at Minty's event.'

'I'd like that,' Elliot says with a modest smile.

'You make us some coffee, I'll open the door. Oh, and there are two gingerbread cookies in the café. I saved us some, in case you came back.'

'I said I would, if I could.'

His palms are still spread around my shoulders and the heat seeps into my body, weakening my core. Neither of us move.

'I loved being here with you. I'm sorry I blew it,' he says.

'You couldn't help it. And you didn't know if you could trust me with your secret, and deep down I think your instincts were right. But you could have told me when I asked you to. By then, I'd have believed you. I could have helped you, come to court with you. But I know now. That's all that matters.'

'I was never afraid of anything until I came here. I'd always looked after myself, relied on myself, and I worked hard.'

'Worked out,' I say, trying to get him to smile.

'True, I did a lot of that too. And I was standing on my own two feet. Even when I lost everything, I wasn't afraid, not really. I had this faith that everything would come good, and even if I had to go to prison, I knew I'd survive it because I was in the right. I'd have been let down, but I was sustained by the feeling of knowing I hadn't done anything wrong.

'But then I came here and from the first second I saw you, I was afraid. Afraid of what you'd think of me if you heard about the trial.' He raises a hand and runs his fingertips down my hairline to my temple. The sensation makes me close my eyes. 'Afraid that I couldn't keep my promise to myself to stay away from you.'

I feel him take a step closer so our bodies are almost touching. All my nerves jolt and buzz at the proximity.

'And when I left to go to court, I was terrified I'd never see you again.' Slowly, his hand slips around my waist and behind my back, his fingertips coming to rest in a soft line at the base of my spine. I fill the gap between us, leaning into his body, my eyes still softly closed, and I hear his shuddering breath in response. His voice is low, whispering now. 'I was terrified I'd get back here and you'd be gone already, or that you'd refuse to see me, and I'd never, ever be able to kiss you again.' He raises my jaw with the lightest lift from his fingertips and I tip my head back to meet his mouth lowering to mine, so slowly it makes me ache for it.

He breathes against my parted lips and the wanting inside me burns harder, making me spring onto my tiptoes and press my lips to his, and this time there are no secrets between us, and no uncertainty, and I let him kiss me until I forget this is our last day together, until my head swims, and all thoughts of driving home to Marygreen tomorrow morning are silenced.

When Elliot at last pulls away and my vision rights itself, I see him emerge from the blur into sharp focus. Amber eyes and a silver scar, black hair tumbling over cheekbones and a jawline that would always weaken me, no matter how long I gazed at him. He's smiling, awkwardly, a little abashed.

'We're not going upstairs?' I ask.

He leans in to kiss my forehead just the once.

'I want to take you to bed and do all the things I've missed doing with you, and I will later, if you'll let me.'

I'm pouting a bit, but the gravel in his voice and the blaze in his eyes soothes away the sense of being rejected. I pretend I'm thinking about it, unsure if I will let him, and he laughs.

'We never got to sell books together,' he adds. 'Let's just do that. Let's just be booksellers for a few hours.'

So that's exactly what we do. The kettle boils all afternoon keeping us in fresh coffee, and we sort through books and restock shelves. I work the pricing gun, and Elliot dusts the high shelves, and we serve precisely two customers (selling one postcard, and a *Wolf Hall*) and it's perfect.

Jowan calls in just after three with Aldous on his lead and a new crate of books that we need to find homes for, and he shakes Elliot's hand. He'd heard how Minty had shouted at him earlier, and she'd told him this morning about the hunting case, and so he'd got online to check the news from the courts and read all about Elliot being acquitted.

He said he'd wasted no time in updating Minty on the situation and she'd been decidedly ashamed and sent her apologies, but she was still too busy at the fun day to come to say sorry in person.

Elliot had smiled and said he didn't blame her, and I could see he meant it. Jowan looked reluctant to leave and after a moment perusing our faces – where he must have seen the whole of our love story written, including how sad we were about parting in the morning – he walked over to the shelf where Isolda's John Donne lived and he turned a few pages before reading aloud.

Absence, hear thou my protestation
Against thy strength,
Distance, and length;
Do what thou canst for alteration:
For hearts of truest mettle

Absence doth join, and Time doth settle.

Elliot walked over to Jowan and the elder man silently pointed to another passage of the same poem, before handing over the book with a smile, taking a little bow and walking out the door. We watched him go, before our eyes met and Elliot continued the reading.

By absence this good means I gain,
That I can catch her,
Where none can watch her,
In some close corner of my brain:
There I embrace and kiss her;
And so enjoy her and none miss her.

Elliot closed the book and placed it carefully back on the shelf. 'Do you think Jowan's telling us his secret? How he keeps Isolda close? She lives in his memory, in a corner of his brain where he can always find her and kiss her so he doesn't always have to feel her absence? He can bring her back?'

I smile and wipe away tears. I don't have to say anything else. This is the answer to how we'll manage without each other, starting tomorrow.

And that was how our last afternoon as the proprietors of Clove Lore's Borrow-a-Bookshop played out; a warm, emotional, caffeine-fuelled afternoon. The sunny weather held out all day until clouds rolled in at closing time bringing a lowering grey pall to Clove Lore.

'There's one last job to do, Elliot, before we lock up,' I told him, and he looked at me quizzically while I cleared away the last few spy novels on display by the door. 'We need to make our mark. But with what, I don't know. I've been racking my brains about our display since I arrived.'

The first of the raindrops hit the windows as I spoke and Elliot joined me by the door. Our little square outside was empty, and Clove Lore utterly still and silent, waiting for the downpour.

'We have to do something that tells the next proprietors about the things we love?' asked Elliot.

'That's the idea.'

We both looked over the empty display table, when a clattering sound drew our eyes to the door.

'What was that?' I started.

'Something by the bins,' Elliot said, and we both peered out the shop door.

At first there was no sign of it, except for the litter strewn around and blowing in the rising wind coming in off the Atlantic and whipping Up-along, bringing the slightest hint of September with it. Then, like a magical creature revealing itself to us mortals, a little black snout brushed with white appeared, with whiskers working in the cooling air, as out peeked a gangly cub from behind the great terracotta pot at the centre of the little cobbled square.

'Look!' I whispered, knowing that Elliot was already behind me, his head craned over my shoulder, gazing at the tiny thing. 'A young fox!'

'Stay still,' Elliot whispered back, slipping a hand around me, letting it rest against my stomach and I leaned back into his body, eyes fixed on the scene outside, as the mother raked through the rubbish, scraping for food scraps and finding none. The pair skittered across the square together, the spring-born youngster tumbling at his mother's feet, wanting to play. The vixen sniffed the air and cast her diamond eyes all around, cautious and alert.

'They're so beautiful,' I whispered and Elliot only pressed his flat palm against my stomach softly, stealing my breath for a second at the pressure, and the promise of this evening.

The pair were almost out of sight at the turning onto the steep slope leading down to the sea when the vixen turned her sleek head back towards the shop fixing bright eyes straight at us, framed inside the doorway, staring back at her, agape. Then she was gone, leading her cub safely to their next foraging spot.

'Wow, that was amazing,' Elliot whispered into my neck once they were out of sight.

'That was the most beautiful thing I've ever seen,' I said, struggling to voice the words.

'That was the *second* most beautiful thing I've seen,' Elliot said, and I heard the smile in his voice. I didn't move, only letting his hands roam over me and his lips brush at my neck.

'Foxes!' I shouted, making Elliot straighten and back away a little.

'I'm pretty sure they're gone now, off to find another bin to ransack.'

'No, let's make our display about fox books!'

'I like your thinking,' he said. 'We've definitely got a copy of Roald Dahl's *Fantastic Mr Fox*. Hey, we could make it a display for kids?'

So we spent half an hour plucking books from the shelves – *The Tale of Mr Tod*, *The Animals of Farthing Wood*, *Rosie's Walk*, Aesop's *The Fox and the Crow* – and laid them out on the table, all colourful and inviting.

'That doesn't look bad at all,' I said to Elliot as I walked to the door to turn the sign for the last time, stopping to look out at the rain falling steadily and making the cobbles shine. 'It was raining on the day you arrived,' I said, low and quiet, and Elliot joined me at the door, reaching his arms around me once more, just as we had stood looking through the glass watching the foxes earlier.

'You didn't like me much then, did you?' Elliot said, mussing my hair with his jaw and lips before pressing a kiss on the top of my head, making me feel tinier than usual and very, very safe.

'I wasn't keen, no,' I smiled, watching him reach for the key and turn it in the lock. 'But a person can grow on you.'

I felt him laugh and wrap his arms around my stomach and we watched the rain in silence, smiling contentedly.

A flash of rainbow colour drew my eye to the turning for Down-along, and there, under a golfing umbrella was Mrs Crocombe, frozen in her tracks and grinning broadly at the shop door. I watched her reach into her apron pocket and draw out her betting book, throwing us a cheery wave and bustling away again, presumably to let the entire village know that all bets were back on.

'She saw us, didn't she?' said Elliot.

'She did,' I replied, inhaling through gritted teeth and shaking my head sagely. 'She's just won herself a tenner.'

'Good for her,' he whispered, turning me to face him, and without another word he lifted me, my body wrapping around his instinctively, and I kissed him all the way up the spiral stairs and onto our bed.

Chapter Thirty

'Oh, Diane! You wouldn't believe the adventure I've had,' I announce as I clip my seat belt. I'm still out of breath from trundling my case and bag down the hill.

Maybe that's not the only reason I'm breathless. There was that view of the bobbing hollyhocks in the gardens all the way Down-along and over the glistening roof tiles in the late-August early morning sun, and the sparkling Atlantic the colour of a starling's egg, speckled with frothy white wave crests and dotted with little black fishing boats far out to sea. And of course, there was Elliot, standing at the top of the slope, with his arms crossed and his feet planted wide, waving one hand every time I stopped to turn back – which was a lot of times.

I'm surprised I haven't cried, although I think Elliot and I did enough of that this last fortnight to last a lifetime, and actually, I'm more inclined to smile at the memory of him this morning, wrapped in crisp white sheets, his lips swollen from kissing me and eyes tired from an almost sleepless night. I shiver at the memory of his hands on my skin and the way he'd made my body sing at his touch, and it is definitely the good kind of shiver.

I'd made him promise not to come all the way down to the car park, saying I wanted to remember him standing there by the turning to our little shop, and I wouldn't let him say goodbye either, and even though he'd frowned, he'd done as I asked. I want to hang onto the notion that he'll always be right there where I left him, handsome and strong, standing solidly, if a little ravaged-looking from the night before, with wild hair blowing in the breeze, and always watching for me, like poor, sad Captain Benwick in *Persuasion*, in his little cottage by the sea, reading poetry all day and dreaming of his lost love.

Except Elliot's not sticking around; he's going for a run this morning to clear his head before cleaning up the shop and café and returning the keys to Jowan. Then he'll be off down South to try to make amends with his faithless parents, cold fish that they are.

'Oh no, Diane, no tears now. Come on, let's go.'

As we attempt a fifteen-point turn in the car park, busy today with the Siren's overnight guests' cars, I can't help picturing my lovely little shop and Elliot behind the counter, and the way he'd have to stoop to get through the little door to the café, and the way he couldn't make a fairy cake to save his life, and how he'd put on his reading glasses, magically rendering himself one hundred times more handsome every time he picked up a book around the shop or worked the till.

I press my foot to the floor, powering Diane up the winding hill towards the main road. She protests a bit after her long sleep in the car park while I was off falling for Elliot and Clove Lore.

I try to distract myself with thoughts of home, and the new bedroom waiting for me, and how nice it'll be to see Gran, but instead, through eyes misting with tears, I picture Elliot, and Jowan, and nosy old Mrs Crocombe, and little scruffy Aldous.

No, I can do this. I'm not crying. I wipe my tears away and sniff back the emotions. Life goes on. We talked through our options in the middle of the night, and came to the conclusion we didn't really have any options. Elliot wanted to protest, to conjure up some plan so somehow we could stay together, but in the blue light, stars still shining down on us, gulls singing after the dawn boats, I knew that while our adventure had been utterly magical, that magic was the very reason why it could not survive in the real world where money needs to be made, bills must be paid, and adulthood embraced.

I fell for a magical illusion once before, the promise of a romantic, bookish, happy life with Mack and look where that got me.

'No, we'll be sensible,' I'd said, trying not to spoil the quiet wonder of the night and Elliot's soft eyes upon me. 'We'll go back to our lives.

You and I are from different worlds, and we met here and had a really special connection but it wasn't going to be forever. Two weeks was all we had. You have family and friends and colleagues waiting for you; your name's cleared and your old life is ready to pick up again. And I've still got to *start* my life. There's a home for me in Marygreen, and my parents, and Gran, and Daniel. There's my entire foundation, my starting point. I'll go home and begin something new.'

Sitting here in Diane I daren't admit to myself I still have no clue what that new something could be, and going home doesn't appeal nearly as much as it should, but it's the sensible decision, the mature decision, and Elliot accepted it all, even if it did look as though his heart was straining in his chest and he had gulped down words until I kissed him again, making the most of our last dawn.

Still, it hurts. I'll miss baking every morning, and seeing Izaak settling into life here with his beautiful man, and I won't get to see Jowan's fabled Christmas light display in the harbour that must be amazing, given that Minty has a hand in it – if her family fun day hunt organising is anything to go by. I'll miss seeing what the Siren's like in the autumn with the fire lit and the windows steamed up, and there'll be no more of Bella and Finan's Sleuthing Club for me, sadly.

I turn Diane onto the main road and the morning is bright and damp after the night's rain and from up here I can see nothing but wild and verdant late-summer greenery and ancient stone walls lining our route.

My thoughts are cut through with an image of my fingertips tracing the lines of Elliot's tattoo, a wild red fox casting stars behind it as it dashes across his broad back, and I try not to let my mind wander to his taut waist and the broadening muscles up his sides that jumped and shook when I skimmed my hands over them. 'I'm ticklish,' he'd said, pinning me down, grinning at me, his hair hanging over his face.

Concentrate, Jude! I'm not going to make it to the motorway at this rate. I'll end up wrapped around a lamp post or in an ancient Devonshire hedgerow.

I'm just losing sight of the visitors' centre in my rear view mirror when it all gets too much and I have to flick my indicator on and pull off the road.

I'll just sit in this lay-by for a second, letting the holiday traffic stream past me. I'll take a few deep breaths and have a word with myself about how this was a holiday romance and now that it's over I'll just have to be glad it happened, consider myself lucky, like Gran said.

If Elliot gets his job back at Cambridge – which surely he will now that the trial is all over and he's been vindicated – there'll be three hundred miles between us, and the small question of my future career to settle, but at least I'll have Daniel by my side, if he's not too busy with Ekon. Anyway, what Elliot and I had was gorgeous, perfect, amazing, and now the adventure's over, and that's fine. I'm fine.

Oh God, I'm sobbing now and rummaging in Diane's glove box looking for a tissue. 'I can do this,' I tell myself, but the tears won't stop.

After ten minutes and lots of big heaving breaths, I'm ready to go. I'm tired already from lack of sleep, so I'd better get this long trudge home over as soon as possible.

I'm reaching for the ignition once more and checking my puffy red face in the rear view mirror when I see it, a moving dark shape in the far distance behind me. I squint and rub my eyes, and turn to get a proper look out the back window in case I'm imagining things, but it really is him, black hair flowing from under his black cap, pounding along the verge, coming after me.

Without thinking, I'm out of Diane and running too, and the gap is closing between us and I watch Elliot's desperate, determined expression turn to a grin as we collide and he sweeps me into his arms and swings me round, kissing me hard.

When he finally puts me down his eyes are shining. 'Mrs C. doesn't win her tenner until we've settled down here in Clove Lore.' He's gasping between the words, breathless from running after me.

'What?'

'You have to stay. *We* have to stay. Or she'll lose out, you see?'

'Oh, right.' My mind's reeling, offering up plenty of good reasons why that idea isn't at all practical or well thought out. 'It would be a shame for her to lose the money.'

'Anjali mentioned the possibility of working at her practice, as a partner, if I wanted to stay.'

'She did?'

He nods. 'Just got off the phone with her. Would you be happy, sticking around for a while, living with me – if we can find a place you like, that is?'

Yes, my brain screams. *Yes, yes, yes!* 'What would I *do*?' I say, ever the stubborn one.

'Whatever you wanted. Whatever makes you happy. And I promise I'll take care of you, and I'll make you as happy as I can.'

'We'd take care of each other,' I say, and his hopeful, pleading expression melts away into relief, and I reach up to him once more, kissing him as though we don't, in fact, have all the time in the world.

Chapter Thirty-One

Clove Lore is busier tonight than it ever was in the summer months. Everyone's out on the beach and harbour wall, waiting for Jowan's announcement.

The moon shines down on the crowds and the speakers crackle and buzz. There's woodsmoke from the cottages' chimneys in the air and the coldest of winds coming in off the still, black sea.

Every window at the Siren blazes with light and someone's calling out from a smoky brazier down on the beach, 'roasted chez'nuts, roasted chez'nuts', and if this is what the rest of winter in Clove Lore is going to be like, I never, ever want to leave.

Elliot muscles back through the crowds towards me carrying two steamy mugs of mulled cider.

'Sorry about that, the queue was a mile long. Nothing happening yet?'

'Any second now.' I take the cup from him, as well as a kiss, and I smile into his eyes.

'What is it?' he laughs. He's wearing a puffy outdoorsy jacket over his zipped-up hoodie, scarf and beanie and I'm finding the fact he's wearing fuzzy black gloves too adorable for words.

'I don't know. Nothing really. I'm just happy, that's all.'

'Good. Me too.' He pulls me close, and I lean into his warmth, looking around the harbour, sipping the spicy, sweet booze.

There are two donkeys in knitted jumpers down on the shingle with pannier baskets over their backs collecting money for their stabling. Elliot told me recently that they're struggling for money

237

this year so he and Anjali had waived all their veterinary fees for the foreseeable future to help them out.

He was worried the court case might have hardened him but if anything it's made him softer. Even if things with his parents aren't perfect right now, he seems contented with life.

I'm hopeful his mum and dad will, in time, be able to apologise and things can get back on track. Right now they're still not taking his calls. He thinks they'll come around, it's just they're not the sort to admit their failings. I'll look forward to meeting them whenever they want to come see us here.

I give Elliot a squeeze and glance up at him drinking his cider. He's smiling and staring out over the scene. He's valued and loved here by the community already and he's very popular at the practice with the clients, and that means a lot to him, I know. His college did offer him his old position once again, but he wasn't inclined to take it.

There are children with sparklers down by the boats on the shore, and I can hear Finan from the Siren, playing a guitar and Bella singing through the open door of the pub, and there's someone else shaking some sort of jangly stick instrument that looks *very* local, like it's made of bottle tops stuck to a branch, down on the beach. I smile at the sound. I've learned it's best not to question Clove Lore traditions. You just have to go with it.

Not that we're *technically* Clove Loreans. Our little house is way out along the main road, but still it's in a nice green spot, with our garden full of bird-feeding stations, natural little hidey holes for hedgehogs, piles of logs for the beetles and bees and a little bench just for us. Elliot calls it our Garden of Eden.

I can't wait for Mum and Dad, Daniel and Ekon to come and see it at our house-warming party slash Christmas day festivities next month. Gran's looking forward to it too; she says she's counting down the days until then, not that she's been lonely. In fact, she's bringing Avi with her, the poker-playing silver fox who lives three doors down from her apartment in the east wing.

Mum sent me the local paper last week and the front-page story was about a stealth Christmas yarn-bombing campaign that transformed Marygreen's High Street. Every single shop doorway, railing and lamp post was decked out in crocheted holly and mistletoe. The report was accompanied by a picture of an overstuffed chunky-knit robin perched on top of the post box with a note in its beak – something about reclaiming the town from greedy developers and resisting the march of capitalism.

Nobody knows where the woolly décor came from. It appeared overnight and images from the only CCTV camera that could have identified the culprits had been obscured by what the investigating officer believed to be a thick layer of Brylcreem.

In a side column on page two I noticed a report on the mystery of a stolen mini bus belonging to New Start Village which had been safely returned to its parking space only three hours after it was reported missing shortly after midnight on the twentieth of November. Gran's been characteristically tight-lipped about the whole topic, only chuckling secretively when I asked her if she knows anything about it. New Start Developers better beware; they have no idea they've a secret anarchist living in their midst.

Gran's not the only one who's been keeping busy.

It was a bit of a scramble to get the forms filled in back in August, and then there was the interview over in Exeter, but now that my Master's course in book conservation has started, I'm loving it. I spent my thirtieth birthday on a class trip to the British Library to see the *Beowulf* manuscript (which was mind-blowing, by the way) and in January we're all off to the Gutenberg Museum too. It's in Germany, so you see, my new passport *is* going to get put to good use after all and I'll be taking to the skies for the first time in my life.

There's six of us on the course, a happy band of book nerds pursuing our love of print into postgraduate life, learning all about papermaking, printing, bookbinding and repair. Turns out I'm a dab hand at a saddle stitch through paper and Japanese bookbinding is my forte. Two of the group, Vita and Leo, are already firm friends to me and Elliot and they come round for drinks some weekends when

Elliot isn't working, and there's always someone from the group ready at a moment's notice for a study session via FaceTime that invariably starts with good intentions and cursory glances over our textbooks before we end up enthusing about the latest paperbacks we're reading.

Anjali calls around too and she and Elliot talk shop while the three of us cook and drink wine in our cosy kitchen. Our oven's big enough to bake multiple batches of gingerbread cookies and scones three times a week, enough to keep Minty's estate tea room in yummy bakes and to keep me in pocket. That's my new job, you see? So, yeah, I am living a life of my own, with zero distractions to throw me off course. It's more *Jude the Awesome* than *Jude the Obscure* these days.

'Friends and guests, welcome to the Clove Lore Christmas Lights switch on,' Jowan's voice booms out over the harbour. He's standing on a scaffold wearing a Santa hat and Aldous's fuzzy head is peeking out the collar of his buttoned-up coat. They're both enjoying a new lease of life now Aldous has moved into the B&B with his master. His brush with doggy death in August forced him to act more like a pet than a wild cheddar-munching monster and has turned things round for him. Jowan, Elliot and I walk him on his lead on Sunday afternoons all the way to the Siren for lunch with the Bickleigh brothers and whoever else happens to be in the bar that day, and not one of us will order the cheese ploughman's or chicken soup out of respect for the little mutt's feelings.

'I'm going to hit the switch any second now. Are you all ready?' Jowan's voice carries around the harbour.

A great cheer rises up into the cold air, and Elliot turns to me and smiles excitedly.

'Are you warm enough?' he asks.

'I am.'

Jowan's voice sings out again. 'But before I switch on the lights, I'm going to ask you to look around you at our beautiful harbour, and our special community. We've clung to the rocks here in Clove Lore for centuries, and gradually the village grew and prospered, and it shrank and struggled too as the years passed, but we keep our little light shining, and our doors open, and we welcome our guests and friends from the world over to our tiny village. Sometimes I worry we won't be able to cling on much longer here, life is so expensive, and so difficult...'

I find myself thinking that Jowan might well be right, maybe life at Clove Lore has changed unrecognisably over the decades, maybe it *is* harder to survive here than in other parts of the country, being so cut off and dependent on visitors, but I don't think he should worry too much. The camellia displays in the estate gardens promise to be more beautiful than ever next summer under Leonid's expert green fingers, and Minty's already got him roped in to host a Camellia Day festival in June, another new way of keeping old traditions alive up at the estate. I'm looking forward to trying out some pink and white iced shortbread camellias for the event.

Izaak and Leonid now live in an apartment full of books and plants in what was once Minty's great grandfather's nursery and the governess's rooms. They still read to each other every single night in a mixture of Polish, Russian and English.

So the estate's not going anywhere soon, and neither is Borrow-a-Bookshop which is presently fully booked for the next two and a half years with a long line of eager book-lovers dreaming of their chance to sell books by the sea. Elliot and I help out with the trust. We're currently trying to modernise the booking system and encourage many more singles to sign up. I'm not saying we've turned into matchmakers to rival Mrs Crocombe, and I'm definitely not playing along with her betting syndicate, but there's nothing wrong with encouraging a few more bookshop love stories. I think of the long waiting list and smile. They won't know what's hit them when their patience pays off. Lucky people.

On the way Down-along tonight Elliot and I peered in the darkened windows at our beautiful bookshop. Its current occupants must already have been down at the harbour side.

I could just make out the display by the till of Grandad's recipe book. It's just a pamphlet really, nothing too fancy, yet, but Minty knew someone who knew a designer and she twisted their arm to help us out. I think she felt bad about judging Elliot so harshly and was trying to make amends.

Now Dad has the treasured original notebook back in his possession and there are a few hundred copies of our family's recipes stockpiled and ready to sell on the bookshop shelves. So even though Marygreen bakery is gone, redeveloped in the world's unstoppable appetite to wreck and rebuild, it lives on in print, with my grandfather's dedication to my dad, the best thing he ever made, reproduced in a beautiful curling font inside every fly-leaf, forever.

I try to tune back in to Jowan's words.

'… but we managed to shine on for another year,' he's saying. 'And we'll keep on shining here in Clove Lore in the year to come, and the next, and the next, and for as long as we can.' The crowd applaud as hard as they can through two hundred pairs of winter gloves. Jowan's voice rises again above the cheers. 'So, without further ado, let's light up our little harbour for winter. This is for all of us, and for my darling Isolda, who is never far away.'

Lightbulbs flicker into life all around the waterfront. First, the chains of lights that run the length of the harbour walls and all down the path to the beach burst into multi-coloured magnificence, and then one by one, bright displays on boards floating in the water are illuminated – a mermaid, a Father Christmas and a Clove Lore donkey with long pink ears – all bobbing on boats fixed close to the shore, and finally a tall Christmas tree by the lifeboat house gleams in gold and silver.

The local school choir erupts into festive song over by the great lantern at the end of the harbour wall, led by a bobble-hatted Mrs Crocombe and her daughter, their headteacher. The Burtislands are there too, looking every bit like a family in a brochure for luxury festive getaways.

Elliot and I are firmly in Mrs C.'s good books now that we're locals, even if we don't have plans to help swell the numbers of that school choir any time soon.

In the applause that follows, I find myself sighing happily and thinking that for once I don't feel the need to compare my situation to any character in any novel from long ago. I'm not like Anne Elliot waiting for love to come to her, or some old Thomas Hardy creation dreaming of success and escape. I'm Jude Crawley, I'm thirty years old and I made my life happen, just like Gran knew I would. All I had to do was believe in myself a little bit and take that first step towards living a life of my own.

Elliot catches me smiling at my thoughts and he casts his amber eyes over my face, grinning back at me. I let him turn me towards him and I know exactly what he's going to say, so I beat him to it.

'I love you, Elliot.'

'Me too,' he says, and he kisses me as Clove Lore shines its lights out into the darkness, celebrating and singing, and dreaming of Christmas.

Yes, I am absolutely fine. I'm home.

A letter from Kiley

Hi! I'm Kiley Dunbar! Welcome to my fifth novel. I hope your visit to Clove Lore makes you happy and helps you escape real life for a while.

If you find you've fallen in love with Clove Lore, there's a place not too far from here that bears a bit of a resemblance to the village, Clovelly in North Devon, where you'll find breath-taking views, a steep picturesque main street leading down to a historic harbour, a beach with a waterfall, and there's also a Visitors' Centre, a beautiful garden, and even some donkeys, much like Clove Lore, but that's where the resemblance ends. I love to take a beautiful destination that means a lot to me and add my own sparkle and magic, making it my characters' own.

Clovelly does mean a lot to me; it's the place a lovely man swept me away to on our first weekend together, twenty-one summers ago. I'd never seen anywhere like it and fell in insta-love with the location, and with him. We celebrated our twentieth wedding anniversary at Christmas and we can't wait to get back to Clovelly again, which we've visited many times over the years, but we've never taken our kids or our little Bedlington, Amos (the inspiration for a certain grumpy someone in this book). Hopefully, 2021 will be the year we return and if that's not to be, I'll hold memories of that beautiful place in my heart a wee bit longer until we get there.

I drew on my own experience in other ways writing this book, letting my lifelong troublesome relationship with maths and numbers resonate through Jude's life. Like me, it took Jude a while to realise it's OK if your teachers thought you were a mathematical lost cause and calculations still bring you out in a cold sweat even now; we've all got things that feel insurmountable and embarrassing, but when we ditch the shame and love ourselves, and support each other to identify and emphasise our strengths, life gets better and better.

Jude's strength comes from the thing she loves most in the world, reading, just like me. She's a woman who understands the power of books to transport and transform people. What she doesn't know is that she's about to have a literary life transformation of her own.

I hope you love watching Jude on her adventures, and if you've enjoyed her journey I'd be really grateful if you could leave a review on your favourite reviewing platform, even just a few words to let your friends and followers know what they might like about the story would be amazing! Reviews help readers find authors and every single one helps.

Finally, you'll see I dedicated this book to you. It is for readers, reviewers and bookworms everywhere. Thank you from the bottom of my bookshelves to the top of my towering tomes for your encouragement and kind words, I'd be nowhere without you.

If you're a book lover looking for a bookshop of your own to borrow, there's always The Open Book in Scotland's Wigtown, a place, sadly, I've never been.

Oh, and just so you read easy, I don't suffer from the compulsion to have every elderly person in my books hanging onto life by a thread. Gran is there at the start of this book and she's there at the end, loving life, OK? Great!

Happy reading,
Love, Kiley x

Acknowledgements

My heartfelt thanks are sent to the following lovely people who kept me writing and smiling through lockdown.

Lindsey and Keshini from Hera Books, and all the Hera family, including Jennie, Vicki and Diane. Thank you for everything.

My darlings, Nic, Robin, Iris, and Michael. You are all angels. I love you more than I can ever express. Thank you for loving me. X

I couldn't have coped during 2020 without the Dream Team, little and big. I love you guys.

Vicky and Lisa, you got me through lots of long days battling with the words. Thank you so much! Lisa, thank you for your help with the comic place names!

All my lovely friends, family and colleagues – I'm grateful as always for your support and love, especially Kelly T, Laura J, Lizzie F, Roxanne, Ritu, Alana Oxford, Imogen, Jo, Angi, Orlagh, Susan and Kerry, Nicola B, Sara and Rhian. And thank you so much, Catherine, Usma and Paul. It was lovely co-teaching with you.

Thank you to every person who joined the blog tour for my last book *One Winter's Night*, you're all *so* much appreciated, and thank you, Rachel for organising another absolute smasher of a tour. Thank you Jo Selley Cake Artist in South Cheshire for the best book cake ever made. Check it out on her insta!

I'm hugely grateful to the Romantic Novelists' Association and especially thankful to have been shortlisted for their reader-voted awards in the category of best Romantic Comedy Novel 2021 for *One Winter's Night*. It feels lovely to have my writing acknowledged in this way. I'm very proud to be a member of the RNA's 'Rainbow

Chapter' for members who identify as LGBTQ+, their allies and those who are writing novels featuring LGBTQ+ characters.

Thank you to LC at the *ChickLit4Life* podcast for filling my ears with loveliness, keeping me company with bookish (and BTS) chat and making me laugh hard during lockdown. I wholeheartedly recommend the podcast to all of you! Same goes for the magnificent Kelly at *Boobies and Noobies* podcast. Jared Goode, I promised you I'd give you a little Dolly Parton tip of the hat in my next book. x

Nantwich Book Shop have been hugely supportive of me this year, even giving me a window display of my own! Thank you so much Steve, Denise, and all the family and staff there. Indie bookstores are vital community resources and a source of friendship and comfort. Dickens knows I LOVE eBooks and wouldn't ever be without them (and I have a digital To Be Read pile long enough to last me a happy lifetime) but our high streets would be a sad place without our bookish treasure palaces. Let's all take good care of our local booksellers and the shops they curate for us.